The Three Ravens

By
Ed Kirwan

KCM PUBLISHING
A DIVISION OF KCM DIGITAL MEDIA, LLC

CREDITS

Copyright © 2017 by Ed Kirwan
Published by KCM Publishing
A Division of KCM Digital Media, LLC

All Rights Reserved.

This content may not be reproduced in whole or in part, in any form or by any means, electronic or mechanical, including photocopying, recording, or by any information storage and retrieval system now known or hereafter invented, without written permission from the publisher.

This is a work of fiction. Names, characters, businesses, places, events and incidents are either the products of the author's imagination or used in a fictitious manner. Any resemblance to actual persons, living or dead, or actual events is purely coincidental.

The Three Ravens by Ed Kirwan

ISBN-13: 978-1-939961-58-7
ISBN-10: 1-939961-58-0

First Edition

Publisher: Michael Fabiano
KCM Publishing
www.kcmpublishing.com

> Susan
> Pleasures are many, but none more sweet than making new friends!
> — Jul and Ken

To my dad, who taught me that when it is written, the
text of every man's life is two things; honor
and footnote.

Table of Contents

Chapter 1: *Lake Huron* 1
Chapter 2: *Fairfax, Virginia* 6
Chapter 3: *Bethesda, Maryland* 13
Chapter 4: *Havana, Cuba* 16
Chapter 5: *Upper West Side in Manhattan, New York* 19
Chapter 6: *Bethesda, Maryland* 26
Chapter 7: *Fort Myers, Florida* 29
Chapter 8: *Reno, Nevada* 33
Chapter 9: *White Sulfur Springs, West Virginia* 38
Chapter 10: *CIA - Fairfax, Virginia* 42
Chapter 11: *New York City* 57
Chapter 12: *San Juan, Puerto Rico* 61
Chapter 13: *Culebra Island, Puerto Rico* 65
Chapter 14: *Teterboro, New Jersey* 69
Chapter 15: *Culebra Island, Puerto Rico* 72
Chapter 16: *Oscoda, Michigan* 74
Chapter 17: *Pokolov Safe House* 76
Chapter 18: *Huron National Forest* 81
Chapter 19: *Twenty Nautical Miles outside San Juan, Puerto Rico* 83
Chapter 20: *Huron National Forest* 87
Chapter 21: *Oscoda-Wurtsmith Airport* 91
Chapter 22: *Capital Regional Airport Lansing, Michigan* 95
Chapter 23: *Boat Harbor Rogers City, Michigan* 99
Chapter 24: *Katy - Rogers City Marina* 105
Chapter 25: *Aiden - Rogers City, Michigan* 109
Chapter 26: *Asidilov - Rogers City, Michigan* 113

Chapter 27:	Teterboro Airport, New Jersey	117
Chapter 28:	Fifty Two and a Half Barrow Street New York City, New York	121
Chapter 29:	Brussels Airport, Belgium	124
Chapter 30:	Molenbeek-Saint-Jean, Brussels	129
Chapter 31:	Omar Molenbeek-Saint-Jean, Brussels	136
Chapter 32:	Fifty Two and a Half Barrow Street New York City, New York	140
Chapter 33:	Barrow Street, New York City, New York	145
Chapter 34:	Oval Office Washington, D.C.	151
Chapter 35:	Hotel Lombardy Washington, D.C.	153
Chapter 36:	Washington, D.C.	158
Chapter 37:	Phoenix, Arizona	162
Chapter 38:	Downtown Phoenix	168
Chapter 39:	Phoenix Convention Center	171
Chapter 40:	Phoenix Sky Harbor International Airport	184
Chapter 41:	Barrow Street, NYC	187
Chapter 42:	Alexandria, Virginia	192
Chapter 43:	Barrow Street, NYC	194
Chapter 44:	Jersey City, New Jersey	202
Chapter 45:	The Incursion - Jersey City	209
Chapter 46:	Minus One - Jersey City	212
Chapter 47:	Take It All - Jersey City	219
Chapter 48:	Barrow Street, NYC	223
Chapter 49:	Believe It - Barrow Street	228
Chapter 50:	The Hourglass - Barrow Street	232
Chapter 51:	The Forger Fifty - Barrow Street	235
Chapter 52:	The Passenger - Barrow Street	239
Chapter 53:	The Dupe - Barrow Street	245
Chapter 54:	Lower Manhattan NYC	249
Chapter 55:	Barrow Street, New York City, New York	256
Chapter 56:	Waiting - Barrow Street	259
Chapter 57:	Barrow Street, New York City, New York	264
Chapter 58:	Financial District New York City	268
About the Author		284

The Three Ravens

Ed Kirwan

Chapter 1

Lake Huron

The summer wind on the lake plays with your hair, the winter wind on the lake plays with your nerves. It was a winter wind blowing on Lake Huron this November night. For the people on the boat, frayed nerves were only a matter for those with hope.

The first real bitter wind out of the north was announcing its ungraciousness and it wouldn't take no for an answer as it cut through the clear November night to lay claim to the water. It was a night so cold and harsh that it beat the beauty out of the full moon, a night on the lake where everywhere did its level best to be elsewhere. It was a perfect night for nothing other than smuggling human cargo from Canada into the United States by boat.

The boat's skipper was an odd sort, a hard sort, part Boo Radley and part Quint. His given name was Rustam Asidilov. The townspeople called him Rusty, a nickname the skipper hated but never challenged. The Chechen American had moved up to Rogers City on the lake from Lansing, Michigan three years earlier.

From his first day in Rogers, Asidilov came and went as a solitary man of the water. That's how he was perceived by the folks of Rogers and that's how he wanted it. He wanted to stand out only enough to be recognized but not enough to be included, or remembered after he left.

Asidilov was a lizard leather hard-looking man, with cold black crocodile eyes and a serpent's disposition. He rarely smiled. He moved about his business under a white seafarer's beard and mustache covering a four-inch scar on the left side of his face, which he didn't show off but didn't hide either.

He stared out over the bitter cold moonlit night from the open canopied bridge on his non-descript 1990 thirty-one foot Cherokee 310 Chief, a vessel with a sturdy eleven-foot beam. He had made this fifty-mile trek so many times he knew the bearings by heart. He could get from one point on the lake to another and get there within a three minute window; however the weather bet against him. He knew how to avoid U.S Customs and Border Protection and their Canadian counterparts.

For more than two years he had ferried many illegals, almost exclusively Eastern European men, four and five at a time into the sleepy U.S. harbor at Rogers City from the sleepier still Canadian port at Kincardine, Ontario.

He perpetrated his illegal smuggling by employing a series of local boaters on either side of the border who were paid very handsomely. The peripheral accomplices, once tethered to his operation, were kept in line by his steely promises of swift and final retribution should they ever feel comfortable enough to mention his name.

He had perfected the timing of his travel with routes that were meticulous. He had mastered his own visibility when he wanted to be seen and a flawless method of evading any detection of his activities when he didn't.

Asidilov was fearless, but never careless. He was an intelligent, meticulous human smuggler, who fetched an extraordinarily high price for his unblemished services.

Tonight however was different, quite different, once in a lifetime different. All the previous smuggling had merely been rehearsal for this transport. Tonight there was no charge for bringing the human cargo across the lake.

The plan for this cargo had been imagined in 2001 but it was only a sick dream, a perverse fantasy, until the 2008 American presidential election made it all possible. Tonight was the beginning. Tonight many would die and, in the minds of the fanatical, many would be glorified. Tonight a 14 hundred year prophecy would finally come to be. But they had to get the cargo into America first.

The sea worthy, thirty-one foot vessel normally traversed the lake with five or six total passengers aboard, maybe seven or eight max, if the price was right. On this bitter cold early November night it sailed with twenty-three aboard; Asidilov, two heavily armed Middle Eastern men guarding twenty other Middle Eastern men, each bound, gagged, and lying face down, one on top of the other like rolled up rugs, some in the galley below and some in the V-shaped berth.

The boat docked at 10:40 pm in Asidilov's harbor slip in Rogers City, Michigan. He turned the boat dark. Everything looked exactly how it had every night for the past thirty-six months.

Once the boat was tied in, Asidilov immediately went through his nightly paces. A scripted and repeated routine he had developed and etched into the normalcy of the town's expectations of him every day for three straight uninterrupted years of nights. He went to the local bar across from the dock, as was his custom, for the better part of two years. He sat down to a shot of Irish whiskey and a pint of Pabst Blue Ribbon beer. He was such a creature of habit the bartender didn't even have to wait for him to order the drinks. He simply set them down in front of the stool reserved nightly for Rusty.

He fired the shot of whiskey into the back of his throat and savored his beer only slightly longer than that. He left a two dollar tip on the bar, said his guttural hellos and abbreviated goodnights to the few patrons still in the gin mill, and left, just as he had done the night before and a thousand nights before that.

Comfortable neither he, nor any movement on his vessel, had stirred any unwanted attention he headed back towards his boat.

Among the cars in the parking lot of the Roger's City Marina sat two unmarked, dirty white vans, each with two men, each waiting for Asidilov's signal to move. As Asidilov passed through the marina parking lot he removed his black Greek fisherman's cap from his head and slapped his thigh with it. The signal to move had been given. The drivers of the vans both turned their ignition keys.

The prisoners in the boat were shuttled, with their hands still tied behind them and their mouths gagged airtight with duct tape, ten into one van, and ten into the other. Each van's ridership was finished off with one additional heavily armed guard. The vans quietly disappeared into the night.

Asidilov went home.

If the bitter November night winds keep folks off Lake Huron, it just as certainly keeps them out the woods of Northern Michigan.

Forty-five minutes into the drive away from the marina the driver in the lead van pulled off the unlit, one-lane road onto an even more desolate road leading into a remote area of Huron National Forest. The second van followed dutifully.

Twelve minutes into the trek through the forest the van driver whipped the van off the road onto yet another dirt road. Again the second van followed.

Several hundred yards further along both vans came to a stop and the drivers and the guards exited the vans. The armed gunmen opened the backs of their respective rolling prison cells and ordered the human cargo out.

There were now four armed men with what looked like AK47 machine guns barking orders at the twenty terrified, confused, bound and gagged men. The prisoners meekly complied with their captors' orders, spoken in Farsi, to march in line into the darkened forest.

Colder and more foreboding by the yard, the prisoners followed one another. Every step deeper into the woods was a step deeper into each man's own despair.

The timorous, sidling prisoners, dressed in traditional Muslim garb, some with only sandals covering their bare, stinging feet, were ordered to halt in a grassy opening just big enough to fit all twenty-four men afoot amongst the otherwise thick trees.

Just as they had in their countless dry run rehearsals, the armed men separated the prisoners into four groups of five. Each group of five was separated from the other by an exact number of feet. One armed guard was assigned to each group of five prisoners. Should any man in any group even hint at noncompliance he was to be summarily executed, no questions asked.

The prisoners were ordered to sit and huddle tightly to one another. Again, the terrified men did exactly as ordered. Nothing strengthens authority quite like acquiescence. Nothing compels acquiescence quite like four men pointing automatic weapons at you.

As soon as they were all seated and snugly pressed against one another in the four arranged groups, the captors took a moment to look at each other. There wasn't a hint of remorse for what they were about to do.

The stoicism of mass murderers in the moments before a kill sure does mask their fanaticism. Each armed man gave a nod of his readiness. The carnage was prolific.

Twenty young defenseless men were killed in the first few seconds of the machine-gun fire. It wasn't enough. The killers had very specific orders. They were to keep firing until their clips were emptied into the dead men. They had orders then to unload their clips, reload and unload a second clip into the dead bodies. It wasn't a kill. It was a statement kill, a statement meant for mankind to record.

When the second clips had been emptied into the bodies the assailants each pulled from their assault gear a flashlight and a camera. They began snapping pictures of the sickening pile of blood-soaked dead with the same callous aim as they had with their weapons.

Auschwitz's blood-thirsty murderers could never have left behind an uglier sight to behold, nor could their evil purpose leave a more horrifying reminder as to what humanity could prevail upon itself by itself.

Chapter 2

Fairfax, Virginia

*H*ome to the warrior isn't a place; it's a reason.

The piano keys bounced off the corners of the dimly lit bedroom. "You Are So Beautiful", the throaty song carrying Joe Cocker's raspy singing voice, pined and pulsated along the high ceiling giving it an almost concert feel to it the intimacy.

The three dozen white roses and three dozen red roses which he brought home with him, along with her air of delicious perfume, filled the entire house with a fragrant sweetness reserved for botanical gardens, flower shops, and dreams.

The atmosphere was perfect. The longing seventeen months unabated. The atmosphere was better than perfect.

There are two kinds of sex: One which lives on the flesh and perishes there, and one which lives far from the flesh and unrelentingly seeks deeper and deeper for the soul. This never perishes. The first is an act which endures the length of the act. The other is a truth which persists for the length of all coming time.

There may be no greater way to measure how humans waste their lives than to count the things they allow to get in the way of living it. There may be no greater way to live it than in the passionate arms of a true love.

There are countless reasons people feel the desperate deprivation of sexual bliss. People often living under the same roof reduce sex to the physical act and measure it as a calculus of what it is not, of what is unmet.

Many who are trapped in its despairing grip think sex is the first kind, the stuff of the flesh. The wife calls it work; the husband thinks it bland.

Then there are couples with troubles, financial trouble, kids in the way, selfish wives, selfish husbands, lazy wives, lazy husbands, husbands who don't measure up to the actor on the silver screen, wives who don't measure up to the actress on the porn screen. All these leave varying sizes of gaping emotional holes in the precious human experience. Too bad.

Then there is another kind, the deprivation which comes from being separated from the object of one's desire. In the spaces between comes a particularly pressing physical longing to accompany the physical human need unmet.

Then there is yet a deeper kind. This is the deprivation of separation with true love attached to it. This places a peculiar anguish alongside and a barren earth kind of longing, to go along with the heavily weighted physical hunger.

And then finally, lastly, there is deprivation only a few men know of. This belongs only to the warrior soldier.

This is the agonizing destitution of the warrior in war when he contemplates why he must survive, why he must endure and return to his one true love. It's the most intensely desperate kind of sexual longing a man can know, and once felt, makes up the larger part of why 'war is hell.'

Ah, but to the survivors, upon deliverance home, his drive to live so near again, after the fundamentally primal urge to make it back, can become the most intensely satisfying kind of love-making a man can experience. It is all the one and all the other, all the flesh and all the soul.

Ernesto Suarez knew such an urge and such a love. And tonight he would assure the world that Winston Churchill's declaration asserting "Nothing in life is so exhilarating as to be shot at without result" was wrong. Way wrong. Nothing in life is so exhilarating as to be shot at without result and then making love to the reason you live.

With every broken, emoting voice inflection echoing in his ear his want for her grew sharply deeper. He heard every slightly unreachable pitch the soulfully sincere troubadour got near but could not reach. Ernesto knew to his core that he was where wanted to be, where he should be. He was genuinely alive at this very moment. The atmosphere was better than perfect.

"You're everything I hoped for, you're everything I need," crooned the irresistible throat with the undeniable depth of soul.

He loved her so and, without the words to express how deeply, he had only the soft touch of his fingertips, the affirming manly power in his hands and his lips with which to prove it.

It was time.

Her raven hair draped on the pillow, his chest to her chest, his cheek, her cheek. He wanted not to move. This was his Heaven. Tomorrow would be for sex; tonight was for making love, once in a lifetime love making. He wanted not to move.

He had been away for what seemed an eternity and God she was beautiful. It was time.

The phone rang. The timing couldn't be worse for hell to intervene.

"Don't answer that phone," she softly demanded.

A second passed. A second ring. They both knew it would ring yet both felt a tinge of startle by it. She didn't say a word. She didn't have to. Her eyes and eyebrows spoke, "Don't…please."

The tall, dark-haired, dark-eyed man, half Hispanic and half Irish, with skin near black from months hunting ISIS terrorists in the blistering Syrian Desert, knew he couldn't honor her wish…or fulfill his own.

In the three years he owned a "company" phone it had never rung more than twice. If it was ringing it meant someone, somewhere, was either dead or about to be dead, unless he answered it before a third chime. Ernesto's eyes drew one last look at her legs.

It was well over a year since Ernesto had been with his wife. He wasn't selfish. He knew there was a peculiar longing she must have felt as well. It had been well over a year for both of them.

Those legs, those legs, those lips, those lips…God those legs!

He was a sensitive man, a feeling man, an empathetic man and he was physical person. He wasn't just about love's higher ground. Those legs were supposed to be his night, his weekend, his bliss.

He pushed his fingertips along the inside of her thigh, over her sheer black stockings as gently as a man could brush his hand over his lover's thigh. He stared at his hands as they paused ever so close to the place where the road of passion had so long reminded him that beauty indeed existed. It's beckoning kept him sane when he was in the terrible places.

It was her alone he thought about on the countless lonely nights. She was the place of pleasure and the place of peace. In the moments after the bloody hand to hand kills had been washed away, she was the promise that his hands would know gentility again.

He wanted her…badly, but he lifted his fingertips and brushed his palm back away from what he wanted towards her knee, pressing his palm firmer as it traveled away from the pinnacle of passion. His mind was hardening.

"Don't answer that phone," she whispered as she grabbed his thigh with her own powerfully pressing fingers. It pushed a rush of blood from her fingertips to the nape of his neck.

He shivered. She trembled.

He answered it. He had to.

"Suarez" was all he said when he answered the phone, as his head dropped like a stone until his chin crashed into his chest. The voice on the other end said but two words, "Three Ravens."

"Ah, c'mon. It's been seventeen friggin months since I've been home. Three Ravens? Are you sure it's like that?"

The clerical woman's voice on the other end of the line refused his plea. "The big man called, "Three Ravens."

That was it. Those three words were all it took. Ernesto Suarez knew it was serious and whatever it was, wherever it was, it was a matter of national urgency.

The Big Man was their call sign for the President of the United States. When The Big Man called the "Three Ravens," it was a matter of life and death and it was going to be an operation outside of law enforcement or military channels and quite possibly outside the law.

Ernesto forgot about his nearly naked wife lying within arm's reach. He was about to hang up when the voice spoke.

Ernesto became visibly agitated and he blasted the voice on the other end. "He's not my brother. I don't know where he is. He's where he always is, underground, off the grid. All I know is when I last spoke to him he said he didn't want any part of this anymore."

The voice interrupted, he interrupted back, "No, I won't find him because I can't find him. You find him. I'm on my way."

He abruptly hung up the phone and muddled to himself, "Fucking Rolly.... find him? Really...you work for the damn president. You find him."

Ernesto trained his eyes upon his wife's disapproving eyes. Then knowing he would be behind the wheel of his car in six minutes or less, and surely in grave danger with thirty hours or less, turned his glare at the black sheers he had so longed for and so nearly had the pleasure. If he was to die, he was going to take this last image of his wife with him.

"Sorry... Shit!" He let go of her thigh.

"You gotta go? Now?" she whispered rhetorically. "And they need Rolly too? I thought he quit. I thought he hated the president?"

Ernesto tried to look as sheepish as he could but she knew better. When the big man calls there's no delaying, no negotiating. There's was only doing.

If they wanted Rolly, they wanted Aiden Palmer too. They were the team.

The Three Ravens.

When these three men were assembled to do a job, it meant something awful was happening, the worst of the worst. It meant the unimaginable. His mind raced as he thought about it. He grew more agitated as he moved. His pace quickened. He almost forgot the gorgeous woman in the black sheers was in the room.

For her part, Ernesto's wife tried to look as scolding as she could but she knew in her heart he had no choice. She didn't want him to remember her face with a furrowed brow. There was a fire somewhere on earth and he was going to get there and put it out. Surely lives were at stake. Ernesto's team was as special as special gets. She knew it. She would never know the circumstances, never be told the why of his leaving her. But she knew if they called him it was that deep and that important, and that secret.

She felt a profound pride in him and his service to his country and humanity, but to her, despite all the nobility, it sucked.

Ernesto cursed circumstance itself. The impulse of woe lasted less than a second. There came over him an air, that thing she saw before, purpose. It was the thing she loved about him, but the thing she hated now, at this moment.

The next five minutes saw him scrambling to put a suitcase together. She offered her assistance but he was already gone. He didn't answer her. She sat back down on the bed, head bowed, a prayer, a tear, another prayer. Her five minutes were up. He stood at the door. He tilted his head, placed his hand over his heart. He was gone. Her eyes overflowed.

Ernesto Suarez was tall for his country of origin, Cuba, but not for his family. He was six feet tall and then some, but his father was six-foot-eight. There was never a time in Ernesto's life where he wasn't in perfect shape. He worked at it diligently, fanatically, and it showed on every muscle. When tense, his arms looked like elevator cables. There wasn't an ounce of fat on him.

His father, an immigrant from Cuba, always preached to him that success was a measure of outworking his opponents and that most of the time that opponent was himself. He'd say, "God dishes out two kinds of talent: the talent he gives at birth and the talent he gives because you are willing to pay a price in sacrifice and practice."

Ernesto would use his father's words on the football field to make himself an All-State New York quarterback and outside linebacker at Cardinal Spellman High School in the Bronx. After high school Ernesto would take that same determination, focus, and dedication to Marist College where he would elevate himself to team captain and All-Conference linebacker.

Under his captaincy, Marist won the only Division 1 Football Conference Championship in its fifty years in existence. He credited his athletic success to his father's advice. He would employ that advice in everything he did on the field. When asked by a local upstate New York newspaper about Ernesto's fifteen tackles in the championship game, the Coach responded, "Ernesto just outworks and outlasts everybody. He's the most loyal and sacrificial player I've ever coached."

When that same reporter asked Ernesto about his fifteen tackles in the championship game he replied, "I got the statistics but the guys who spilled the lead blockers made the plays."

After his football days at Marist College, Ernesto was admitted into Columbia Law School in 2003 at the age of twenty-two, where he went on to graduate near the top of his class.

After graduating law school in 2006, he enlisted in the United States Navy largely because of his uncle, a Cuban immigrant waiter, working in a roof top restaurant at the World Trade Center on 9/11, was burned alive by jet fuel. Minutes later, another uncle, this one on his mother's side, was crushed beneath the rubble as he sat on the Path train when the Trade Center Tower Two collapsed. The senseless inhumanity had haunted him all through his school years. It didn't sit well with his character that it was other boys, from other families, who were fighting and dying to avenge the murders of his family. He was determined to get in it.

He became a member of Seal Team Six in his fourth year of service. He would go on to become an expert sniper with expertise in explosives, counter terrorism, espionage, and close combat. In time he would be able to speak five languages. In combat situations he distinguished himself as a genius at adaptation.

Ernesto Suarez became one of the finest fighting machines in the United States military. He never lost his sense of purpose. If there were dire situations, if there were awful situations with the highest urgency and the most at stake, Ernesto was there. If he wasn't there, he was called upon to get there.

He was by all accounts, a phenomenon. If he was looking for you, he found you. If he decided you weren't going to live through the day, your life insurance policy would be paid out the next morning. He was a bad dude, and people were soon to find out just how bad.

Chapter 3

Bethesda, Maryland

It was just after 8:00 pm in Bethesda, Maryland. Days were getting shorter and shorter in the Eastern time zone. Sunset officially began at 5:11pm. Dark of night, as depressing as it was, fell over the town at 7:16 pm. To make it worse still, a drizzling rain had been falling all day and continued apace.

Two former Spetsnaz, Russia's equivalent to U.S. Special Forces operators, sat in their black Range Rover and watched the house through the stabilized rangefinder of their Russian military binoculars. Tonight was the third night in a row they staked out the house. It was a wealthy street so no one took notice of the ostentatious truck.

Over the decades Spetsnaz commandos have earned a terrifying reputation for brutality. Spetsnaz commandos don't fight. They destroy. To Spetsnaz wherever they stood was martial law, and for the commando, there is no concept of collateral damage. Whatever the two were looking at through their lenses it was a means to an end. For the target, it was almost certainly the end.

The two overweight middle-aged men, jaded by long careers in the business of killing, didn't know why she had been chosen, but they were being paid a truckload of money to put her down.

"Why do they want her dead? She's old lady, not important," one asked of the other.

"I don't know why. The right-wing Americans hate her or something. She did bad to some people not long ago. She's in newspapers. They think she'll be a good statement," came back the answer.

"They should pick someone better. Someone like the others. I don't like killing women. I don't like killing old lady. Is not good thing."

"They have to be cruel to show seriousness or they achieve nothing. Well, anyway, is too late. We are here. We took half money. We cannot fuck up it. We must finish job to get rest of pay."

"But…"

"Shut fuck up. There she is with dog. Do you have it?"

"Dah."

"Show me."

The man held up a small yellow sheet of paper.

"Good. Remember as soon as I put her down you put it on her and get out."

The older woman walked along the sidewalk with her snobby manicured show dog, just as she had done the previous two nights. She was two blocks from the Range Rover. The man in the passenger side of the Range Rover exited the vehicle and began walking in the direction of the woman but on the other side of the street. It was a quiet part of town with near million dollar homes and zero crime statistics; it wasn't unusual for people to be out walking at the hour.

She took no notice of the strolling man. If she did notice him, she was not at all concerned by his presence.

The driver of the black truck assembled the attachments on the front of his weapon and affixed the silencer. When it was attached securely he exited the vehicle and aimed the gun at the old woman with great calm. Clearly he had killed before, many times before.

As the woman passed by a thicket of intentionally uncut hedges and had reached the exact spot they had chosen for the assassination, he fired the weapon hitting the old woman. It was a perfect shot made by a professional. It cut through the T-line, the area in the center of the face between the upper lip and the bottom of the nose, hitting the brain just above the base of the woman's skull. The shot made no sound. She never knew it was coming and she didn't feel a thing.

As soon as she collapsed to the ground the tiny Norfolk terrier, sensing something terrible was happening, took off running.

The approaching man, now a mere twenty yards away, sprinted towards her. He grabbed the dead woman under her arms, lifted her and dragged her body behind the thicket of bushes exactly as planned. He came out of the bushes as if nothing was happening. The man who fired the shot made a left at the corner and pulled over. His accomplice climbed into the truck and calmly put on his seat belt.

"I hate we have to kill old woman. Nice shot in the rain though," he said in a thick Russian accent.

The Range Rover was gone.

Chapter 4

Havana, Cuba

The early, orange-hued evening sights, rhythmic sounds, and traditional smells of Havana in November were different than any other place on earth. The sound of the waves had, rather than a rolling and crashing earthly glory to its sound, a deadened matter of fact bluntness to them, carrying both a hopeful wish and a hard truth about the island. Out to sea and back in again, they thumped against a manmade sea wall caked with a hundred years of mildew and fifty years of waiting on it.

The unrelenting tempo of the waves reminded again and again, there was a promise of joy out there somewhere beyond the shore. But there was also stark knowledge that many a brave wayfarer who took on the tides and tumults of the ninety mile ocean journey seeking that better life, found instead only the crushed futures of what lay on the ocean floor.

A couple arguing in Spanish in a seedy dank alley could be heard mixing almost naturally with guitars and lilting voices singing over a syncopated drum rhythm as if the arguing and the music were planned that way.

The setting sun rays sent ricocheting orange, yellow and azure darts against decaying lead laced faded paint facades. The neoclassical structures, suffering from a half a century of withering neglect, each with foreboding wrought gates and window boxes, appear to be defending themselves from the ever present diesel fuel coughing out of the tailpipes of rickety, clanking, old bus engines and burning leaded gas from the carburetors of a thousand 1950's automobiles.

Wonderful smells of grilling plantains and boiling pots of seafood enchilada waft from open windows and mix intermittently with the ancient odors of the ocean's seaweed and salt air which seem to offer a hope against the city's decay.

No one could have imagined a place like Havana, Cuba. It is absurdly contradictory, always arguing with itself over whether it is audacious or meek, heroic or stupid, beautiful or abhorrent.

Something about its energy is Hemmingway-esque. It has a peculiar, indefatigable, swashbuckling, survivalist nature, always with seemingly no idea where its next meal was coming from. It is beautiful, ugly, heroic and pathetic together at once.

A handsome, bearded, light-skinned man in a native Guayabera shirt and white fedora, who had been loitering against a parked dirty Russian Lada watching Odette Khan intently for twenty five minutes, approached her diagonally from across the street and moved in an angle which placed him directly behind the sixty-something woman sitting at her accustomed bistro table curbside of a sparsely populated sidewalk café. It was her daily routine. Each night she sat there reading the latest issue of the *Juventud Rebelde* (Rebel Youth), a Cuban newspaper of the Union of Young Communist, which Fidel Castro described as 'a paper devoted mainly to youth, with things of interest to young people.' She sighed as she reflected on her escape from justice and her escaped youth. She had no way of knowing what was about to happen but long suspected the day might come.

As the man approached Odessa Khan from behind he took measure of who might witness to what he was moments away from doing. The coast looked clear.

Odessa Khan was born Alice Carter in 1947. She was a member of the Black Panthers and the Black Liberation Army in the very early 1970's. Khan had been convicted of a number of serious crimes but none more serious than the murder of a New Jersey State Trooper in 1973. She spent six years in prison when she escaped and fled to Cuba where Fidel Castro granted her asylum. In 2013 the FBI added her to the Most Wanted Terrorist List; the first woman to be so listed. On that very same day, the

New Jersey Attorney General offered to match a $1 million FBI reward, increasing the total reward for her capture to $2 million.

An Eastern European voice whispered in Odessa Khan's ear, "This is for the policeman you killed, you fucking animal."

The two muffled gunshots in the tight alley had a hollow whistling to them like the sound you'd hear swinging a cardboard Christmas wrapper tube, Fffft-Fffft.

Khan never saw the bearded man and never felt the bullets. Her head pitched forward then back and then forward again crashing hard into the aluminum bistro table top. Her weight took her sideways and she crumbled to the ground, taking down both her own table and the table next to her. An inch and a half piece of skull fragment could be seen bouncing on the ground settling beneath the rear wheel of a rusting 1962 Ford Fairlane parked at the curb twenty paces to her front.

The assassin calmly disappeared into a nearby alleyway.

A terrified woman, hands trembling and voice breaking, with tears rolling down her cheek, explained in Spanish to the Policia what happened next. "The man in the white hat rolled her over face up. She was already dead, her head pieces were shot everywhere, but he took a yellow piece of paper from his pocket and laid it on her chest. He took out a knife from his pant leg and stabbed her in her heart right through the yellow paper. He never ran. He stood and calmly walked down that ally over there. He left the knife and paper pinned to her. Who does such a terrible thing?"

Chapter 5

Upper West Side in Manhattan, New York

Karma teaches many lessons. Among the foremost is the realization that it is impossible to build one's own Utopia on the misery of others. The misery you create comes back around. It comes without a timetable, but it comes around just the same.

The newly retired septuagenarian professor hit the floor like only a man who had been shot in the kneecap hits the floor.

First it appeared as if the bespectacled criminal activist stepped on a live wire, like a man who had just been electrocuted. The human body, even one of a seventy year old, has a remarkable ability to move before the brain tells it to. But the brain catches up. The English professor wasn't jumping at all; he was collapsing to the floor. Whatever the physics, Will Myers' seventy-one-year-old body hadn't moved this quick in over four decades.

Before the disoriented one-time weatherman could scream, one of the two burly men who had been waiting for him inside the lobby of his Manhattan apartment building punched him quickly in the face with the fighting skill of a professional MMA fighter who pounds his opponent after he hits the canvass. Only for Myers, there would be no referee to stop the bout.

The same muscular, fat-fingered, tattooed man then thrust a tee shirt deep into a dazed, nearly knocked out, Myer's mouth. With an almost dance-like rhythmic movement the controlling assailant placed the cold silencer extension of his black pistol square in the middle of Myer's forehead. He had clearly done this before.

He put one finger up to his own lips and pushed the air through them, "Shhhh." He then calmly assured Myers in a thick Slavic accent that he would kill him if he "Make a fackin sound."

Myers was an infamous 1960's radical academic who lived his adult life in the whimsical world of intangible thought and personal unaccountability. His was a phantasmal existence, a fantastical Utopian brew of glorious socialist possibilities and communist political theory. His was a life of demanding tolerance by intolerance, love thy neighbor in that house or I'll blow up your house sort of philosophy. But something told him, in no uncertain terms that this wasn't the theoretical world of liberal higher education, Trotskyism in weekly wine bottle meetings and editorial letter writing. Something profound spoke into his ear. Something desperately real life told him these were professionals and he was in real trouble. His circumstance spoke but a single word…karma.

Myers tried mightily to retain consciousness but he was quickly falling into throws of shock. Even though the voice in his now throbbing head was saying 'karma,' he didn't yet realize how much existential trouble he was in.

He was trying to manage events and mentally grapple with the possible why of it all, but despite the quickly escalating pain, something told him not to move.

Myers was stuck in between the human instincts of fight or flight and he was trapped. He didn't know how he knew to remain still or why, he just knew and he was going to comply. Myers, the sixties and seventies dissident bomber of police and government buildings, began praying to a god he mocked and who he swore didn't exist. With an abandoned feeling of unrequited prayer, with an agnostically apolitical cold pistol pressed to the center of his forehead, he went quiet and limp.

Will Myers, for the decades of the sixties, seventies, and eighties, was one of the most hated men in America. As a founding member of the

Weather Underground, a politically far-left, homegrown terror group, he attacked the United States within its very own boarders.

Born in the 1940's he was currently a retired adjunct professor at Columbia University. The visceral nationwide hatred for him came behind the activities of the Weather Underground and their revolutionary activities on behalf of black power and opposition to the Vietnam War. He was a high visibility terrorist, who in the eyes of most Americans, had gotten away with it. Indeed he prospered personally from the unapologetic, unrepentant violence against his own people.

His group of radicals became an internationally supported terrorist outfit which declared a 'State of War' against the United States government, after which they conducted a campaign of destruction, bombings, and rioting through the mid-seventies. They were responsible for roughly seventy bombings of government buildings and banks, one of which destroyed a statue dedicated to police casualties.

They had a self-described cause of peace and for it they were willing to kill. For the bombing of the United States Capitol on March 1, 1971, they issued a statement that it was 'in protest of the U.S. invasion of Laos.'

For the bombing of the Pentagon on May 19, 1972, they issued a statement that it was 'in retaliation for the U.S. bombing raid in Hanoi.'

For the January 29, 1975 bombing of the United States Department of State building, the group stated it was 'in response to the escalation in Vietnam.'

The group would go on to bomb a San Francisco Police Department building after which Myers himself offered an explanation as to what the Weather Underground was all about: Kill all the rich people. Break up their cars and apartments. Bring the revolution home. Kill your parents. That's where it's at really.

As he lay on the dirty, cold, black and white tiles of his turn of the century apartment vestibule, all of it was swirling around, coming back to haunt him in his moment of agony was a internalized perverse awareness of karma.

Seeing that Myers was fully under the control of his muscle man, the dark-haired, dark-eyed man who fired the bullet into his knee emerged into view from the Alfred Hitchcock-like shadow of the marble and black iron stairwell, closing in with a wry, remarkably unfeeling smile. He moved slowly and with a certainty of power reflecting the confidence of a man knowing he was indisputably in charge of events and upon speaking, confirmed to Myers his assumption of the professionalism with which the supine professor was dealing.

Getting at least part of his wits about him, he did everything he could think of not to move despite the realization of steadily increasing physical pain. In a bizarre moment, within a bizarre series of moments, Myers couldn't help but notice how thick, how black, and how unkempt the eyebrows of his captor were. This was surreal. This was real. The thought quickly passed.

The beastly shooter leaned directly over Myers, and in the same eastern European tongue as the man currently pressing the pistol to his head, said, "I'm a police officer. I'm not from this country. I have been paid many thousands of dollars to come visit you and do this to you today, but I want you to know I would do it for free."

The assailant's voice got tighter and more angry. "Look in my eyes. You hate police, right? You tried many times to kill police, right? You didn't care about their wives, their children, right? I'm a police officer."

Pointing his pistol at Myers' bloody, shredded knee, the Slavic cop's voice softened. Ever so cavalierly he asked rhetorically, "It hurts, yes? Do you know why I shot you?"

Myers didn't have an earthly clue how to respond so he did what anyone would do; he shook his head with a sort of begging confusion, side to side in demonstrative fear, while simultaneously inhaling whatever air he could suck in through his grimacing cheeks and gritted teeth in a feeble attempt to manage the pain of the gunshot wound.

He kept asking himself why it was that he was in the position he was in. How did it come to this? This is America he assured himself. Cruelty like this happens in communist regimes he thought to himself. The irony was apparently lost on the injured, geriatric man lying in a growing pool of his own escaping blood.

'Where is law enforcement?' he hoped against all hope. Surely they heard the commotion. He begged internally of circumstance itself, 'please get me out of this somehow.' But he'd been thumbing his nose at law enforcement and the law, at circumstance, for decades. Somehow he had thought the very nation of laws he flouted would be there if ever he needed it.

Deep down, he now knew otherwise. The instant his assailer identified himself as a policeman he knew neither the country he so loathed but thrived in, the god he so dismissed as fantasy but cried to now, nor the cops he tried so often to kill, would protect him from this man and this moment. He was up against karma alone and he had to answer for his crimes.

The man asked in a thick, guttural throated accent a second time, "C'mon professor, don't piss me off. I ask you a question…I don't have time. I cannot stay here. Do you know why you are in the shit?"

The rugged overweight cop reached down and slapped Myers face, hard with an open hand. Myers head slammed into the dirty tiled floor. Myers thought he smelled the dank smell of urine in the dirty shadows under the stairs. He had. He just didn't realize it was his own.

Myers couldn't figure out what to do so he did what came naturally. He shook his head no.

Before Myers intended negative head shake came fully to a stop, the vicious man fired a second bullet into Myers same knee. Flesh, blood and bone spit from the limb and spattered on the subway tiled walls of the vestibule. Myers noticed the blood splatter on the wall. It all looked like a bad movie where the blood leaves a symmetrical clue for investigators. His back went violently rigid and his eyes bulged. He screamed with a force so aggressive it felt like his chest would explode. The muffled rebel yell didn't do a thing. The tee shirt being forced even deeper into his throat rendered it mute.

He knew he was out of options and sensed he was out of time. He instinctually tried to get free or perhaps, in some small way, it would be a victory just to get up off the tile.

He screamed again but this time with a far less intense thrust to his voice. This time it had a combination of utter agony, a plea for mercy, a fateful resolve and a final sense of exhaling terror only a man believing he was in the course of dying could understand. No one heard except the two men in the vestibule and they weren't interested.

The muscle man let Myers wiggle for a second. Then he yanked Myers back down to a supine position on the floor and jammed his knee into Myers chest, resting the weight of his two hundred and thirty pound frame on his enfeebled prisoner.

Myers couldn't help what he was doing. He writhed in pain and struggled to get free but it didn't matter. He was pinned and he knew it. The muscle man had clearly done this before, many times before. He was just too powerful and Myers was weakening fast from the blood loss. Like a struggling weasel caught in a bear trap, exhausted, he was out of fight. He could feel the calluses on the hands of the muscled man restricting his arms. Rendered motionless, the weasel exhaled and went limp.

Before he could finally pass out, the shooter violently grabbed Myers cheeks and drew his face closer to his own grimacing, menacing face.

"I assume you already know why I shot you Professor…now twice… but I want to be clear. I want you to know. I shot you because you a coward piece of shit. I wish I had more time to make you suffer. You tried to kill cops with bombs as they slept, not my cops, but cops, not my brothers, but fathers and brothers. When you blew up that police station and planted all those explosives you did not care who died. You ran away and hid. You are a coward and deserve to die this way."

Staring now into Myers soul in a quiet state of rage, the Slavic officer reached into his back pocket and pulled out a yellow piece of paper. He unfolded it, held it inches from Myers eyes, and told him to read it.

Myers looked at it in horror, not knowing exactly what would happen next, but knowing full well it would cause him great pain to go along with the already unbearable pain he was in.

It read. "You wanted a revolution. Welcome to the revolution."

The man with the pistol, the cop from some other place on the other side of earth, held that yellow statement in front of Myers for a few seconds more. The cop stared directly into Myers eyes so as to make sure the man lying in well-deserved agony, understood every ounce of its meaning.

He stood and pointed the pistol at Myers face. All three men knew this would be Myers last second alive. "Your wife is next."

The killer was referring to Myers' wife, another radical terrorist, Barbara Douglas. She had been in on the bombings and the riots.

A forlorn look came over Myers. It would last only a second, but he thought to himself a terrifying contemplation, that perhaps this instant, this reality, would be the sentient underpinning of all his future eternity. He thought to himself that no one would care. He thought he wished he hadn't said the word, "pig" so often. Could it be that hell is actually dying and realizing you're forever an eternal scumbag?

Maybe the difference between heaven and hell is the last thing you think about yourself. Was it a life of honor or a life devoid of it? Maybe the definition of one's own character is ones eternity.

If it was so for Will Myers on this day, in this last moment, hell would be a reckoning of the two his life had earned. He would find out in a second.

The cop fired a bullet into the bridge of Myers nose.

The shooter handed the muscle man the yellow paper. He had already taken a knife from his pant leg and laid the yellow paper on the torso of Myers faceless body and stabbed through the paper affixing it to his chest.

The men were gone.

Chapter 6

Bethesda, Maryland

*I*t was 7:00 am on one of those cold November mornings where the season's first icy rain snaps and pings on the hands and face not yet ready for winter. It was not quite snow, but too cold to stay rain and the wind pushed it sideways. It was the kind of morning that everyone hates, but old men hate more. It was the stinging bite on the skin which aggravates by itself, but also acts as the unwelcome foreteller of months of winter to come.

For this old man winter is a daily drag to get to tomorrow and a nightly strain to remember what the silk of spring once felt like on his youth. Faith is a talent in winter.

There could be no other reason an old man would be out that early in the morning than his wife's toy poodle needed to relieve himself.

Today the dog wasn't focusing on going. The old man didn't want to be outside in the biting drizzle a minute longer than absolutely necessary and he was telling the dog exactly that with extreme prejudice. "C'mon ya little creep. Ya see it's raining. Let's go."

The dog was distracted however and unusually antsy. He interrupted the old man's scolding by barking in the direction of a group of thick hedges. The old man didn't get the message the dog was sending. He just got angrier.

Then the old man noticed another small dog whimpering about twenty feet away on the other side of the hedgerow at which his own dog had been directing his fuss. The old man approached the stray. "Oh, OK. It's alright pup. It's OK. We'll find your owner. Come on…Come on. It's OK."

The stray circled away from the old man. It looked like he was about to make a break for it and the old man thought to cut off his escape. He walked around the largest hedge and turned to the other side of the thicket.

"What the F..? Oh my God." After a moment, he took out his phone.

Operator: "Hello, 911"

Caller: "Hey, there's dead body in the bushes here on Grove Street. I think it's that IRS lady who was in trouble with Congress. I think she's been shot. She's certainly been stabbed. There's a knife sticking out of her chest."

Operator: "What is your name sir? And where are you? I'll be dispatching a patrol car to your location while we speak. Are you near the body? Is the woman breathing?"

Caller: "No, damn it. I just told you. She's dead. It looks like she's been here all night. There's a dog nearby that I think is hers. And you better get somebody out here quick. She has a God damn knife in her with a note stuck to her. I'm in front of 239 Grove Street."

Operator: "A note? What do you mean a note?"

Caller: "A note! A note written on a yellow piece of paper. It looks like someone pinned it to her."

Operator: "Sir, I know this is traumatic for you but I need to know if she is alive or dead. I need to know what is going on there. Tell me about the note. Is it a suicide note? Are there any markings on the note?"

Caller: "You're damn right it's traumatic. I'm out walking my damn dog and I see this IRS lady dead in the bushes. It doesn't get more traumatic than that. Hold on, I'm not next to the body, I was afraid to touch her. But I'm pretty sure it's that IRS woman, Laura Turner. She's definitely dead, though. Her hands are blue and her face appears to be swollen. She's dead, alright."

Operator: "Are there markings on the note?"

Caller: "Hold on. I'm walking over there now."

Operator: "Very well"

Caller: "Holy shit! Yeah there's writing on the note and it's got a knife right through the middle of it. It says, 'You wanted to single out people for punishment. You just got singled out. Welcome to the revolution.' This is some sick shit here."

Operator: "Can you repeat that sir?"

Caller: "Aw shit, it says you wanted to single out people for punishment. You just got singled out. Welcome to the revolution."

Operator: "Sir please stay on the line. There's a car on the way."

Caller: "He's pulling up now, thanks. Officer, she's over there in the bushes. I think it's that IRS woman, Laura Turner."

Chapter 7

Fort Myers, Florida

"Byrnes, what?" That's how Roland Byrnes, forty-one year old, a long-haired, big-bearded, surly, cranky man, always answered his phone. Most days Rolly, as he was known to his friends, spent sitting behind his house with his feet dangling in his temperature-controlled swimming pool. His quiet time was committed to his mastiff and reading books, as many as he could find, about anything but military operations or anything that had the word "blood" in it. For most Americans escapism was a brief respite from daily living. For Rolly getting away mentally was the antidote to the unrelenting poisoning which no human being can continue long to swallow and still move about free from derangement. Most live life vicariously, Rolly lived in the absolute reality of war. He found books and his mastiff were the only way he could escape his own thoughts, mostly about the last military operation.

"Three Ravens," came back the female voice on the other end.

Rolly's retort was curt and abrupt; he threw his library copy of *Pride and Prejudice* to the ground. "I don't work there anymore." He hung up the phone and picked up his Pabst Blue Ribbon beer and began guzzling.

The phone immediately rang again.

"Three Ravens. The old man called Three Ravens himself. He knows you quit, but he asked for you specifically."

"Tell him to go fuck himself." Rolly hung up again.

Rolly was by all accounts the most dangerous man in the world. As an Army Sniper he had to his credit more than one hundred and thirty confirmed kills. It was said that he killed thirteen men in hand-to-hand fighting. Three of those happened in one tight Afghan kitchen for which he was issued his second Distinguished Service Award, the U.S. Army's recognition for extreme gallantry and risk of life in actual combat with an armed enemy force. Actions that merit the Distinguished Service Cross must be of such a high degree that they are above those required for all other U.S. combat decorations but do not meet the criteria for the Medal of Honor.

When Rolly was in full formal dress he drew the attention of everyone in whatever room he was standing. Multi-star generals would stop what they were doing and jealously stare at the medals, badges, and awards all over his chest plate and sleeves. Everyone above the rank of major knew his name. Most under the rank of major heard some story of his valor. He was a legend.

In addition to the pair of Distinguished Service Crosses, which alone is the glitter of envy for anyone who knows what they are, he had been awarded medals by the people of the United States, "for extraordinary heroism not justifying the Medal of Honor; and the act or acts of heroism must have been so notable and have involved risk of life so extraordinary as to set the individual apart from his or her comrades."

There were medals for achievement, good service, commendation medals, badges for Distinguished Shooter Rifle, Distinguish Shooter Pistol, International Distinguished Shooter, and the topper, the one that made all snipers envious, and respectful, The President's One Hundred Brassard, awarded to the 100 top-scoring military and civilian shooters in the President's Pistol and President's Rifle Matches.

Recruited into the CIA from the Navy Seals, he would prove in any conflict an uncanny ability to "get there first." It was said he had a sixth sense for the bad guy and dispatched justice in lethal light speed.

He was considered a personal friend of the former president, who was called 'Iceman' in his time in the White House, but he felt wholly unloved by the current president.

He in turn hated the current 'Man.' He never referred to the office holder by his call name or even his birth name. He simply and disdainfully called him Man. The hatred of the current president by Rolly, a witness to so many American deaths in Iran and Iraq, grew out of what he felt was the president's cowardice. This sense of the Man came from the specific White House stand down order in Syria in which the initiative of an op was abandoned for fear of collateral damage to a nearby village. Rolly knew this to be a political decision at the diplomatic level concerning the placation of Russia. He was certain it was acquiescence to the Russians. His heroic young men had been sacrificed in a damn legacy deal which carelessly and callously resulted in an attack on the now exposed American position; unforgivably leaving nineteen American soldiers to die.

Upon returning with just seven survivors, and sickened by the idea that he had lost nineteen great individuals, brothers in his charge, Rolly immediately resigned his position at the CIA. The incident scarred him deeply, the depths of which he could not reconcile with himself as their leader. He hadn't slept much since.

The phone rang a third time. "Rolly. It's Nesto. What the fuck is going on? You need to get to the building."

"No. I'm done, Nesto. Fuck them," Rolly snapped back. But curiosity got the better of him. "What's it about, anyway?"

"I don't know the whole story yet but it's serious, the worst kind of serious. The Old Man asked for you directly. He wants the three of us on this, only us. It was he who called for us. We're trying to get Palmer out here too but we can't find him. You need to get here."

"Fuck him," Rolly jumped back into his obstinacy. "I don't work for that fucking coward anymore. Tell him to find someone else he can leave for dead when Putin or the Mullahs rattle their friggin sabers. I'm not coming."

"Dude, forget about him. This is about an attack on the homeland. It's about to happen and it's going to be a thousand times larger than 9/11. That's what I know. I don't have details but I was told the threat is real and already in fuckin' motion. They're waiting till the three of us are assembled."

Without pause between sentences Rolly put down the hammer. "No, I'm done. I'm sorry Nesto, there's no second way. I would never leave you out there alone, you know that, but I can't work for that weak prick another day."

Nesto had known Rolly for nearly a decade. He knew when Rolly said those three words, no second way, the gun had yet to be invented which could break his will. "I'm sorry Rolly."

"Me too, Nesto. I'm praying for you."

Two sips into his newly opened can of PBR, the phone rang yet again. Rolly loved Nesto's tenacity but before he could shut it down he noticed it was a number flashing on his phone screen that he hadn't seen before. He answered it as he had for fifteen years. "Byrnes,…

Hold for the President of the United States." The phone went silent. Rolly hung up.

The phone rang again. "Look, tell the president I'm retired."

"Rolly, hold on a second, it's me," the president said matter-of-factly.

Rolly shocked himself by how fast he instinctively reacted as he jumped to his feet. Never before had the President called him directly.

"I'm calling you directly because the country needs you. I know how you feel about me personally, but I'm asking you to put it aside. It's that important to the nation. To the world, really."

Rolly was a pure patriot more than he was a pure man. To him duty was spontaneous, as common as breathing. However, it wasn't a blind following kind of duty. Many a lesser commander tested him and lost on this point. Following blindly was following badly. The man on the other end of the phone, the leader of the free world, just got himself a face full of it.

To Rolly, honor was the exercise of duty and it pinned its existence on a creed written in his soul. It rested on but two words; "I must" and it superseded everything.

Everything he trained for and everything he believed in, rushed over him. Something huge was happening he was certain of and he was incapable of refusing his service. He was powerless.

"I'm on my way, Sir," softly spoke the voice of a determined soldier, a warrior already fully engaged.

"Thanks," was all the words a sheepish president could muster.

Chapter 8

Reno, Nevada

Calvin Berpa was the shallowest kind of man, a political appointee who lived entirely in the perfunctory. Never were shortcomings more apparent than in his 'I'm here for show' meetings at the Bureau of Land Management's (BLM) Nevada State office.

Berpa so hated the people in those town hall meetings, especially the ranchers. He hated them for their demands, for their stubbornness and for their bluntness. When he wasn't patronizing them, he was calling them morons, hicks, rubes, and assholes when he was angriest. Mostly, he hated them because they were on to him and might very well get in the way of his political ambitions. Although Berpa was raised in Nevada he hated being in the state. Every time his plane landed in Reno his first impulse, his only impulse, was to figure out how best and how soon he could leave it.

The meeting this day was particularly contentious. The ranchers were rambunctious and determined that he answer for the awful behavior of his agents.

Berpa had to be here for this one. This meeting with irate accusatory ranchers was about all the usual complaints. One by one they stood and enunciated their aging grievances: missed court dates and accusations of governmental infringements of their lands and rights. It was as it always was, a continuing exercise of officials overlaying truths with misdirection. But today it was something more. Today the official's main goal was that, with much press coverage, they would not have to address in detail the publicity disaster hovering over them following an armed standoff between BLM agents and a militia group which had gathered from all over the western United States. It was a gun pointing brink of insurrection stemming from what the BLM called 'the cattle gather.'

The federal government's cattle gather, orchestrated under the table and in the shadows, by Berpa and the senior senator from Nevada, involved nearly one hundred of fifty thousand acres of land in Clark County, Nevada whereby the land was closed for the capture, impound, and removal of trespass cattle.

What was so galling to the ranchers was how BLM officials and law enforcement rangers began a roundup of such livestock along with an arrest of a well-known and well-loved rancher. A few days after cattle gather began, a group of protesters, some of them armed, advanced on the BLM's agents conducting it.

The local sheriff negotiated with the rancher and newly confirmed BLM director, Berpa, to release the cattle and de-escalate the armed standoff.

Berpa, a minor man and small-minded political operative for a corrupt state senator, overmatched in the job and in the field, along with his bullying BLM agents, found themselves on the business end of four hundred long guns. They blinked. "Based on information about conditions on the ground and in consultation with law enforcement, we have made a decision to conclude the cattle gather because of our serious concern about the safety of employees and members of the public. We ask that all parties in the area remain peaceful and law-abiding as the BLM and National Park Service work to end the operation in an orderly manner."

He finished the meeting and headed back to his hotel in his rented full-size Chevy Suburban. He showed his face and that was the only goal. He had put in his time. He'd be back in Washington, D.C. drinking gin and tonics and mapping out his political future.

The ranchers and a large part of the American public mocked Berpa mercilessly as a coward and it galled him. It galled him to the core. It wasn't so much the claims of cowardice. He knew he had no courage, but it broke him that the world could so clearly see it.

Embarrassing Berpa was small consolation for the people closest to the land, particularly the ranchers, whose families in some cases had grazed the open land for more than a century. In Nevada, while they hated him like the plague, they had bigger problems. Nevada ranchers considered him public enemy number one and a yellow-bellied bastard, not worth spit. Berpa had to take it in an hour and a half meeting each quarter and then he could run back east to brief the senator and shower off the prairie dust.

At the meeting he was personally accused of massive land grabs in the western parts of the United States. To the ranchers even a blind man could read between these lines. He and the senator claimed the land unsuitable for grazing and cited reasons of endangered species which remarkably were no longer on the endangered species list. The rangers knew Berpa and the senator were pushing them off the land for the benefit of themselves and they wanted anyone who would listen to know it.

Berpa was accused of doing other awful things to get his way. They had videos and film to prove it. They had been using helicopters to run the ranchers' cattle until they collapsed in the heat, which to the fundamental rancher was sacrilegious, an affront to nature herself. It was considered heinous and worthy of scorn akin to that which might be directed at dirty bastards betting on dog fighting in filthy basements. He was accused of using the courts to trap ranchers in inescapable fees and penalties against which their stock would be forfeited for non-payment. This sort of thing was to them tyranny of highest magnitude.

Worse still for Berpa, in the eyes of the ranchers was that he was a weak political appointee, a man with an Ivy League degree in politics, a Masters in International Relations, a man with no real experience and no character. To them, he was the lowest kind of scum.

He had no land management experience. His only connection to the 245 million acres of confiscated open spaces, much of it in the state of Nevada, his resume for facilitating control over that acreage, was his eight years working in the campaign office of the shifty Nevada senator.

Berpa was a bureaucrat, the worst kind of bureaucrat, a bureaucrat with protection who sees a big payday in his future and is more than willing to climb the backs of ordinary people to get to it. To the people trying mightily to get him off their backs, he was a scumbag through and through.

The men of the land knew he was a fraud, a hack, and a shill. They called him out for being the tool of fraud in the Senate, a powerful majority leader with his designs on the land they had occupied for generations. They knew what he was doing and it ate them up inside. They knew deep down they had no recourse but to swallow his injustices. The media was uninterested or worse, complicit. Berpa had the Senate, the newspapers, and the courts. He could feel their disdain or more specifically their hatred but could care less. He believed his insulation to be impenetrable.

The only disquiet a man like Berpa feels has nothing to do with his conscience, less with his honor. It had to do with the light of day. Only that in the light of truth he might not get the prize he wanted so badly. Nowhere was this light shown brighter than in Nevada and he hated the people of Nevada for shining it on him.

"Fuck 'em," Berpa thought to himself. Any discomfort he might have felt under the lamp would be over in a few hours when his scheduled first-class flight back to the cesspool of DC would take him away from the land he hated most, but the land he wanted badly for what it could bring in wealth for the senator and himself.

Berpa looked at his watch for the millionth time. It was 8:40 am. His flight was in six short hours. He'd be back in DC for dinner and he couldn't wait. He had time for a nap.

The tiny Sheraton Hotel cleaning maid knocked on the door in familiar fashion. Knock, knock, knock, "housekeeping," she said in her heavy Spanish accent, the words rolling off her lips five inches away from the closed hotel door. Thirty seconds passed. Knock, knock, knock, "housekeeping." Still no answer came back from inside the hotel room. She waited ten seconds in the event the guest might come to the door.

Courtesies and protocol having been met, the diminutive maid reached for her master key attached to her hip by a string and opened the door.

The guest inside lying on the bed was supposed to have checked out 12:00 but there he was sleeping, fully clothed on the bed.

"Excuse me, Housekeeping...Sir." She took two steps inside the room and let out a Hitchcock movie-like scream so loud it hurt her own ears.

The little lady spun around and thought to run out as something perverse in her demanded she look at the man. The blood was everywhere, almost as if it was intended to be everywhere. The man on the bed was wholly unidentifiable having been shot in the face more than once. She didn't know a thing about the caliber of bullets, but she knew the man had no face. Whoever shot the man was not easily satisfied. It wasn't enough that his face and head was scattered about the room. Whoever did this murder wanted to make sure that whoever happened upon him would know he had been killed and once dead, had been killed again.

The maid leaned in over the man. His body was riddled with bullet holes. There had to be twenty-five bullet holes in the man's body, maybe a hundred the body was so disfigured. Whoever killed him wanted to make a statement. Something more affecting than the killing of a disliked man, something profound.

Whatever that statement was it would be revealed on a yellow piece of legal paper pinned by a knife to the dead man's chest.

The yellow paper with the knife driven through it shook any curiosity the tiny chamber maid might have experienced. This was satanic stuff. She ran out of the room clutching a cross dangling from a thin necklace her grandmother had given to her at her First Holy Communion more than fifty years prior. Screaming and crying she bolted from the room while repeating over and over in Spanish, "Ha recibido un disparo! Ha recibido un disparo!"

She had absolutely no intention of waiting for anyone to arrive nor did she want to remain on the floor until the elevator arrived. Her cracking, high-pitched voice could be heard as it faded and disappeared down the hotel stairs.

Chapter 9

White Sulfur Springs, West Virginia

The sweetest thoughts of the warrior are those not racing towards the kill nor racing from a kill. The quiet mind is rare and rich to the man who knows war.

The tall, quiet man loved the stillness of mornings by the lake. The lake was what sanity looked like and what peace sounded like. If he did nothing else during the day he made darn sure he took the pilgrimage every morning from his bedroom down to the lakeside deck.

He built his beloved house and surrounding deck himself using seven, forty-foot abandoned truck trailers and it was perfect.

The house was built into the lakeside hill using not much more than those containers and his uncontainable imagination for seeing things where no one saw them and building things from what only he could see.

The back of the house, six abandoned trailers stacked three over three, had all the lake side facing metal doors cut away and replaced by floor to ceiling glass, including center glass doors up and down. A seventh trailer led from the lower part of the main house out to the deck. The top of the trailer leading to his precious deck had a wire porch wrap-around on top, reminiscent of the upper deck of a houseboat. The entire house was wrapped in a thin, Scandinavian-style wood siding, giving it clean, and almost Zen-like lines.

From the lake the boaters could see three Victorian spiral staircases inside the house which its builder recovered from the demolition of an eighteenth-century hotel in Richmond, Virginia. When the house was lit up at night, three hundred yards of the lake had a soft yellow orange hue cast over it. On overcast nights it had a wonderful way of appearing as if it was a rare strawberry moon providing the peacefulness.

The deck sat on cement pylons which fed into the lower level of the house and were perched eight feet above water facing east and protruded out sixteen feet into the lake. There sat a single teak Adirondack chair, side table, and a single red-potted plant. It was the place where sunrises went. He had water to the left, right, and front. He had time. He loved sitting there. He recuperated there. He recovered.

It was here on his deck in his Adirondack chair where he spent his mornings. He loved the lake side at sun up. He was tired of the noise, the gunfire, the explosions, men screaming murder as they charged, men screaming for their mothers after the charge. While he was home if there was noise to be made he was going to make it.

From the lake the house had the appearance of a giant houseboat in dock and that was what was he was going for. It was a perfect place to entertain company even though the owner never had company, at least as far as the township people could tell. They all wanted to visit, especially the single women, but none had the courage to ask. The quiet giant was too quiet. He might be dangerous, they said to one another.

It was here that Aiden Palmer believed once again that beauty was possible.

It was Aiden's reminder that beauty and peace were possible; maybe there actually was a God. He thought about that a lot and concluded that a god existed. He couldn't imagine the universe could accidently produce humanity capable of contemplating its own existence and then so much of its energy trying to kill itself off.

He was a religious man, an unaffiliated religious man, and the lakeside was his church. He called it the Church of Agitation to the few lucky enough to call him friend.

He kept his religion and his church to himself. His church was an argumentative place. He took on his god for his underachieving. How could a god claim any throne and allow for so much evil in the world?

Aiden was a big dude, real big at 6'4". He went wherever he wanted at two hundred forty pounds. If the description of stoic ever applied to one man, it was Aiden Palmer.

The kids and teens of the town that saw the bearded giant sitting beside the lake every morning called him Sasquatch. Never to his face of course. The older folks in town, to whom he was exceedingly polite, called him Mr. Palmer. No one knew what the quiet man did when he disappeared for months at a time, but half suspected he was a criminal and the other half suspected he was a noble loner, an errant knight. Whatever he was, he sure was a mysterious stranger.

Aiden had been a Navy brat who was shuttled around the globe, schooling on US military bases wherever his father, Joe, a submariner was stationed at the time. An exceptional mathematician with an unusually creative mind granted him acceptance into West Point to study engineering and physics, graduating third in his class. He was defensive end and captain for the Black Knights football team. An NFL scout wrote of the defensive end, "Palmer has the fastest hands I've ever seen in my three decades of scouting. His stamina is remarkable and he's mean as hell. He appears impervious to pain and while he's obviously not as fast as the running back, he consistently beats him to the spot. He's at the top of his class academically. I highly recommend drafting this player in the third or fourth round." Aiden had other ideas for his life.

After graduating West Point, Aiden achieved the rank of captain and would mark his career with citations for bravery in the face of the enemy, such as a Silver Star, and awards, including a Purple Heart among other medals too numerous to list.

Despite Aiden's many awards and fitness reports which consistently ranked him at the top of his class and reports of his extraordinary intellect, his real gift, first to the military and then to the CIA, was ending things, mostly the breathing of bad guys. Fluent in a number of languages, including Spanish and Farsi, his natural athleticism and expertise with all manners of weaponry, coupled with the slowest heartbeat imaginable, made him a merchant of death.

It was rumored that every Al Qaeda member in Ramadi had been shown a photo of Aiden, told to remember it and report his whereabouts to the Al Qaeda hierarchy. There was a reward of one hundred thousand dollars for the terrorist who could kill Aiden Palmer. Among themselves, the terrorists would say, "If you see the guy in the photo, you're already dead."

As he was enjoying his morning coffee in his accustomed lakeside Adirondack chair the phone in his pocket rang. A female voice on the other end said two words. "Three Ravens."

The large man, as cool as ever, looked to the sky. "Looks like rain" he said to the god he had just been admonishing. He softly sipped his coffee, took a look out over the lake to pin its beauty to his memory should it be the last time he laid his eyes upon it, put his phone back in his pocket, tossed the contents of his coffee cup into the lakeside sand, and turned back to the house.

Chapter 10

CIA - Fairfax, Virginia

Ernesto Suarez and a newly clean-shaven Aiden Palmer were already seated in the outer lobby of the CIA office they had been beckoned to when an also newly shaven Roland Byrnes walked in.

Both men bounded from their seat and the three shook hands in the middle of the room.

The trust in and affection for each other was palpable. Nothing shallow or perfunctory existed between these warriors who had been so often by each other in the direst of circumstances with so much on the line. Men who've been in foxholes together greet each other differently. In the middle of the room the three men took each other's hands while placing their respective off hands on the others shoulder or forearm. They looked each other square in the eye with a piercing affinity. There was no doubt they had been together in the worst possible scenarios and immediately experienced a sense of invincibility just by the act of being together again. They knew the thing only soldiers know about camaraderie in war. The mark of the "band of brothers" is not that they would lay down their lives for one another when the time comes, but that having been proven to each survivor of the deadly struggle together, it never needs mentioning. Its honor needs no faith, its trust no verifying and the universal nobility of each is forever presupposed.

"What do you know, Nesto?" Rolly asked.

"Not much. I know there have been some murders, but there is something else here Rolly."

"Well we'll find out soon enough," chimed Aiden, ever the cool customer.

The door opened and a gorgeous, fiery red-haired woman in a gray, checked pencil skirt, tight silk blouse, and black pumps stood holding the door ajar. "Right this way, gentlemen."

As she led them down a corridor past several glass enclosed offices, Rolly whispered in Nesto's ear while nodding his approval at the feminine figure guiding them, "Whoa!"

"Really Rolly, even now?" Nesto asked rhetorically.

"Hey goober, I'm retired, I'm not dead."

The beautiful red head led the group towards two large mahogany doors. As she approached the conference room doors she turned, "Right this way, gentlemen. You'll be meeting with three people who will brief you. The Deputy Director, one representative from the Office of Advanced Analytics, and an expert from The Office of Special Activities."

"Special Activities?" Nesto queried.

"Yes, the Office of Special Activities is part of our Directorate for Science and Technology."

Rolly moved into the conversation, "Science and Technology, is that even a thing?"

"I'm not at liberty to discuss anything about which you are about to hear. I don't know why you are here or anything about what you are to discuss. Good luck, gentlemen" said the beautiful, fiery red-haired woman as she held the door to the conference room ajar. Then she disappeared.

"Come in, come in. Time is not on our side, gentlemen," a voiced boomed from inside.

"I'm Deputy Director Lou Capps. This is Morty Cantrowicz from Advanced Analytics and that's Katy Quigley from The Office of Special Activities." Everyone nodded their respective greetings.

Other than being overweight, Capps was an almost unnoticeable man, a completely non-descript man of forty none years. He had never been an operative. He had never been in the field nor was he an analyst. He was a political appointee who spent his early years as a campaign operative for a four-term congressman and now a two-term senator. The Ravens knew the type. They could smell a functionary a million miles away.

"Gentlemen, sit down. What I'm about to tell you and show you is obviously top secret. First picture please," Capps called to someone unseen responsible for providing the imagery on an eighty-inch high definition television screen. An image of a dead William Myers as the police found him appeared on the television.

Capps began, "This is William Myers, the sixties radical and…"

"What's that yellow paper on his chest?" Rolly interrupted.

"Very good, Mr. Byrnes. It's a handwritten note which read "You wanted a revolution. Welcome to the revolution."

"Wait a minute," Aiden jumped in. "The William Myers? The William Myers who bombed the Capital Building and the police building in San Francisco? The personal friend of the President? That William Myers?"

"I knew it," an obviously angered Rolly said as he punched the conference room table with the base of his closed fist and wiped away the little bit of spit which had leaped from his mouth in the outburst. "That selfish prick. This is about a damn friend of his. A scumbag to boot who got what he deserved. This is a job for the FBI, not us. I knew it. His fucking friend… Fuck! I hate that fucking guy."

"No Rolly, it's not about a friend."

Everyone turned to the doorway where the president of the United States and his most senior advisor, Hannah Gafar, had quietly entered. Each person in the room leapt to their feet, each to a stance of military attention.

"It's far, far…far more than that," the President said softly, not at all acknowledging Rolly's slanderous, character assassinating remark against him.

"I came by to see the three of you for a moment to tell you how grateful I am in advance of the dangerous mission you are about to undertake and to assure you of its urgency. Don't let us down fellas. Before you leave here you will be issued a number. If you call it will go to two people simultaneously, to the CIA Director and to me. If there is anything you need, you'll have it. Rolly, you have the ball."

"Director Capps anything these men need they're to have it, understand?"

The Director nodded in the affirmative, "They'll have it, Sir."

The President looked deeply into each man's eyes; first to Aiden, then Nesto, and lastly to Rolly, where he held his glare for several seconds. "Good luck, Gentlemen." The president turned and with his trusted advisor, Hannah, walked out of the room.

Stunned silence took over the conference room. Everyone remained standing at attention for several seconds not exactly knowing how to process the gravity of what had just happened.

Aiden broke the ice and tension. "Nice going Rolly. I bet it's been a long time since anyone has called the president a selfish prick to his face." Rolly shrugged his shoulders and nodded his tilted head as if to say 'oops.'

The air having settled back a bit, Director Capps refocused everyone. "Shall we continue gentlemen?" and paused for everyone to sit.

"Next picture, please."

"This is Laura Turner, former IRS employee. She was murdered two nights ago. She had a similar note pinned to her chest. Next picture, please. This is Conrad Berpa, the director of the Bureau of Land Management. He was murdered yesterday afternoon and when he was found he too had a yellow paper pinned to his chest. Next picture, please. This is Odessa Khan, AKA Alice Carter. Khan killed a New Jersey state trooper, later escaped and fled to Cuba where Fidel Castro granted her asylum. She was shot and killed in a café in Havana three nights ago. A similar yellow note was stabbed into her chest. Four murders in three nights all connected by the yellow paper pinned to the victims."

"So you have the murders of some assholes. Why us?" Rolly asked dismissively.

Capps responded professionally, "Gentlemen, this is Katy Quigley. She works for our Division of Special Activities, Science and Technology." His voice went heavy, an octave deeper, and deadpan for affect, "Her expertise is in nuclear proliferation, dirty bomb making, and the black market."

Capps didn't say another word, he didn't have to. It was completely clear now why they had been called. The use of the words "nuclear" and "black market" sent a sober shiver across the nape of each man's neck. Their tongues went dry. They trained their eyes on the girl who looked young enough to still be in college. They were not going to miss anything she was about to reveal, even in the smallest voice inflection which may convey something important, a single syllable from which might reveal an obscure clue which may aid their cause.

Each of the Three Ravens were charged by their country with the task of not allowing this thing to happen, the thing in motion fifty-four hours ahead of them, a thing they didn't know about until this very instant to happen. Each of The Three Ravens glanced at their respective watches and noted the exact time. Whatever it was that she was about to tell them, whatever the awful circumstances, they knew the clock was ticking.

Katy Quigley was a no-nonsense analyst with the tenacity of a hungry pit bull. It seemed she always had her teeth in a bone. She was a natural born sleuth. As a child her overwhelming curiosity and intellectual boredom often got her into trouble. Quigley's academia was protégé stellar. She graduated at the top of her high school at just 14, and got her Master's degree at 18. Computers were her passion. They were her piano keys, her canvas, her introduction.

She came to the outfit as one of the most gifted and intelligent hackers in the world. Within months she found herself consulting on the most difficult technological security problems her country was facing. While most look at their computer screens and see text and pictures, Quigley saw code and secrets. She was the first female to ever give a presentation at DefCon, one of the world's most prestigious gatherings of hackers. At the CIA, she was a frequent speaker at hacking and security software conferences. She shunned the spotlight and grew to value the contribution she was making to her country...in secret. Invariably wherever she went within the CIA she was asked about her "first female" appearance at DefCon, but she would always maintain that she would like to be known for her work, not for being a female in the field.

Currently Quigley specialized in securing data from end-to-end and this had made her invaluable to the outfit as it looks to protect and uncover secrets. She gets loaned out to a number of federal firms in an effort to secure their online databases. When she attached herself to something, it was either going to capitulate to her or she was going to die trying.

A tiny thing, she stood five feet even and had straight champagne hair and never wore make-up to work, which meant she never wore make-up because she was always working. She didn't care if people liked her or not. Almost everyone deferred to her either for her preparedness or her unwillingness to concede anything. If one pulled out an argumentative knife, she drove over them with an M1A1 Abrams tank.

"Slide one, please."

The slide Quigley requested was a gruesome thing. Photo images of mass murder could never be of another kind. This one was particularly eerie and, despite their long history of combat that each man knew even close-in hand to hand bloody affairs, these images turned their stomachs. Scattered about in a wintery forest setting lay the mangled bodies of twenty men, some with their heads severed from their torsos, two burned unrecognizably, several shot, one was hanging from a tree limb. Men had their hands cut off and laid upon their own eyes, one over his own mouth. Tongues had been cut out. These men hadn't been killed in a shootout. These men had been systematically killed, obviously slowly in some cases. This was not a cult thing or a war like thing. The murdered men were all wearing traditional Muslim garb and each eliminated man had a yellow piece of paper affixed to their chest by knife.

Slides two through thirty four were worse. Each image, close-up or wider lens landscape, was more heinous than the last. Quigley described each in detail, in matter-of-fact, cold hard bluntness. When the last image had been shown and the lights in the room were brightened, their faces took on a sickly, slightly sad, wholly worried look. It felt like a line had been crossed, a Rubicon of sorts. This had a pivot to it, a new reality and an historical shift. The three men all had the sinking feeling that it was a world statement. It was exactly that.

Rolly summed up in a fashioned vernacular neither of the other two men would employ, but what each of the three men were indeed thinking. "Shit, it's here. This is the shit that goes on in Syria, in Iraq, not here. Now it's fucking here. It's on us, among us. Only the damn beginning. Shit."

Nesto loved Rolly for his candor and his commitment, but wanted not to go down that road. Pointing to the now blank screen and looking at the pretty neophyte analyst, "You got anything else on this?"

"Anything else?" Quigley asked.

"Got anything else. Any leads? Any intel that can give us a direction? Anything we can use as a jump off?" Nesto asked.

While everyone in the room was digesting the horror of what they were looking at and contemplating what "on us, among us" really implied, and while trying to normalize their breathing, Aiden, ever the cool cat, ever the matter-of-fact processer of data and information, pointed to the screen, "They weren't set upon there. They were taken there," he said. Everyone looked at Aiden waiting for the clue.

"Snow on the ground, no coats, sandals, no socks? Middle of winter but none of them had winter clothes on? Not one? I don't think so. How many photos do you have? Never mind. You have hundreds. I need to see them and I need to get to that site…today. Where is this place?" Pointing to the screen, "Go on."

Nesto thought to himself he was glad Aiden, the voice of calm and reason, was in the room ingesting the dangers into which they were soon to be thrust. How glad Aiden and Rolly would be at his front, side, and back. He turned his eyes back to the cherubic, little analyst.

Quigley glared at her notes although she didn't have to. "The men were found by a hunter just outside of a densely forested place called Huron National Forest. It's about two hundred miles north of Detroit."

Nesto to Aiden's lead, "That looks like a dense ass forest. How were they found?"

Quigley was clearly feeling a little youthful frustration by being interrupted a second time but she was keenly aware of her proper place. She waited a second before continuing, "A hunter saw the smoke from the burning of the two Muslim men and went to investigate."

Nesto pressed, "A hunter? A lone hunter? What was he doing all the way out there by himself?"

A second train of thought crept into Nesto's mind, "Why would they burn those bodies? Who is this hunter? Where is he now? We need to talk to this guy."

A third lane opened up in Nesto's clouded mental highway, "Have any of the dead been identified?"

Rolly chimed in, "Are they Americans or foreigners?"

Nesto climbed over and returned to his yet unanswered question, "Anything else? I'm sure you've had counterterrorism analytic teams on this for the last two days."

Quigley's youth was starting to show. It looked like she knew something, but couldn't say. She looked over to Capps for a bailout.

Capps sensing the staccato questioning was beginning to take the meeting off on a tangent, and away from his control, thought he had to rein it in.

"Our teams have it a significant probability that a right-wing militia group has organized itself into a terror group. We suspect they are primarily ex-military. The killings were textbook insofar as they were organized and the firing lines were triangulated perfectly. They are highly likely to be message targeting. We are focusing our assets in that area. You let us worry about that. It is not the reason you have been brought in."

All three looked at Capps with disdain. They knew a functionary when they saw one and they could recognize a sycophant from a million miles away. Rolly wasn't going to allow this process to be guided. He had enough experience with analysts, "No, we'll worry about that".

To the warrior, among the greatest adversary is his own apparatus of war and when that apparatus is headed by a functionary, they know to be extra careful. When they know that functionary is politically motivated, they know he's not to be trusted. When they know the politically motivated functionary is a sycophantic suck up, usually someone is going lose their life because of it.

They were looking at a forest full of dead Muslims, all dressed in traditional Muslim clothing, all killed by known ISIS methodology and Capps. The political suck up following the current administration's narrative was not even going to look under that rock. He was steering the analysis rather than following it and they knew it.

Aiden, ever curious, ever the analyst out-analyzing the experts, and ever the challenger, wanted to see if he could glean anything from Capp's expression. "Not the reason we were brought in. Are you friggin' serious?"

"Gentlemen," said Capps ignoring Aiden's questioning, talked over the questions with just enough of an authoritative voice to control the conversation without, he'd incorrectly hoped, totally alienating the conversant. "There will be time for all your questions and Ms. Quigley is entirely at your disposal, but I need to introduce Morty Cantrowicz from the Office of Advanced Analytics. He will make it clear why you are here."

As the analyst stood, Capps held up his hand to Cantrowicz as if to tell him to hold on a moment. Capps had spent more than a decade conducting meetings where people were shown or told about dramatic things. He was wise to give the room a second or two to recalibrate and refocus.

"Mr. Cantrowicz," Capps pulled his hand down, "If you please."

Every now and again a man's appearance, his physique, his face, his voice, perfectly fit his occupation. Cantrowicz was such a man. Unlike Quigley, who looked more like a gymnast than a CIA operator, this balding, bespectacled, almost cartoon-like figure with the squeaky voice, looked every bit the analyst.

The little man spoke in an almost feminine lilt, "Gentlemen, what I'm about to tell you is to be kept in the highest confidence. Its national security implications cannot be overstated."

Something resembling dread fell upon The Ravens.

"At the site where these men were found, we also detected exceedingly high levels and low levels, among other things, of Americum-241, Caesium-252, Cobalt-60 and Iridium-192. This portends the distinct possibility that whoever did this, either had with them or stumbled upon it, when they attacked these men what could be, very likely is, the RDD, Radioactive Dispersal Device or, in layman's terms, a dirty bomb."

There it was, the thing that kept every CIA operator, FBI agent, every Homeland Security Officer, and the president of The United States, up at night; the terrifying idea that a dirty bomb was in the open and could be detonated, killing thousands, perhaps hundreds of thousands, of American citizens.

Cantrowicz went on, "In order for a terrorist organization to construct and detonate a dirty bomb it must acquire radioactive material, by stealing it or buying it through illegal channels. There are nine, possibly ten, reactor produced isotopes suitable for radiological dispersal, any combination of which if acquired could become the material for a successful RDD. At the site, we found four of these; plutonium-238, polonium-210, radium-226, and strontium-90."

With but a single guttural sound, 'ugh', Aiden summed up the feeling in the room.

Rolly was first to collect his mind and get himself back from the contemplative doom which overtook each of The Ravens. "Where does this RDD stuff come from? Where the fuck could someone get these isotopes and whatever the hell else is in the damn brew?"

Cantrowicz anticipated the question and began answering it before Rolly even finished asking the question. "Of these sources the U.S. Nuclear Regulatory Commission has estimated that within the U.S. approximately one source is lost, abandoned, or stolen every day of the year. Within the European Union the annual estimate is seventy. There exist thousands of such 'orphan' sources scattered throughout the world, but of those reported lost, no more than an estimated twenty percent can be classified as a potential high security concern."

"Only twenty percent?" Nesto asked sarcastically, not at all expecting an answer. "Well that narrows it down."

Cantrowicz unfazed continued, "Of the elements used in a RDD and crossed against what was found, we believe Russia is the most likely source. Thousands of orphan sources which were lost following the collapse of the Soviet Union constitute the largest, albeit unknown, number of sources, probably belongs to the high security risk category. Noteworthy is the beta emitting strontium-90 sources used in lighthouses in remote areas of Russia."

Rolly couldn't contain himself, "You mean this dirty shit could have come from fucking lighthouses?"

Cantrowicz knew there was no correct answer for such a question so he plowed over the question, "I'm afraid that is exactly the case and in our estimation the most likely source of what we found at the site. In December 2001, three Georgian woodcutters stumbled over such a power generator and dragged it back to their camp site to use it as a heat source. Within hours they suffered from acute radiation sickness and sought hospital treatment. The International Atomic Energy Agency later stated that it contained approximately 40 kilocuries of strontium, equivalent to the amount of radioactivity released immediately after the Chernobyl accident."

"OK," Aiden interrupted, "We know what's in it. How does it get dispersed?"

Cantrowicz had long been thinking exactly that. "Such a speculative, radiological weapon requires combining radioactive material with conventional explosives. The purpose of the weapon is to contaminate the area around the dispersal agent/conventional explosion with radioactive material, serving primarily as a denial device against first responders, leaving civilians to die unattended"

"Nice," Rolly interrupted.

"This kind of weapon, however, should not be confused with a nuclear explosion, such as a fission bomb, which by releasing nuclear energy produces blast effects far in excess of what is achievable by the use of conventional explosives. This is not that. Though an RDD would be designed to disperse radioactive material over a large area, the explosion itself is, by itself, is not likely to use much explosives to produce a large blast. We expect this device to be far less lethal than the hazard posed by the radioactive material we found and inflict manageable damage."

Again Rolly couldn't contain his indignation, "Tell that to the dead and their families."

Nesto overarched Rolly's sarcasm with a much needed dose of logic, "What exactly does happen in such dispersal then, Mr. Cantrowicz?"

"A test explosion and subsequent calculations done by the U.S. Department of Energy found, assuming nothing is done to clean up the affected area and any survivors stay in the affected area for one year, the radiation exposure would be "fairly high" but no longer fatal. Recent analysis of the Chernobyl disaster seems to corroborate this."

Rolly said in sarcastic fashion, "Only a fucking year. Oh…well…that ain't bad. What might this thing look like? "

Cantrowicz came back quick in typical analytic-ease, "It could be anything that holds dynamite. As small as a knapsack or a car bomb scenario. We just don't know. The radioactive traces were pretty solid so we assume it was something smaller than a car, something that could be carried, but honestly we just don't know."

Capps feeling the newly percolating sense of urgency almost desperation and a hint that he was losing control of the meeting, thought it was time to bring it down a notch.

"A dirty bomb is unlikely to cause too many deaths by radiation exposure. Many scientists do not even consider this to be a weapon of mass destruction. Its purpose would presumably be to create psychological chaos and not so much physical harm through mass panic and spread a sense of terror. For this reason dirty bombs are sometimes called "weapons of mass disruption" rather than WMD's and for the same reason we will not refer to this device as a WMD."

Rolly was beginning to boil at the idea that what it is called in the grand scope of things mattered.

Capps continued, "The containment and decontamination of victims, as well as decontamination of the affected areas, might require considerable time and expense, rendering areas partly unusable and causing economic damage. It's this sense of widespread terror that we wish to avoid. And there are sensitive political ramifications."

"Political ramifications?" Rolly had had enough of Capp's cavalier tone and he knew where this was going. "What political ramifications?"

Capps wanted an out but he was trapped, "These men were Muslims, likely killed by Americans."

Aiden's blood was now heating up, "So?"

"So, we have to be careful as we proceed not to adversely affect our perception in the Muslim world."

Rolly was near his breaking point, "Careful? Who gives a shit about perceptions? And the law? What about the idea that there are crazy bastards in this country right now who are capable of mass killings? Fuck perceptions. The dead? What about the dead? Are we wishing to avoid that for perceptions? Oh wait, too late, they're fucking dead!"

Capps couldn't help himself. His academia and condescension had always been a blurred line. "You spent a lot of time in the Middle East and have been fighting a group of people with a particular appearance. Your view of the political sensitivities between Muslims and the West makes it difficult to understand the complexity."

The Three Ravens glanced at one another in disbelief. Capps thought he was dealing with Neanderthal warriors with sticks. He had no idea he was looking at three men who possessed far greater academic prowess than he.

Rolly went right for the jugular, "Look, you fucking mutt, I spent years, not days or weeks, years fighting side by side with Muslims against evil murderers. I fought with great men in Iraq, Afghanistan, and in fucking Syria. Men born there. Muslims, you shit. Men who loved their people and men who died at the hand of other men who looked like they did and who hated their people. Courageous men who fought along with me, not against me or the West or anything else but against evil. Muslims. Fine men who saved my life. So don't talk to us about stupid ass nuanced "appearances" or fucking religious this or fucking that. I don't give a shit about whether they're Muslim or believe in a god that speaks to them from a fucking bong in a closet; this ain't about religion or gods. It's about fucked up men who killed other men in a Minnesota forest, men who are out there still. Oh, and one more thing. If you condescend to us again, I will disregard "complexity" and courtesy and your fucking teeth. I will beat the absolute fuck out of you so you have to eat your sushi with a fucking straw!"

Nesto, seeing Rolly's pressure point had been reached and how close Capps really was to needing a blender to eat, broke into Rolly's diatribe, "Look we need everything you've got on this, who you are looking at, what the counterterrorism guys have, what the nuclear people are saying about what we're looking for, everything the core collectors have, any tradecraft analytics and any analysis you have on the targeted killings. Everything. We'll decide what's useful and what isn't."

Capps responded, "Your job is to find the box, if there even is one. The rest we'll work on. If you have any questions as you go, you let me know."

Rolly's mind rushed back to the reason he had quit the life. He had so often experienced firsthand the fallout when organizational emphasis is placed on secrecy rather than effectiveness. He knew limiting available intel and/or resources always results in operational failure. Operational failure to the bureaucrat sitting at the end of the table meant a blame game. Operational failure to Rolly and his Ravens meant death for them and so many innocents.

"Fuck you, you'll give us everything! And I mean everything. There's no second way." Capps was about to say something, but Rolly bullied his voice over Capps's. "Everything… How'd you get this fucking job?"

Rolly stood. His voice went calm and low. "Look in my eyes you fat fuck so to your core you know I mean what I'm about to say." Rolly paused to allow Capps a moment to connect eyes. "If it goes bad and I get a sense, the slightest bit of a sense, that the reason it went bad is because you had information we needed and chose not to give it to us because of territorial shit, blame insulation, plausible deniability bullshit, or some political agenda, there won't be a place on this fucking earth you'll be able to hide. I'm going to find you, put a bullet in your empty fucking brain and then stick one of those yellow pieces of paper to your chest which says on it, 'This fat fuck killed good people because he didn't give a shit.'"

Capps did what he always did. He relied on the senator. "Mr. Byrnes, Are you threatening me?" Rolly never moved a muscle. Capp's voice began to tremble, "I can assure you I am quite comfortable in my position and so, too, is Senator Schumacher. Look, I know you're the decorated hero type, but what I'm telling you is what my job is, to get as close to the truth about the fallout from such a dirty bomb scenario as I can."

Rolly's hatred of this guy grew exponentially with every word Capps spoke. He still would not recognize the likelihood of multiple American deaths, an anathema to Rolly and the rest of the Ravens, who would each sacrifice their own lives to save a single American life.

All three men knew what this was and what this guy was. They'd seen these lackeys a thousand times before. Whatever this was it was going to be renamed so to protect this administration's open border philosophy and his promise to take in Syrian refugees. This was going to be prioritized behind policy and avoid any risk to the wall of insulation against accepting political blame should these bastards, whoever they were, detonate that dirty stinking bomb. That this man had so low a moral compass disgusted all three men, but none more than Rolly. Capps never saw it coming.

"There is no such thing as closer to the friggin' truth you fucking piece of shit!" Rolly paused for a moment. "Your job is protecting the lives of Americans! Tell the Senator or the President this; there is always either just what happens or there is nonsense. Interpretive whatever is bullshit political spin for we start with an outcome we want and then direct revisions of events and intentions to suit that political outcome. It's the worst kind of corrupt thinking because it supplants the actual truth with your convenient truth to avoid blame and it does no one any good except your damn slithering, slimy, self-preserving, political leeching scumbag selves. God, I hate people like you."

"Give it to him, Rolly!" Nesto thought to himself.

Aiden just ran his fingers through his own hair. He knew there was going to be a lot of killing in the coming days. He just hoped they would be the ones doing do the killing and knew above all else, the sand was fast falling in their hourglass.

Rolly had enough of Capps. He stood up from his chair, walked around to a seated Quigley, reached over her and ripped a blank yellow page from her legal pad. Turning to Capps said, as he held the yellow paper above his shoulder for all to see, "Remember what I said about where this paper will end up."

He aggressively shoved a conference room chair into the back wall. Glancing at Aiden, he nodded and said, "I gotta get out of here before I strangle this asshole right now. I need to make a stop. Meet me at the house," and left the room.

The rest of the occupants in the room fell silent for what seemed an eternity.

Chapter 11

New York City

The Three Ravens "house" was owned by a CIA shell company and hardly the place one would look to find the intellectual epicenter of a CIA location. It was a four-story, cobblestone structure built in 1892 and once served as the U.S. Appraiser's Store, a warehouse for goods waiting customs inspection and later part of the U.S Federal Archive building complex.

The building and grounds were sold and converted to a private residence in 1972.

The structure's frontage had no street exposure. The address of the post-Civil War house showed as Fifty Six and One Half Barrow Street in Greenwich Village, New York City. To access the property one had to walk through a tunneled pathway between Forty Six Barrow Street and Fifty Barrow Street. The corner of the storied building twice housed alcohol establishments which made the address marginally famous for its time; a corner pub originally part of the Keller Hotel built in 1898, later as New York's first leather bar and often cited as the birthplace of disco.

Aiden and Nesto walked through the heavy, clanking door in the courtyard at Fifty Six and One Half Barrow Street and made their way up; first to the three sets of 1892 creaking stairs and then up to the fourth level by way of an ornate wrought iron spiral staircase fit for a fifteenth century palace on the Danube. They entered into an open room of television screens, computer screens, and phone banks all busy conveying images and signals. On one of the phones sat Rolly with his free hand, fist clenched and punching the air in anger.

"Shit. Who else has the story?" He waited until the responding voice had answered his question. "Have they spoken to the White House? Has anyone talked to them about withholding it?"

"Fuck… How long do we have?" Again he waited for his answer, "Thanks."

Aiden and Nesto pretty much knew what it was Rolly was assaulting the innocent oxygen in the room over, but they didn't know how bad it was.

Rolly caught his breath for a second, "OK boys, I've got some good news and some really, really, really fucking terrible news."

Aiden started eliminating possible bad news before he spoke, "Well it's not that the device was dispersed, we'd have heard about it already."

Nesto, knowing what the bad news likely was, needed a positive first, "Give the good news first."

"OK, we have a lead on the Khan murder in Havana. One of our asset guys had her under surveillance at the time of the killing. He got off a clean photo of the killer and ran it. Name is Constantin Pokolov. A Russian and a bad dude too. Ukrainian by birth, he was Spetsnaz, KGB, all the black bag stuff. From what they know of him and what they can gather from events, they believe he was contracted for the hit on Khan."

"The news gets better. We may have an opening. Apparently, Pokolov left Cuba and our man followed him to Culebra Island, a small island off of Puerto Rico. It looks like he keeps a house there."

"Great," a suddenly energized Nesto replied, "Let's have him scooped up."

"No," Rolly abruptly ended that idea. "Any whiff that they've been compromised is an entire breach. We need him to talk to us, alone. We have no idea as to whether or not he's supposed to be anywhere or talk to anyone, so you and I are flying to San Juan in an hour and a half. We're gonna grab this prick ourselves and get him to tell us what he knows… tonight."

Aiden with his arms folded, "And the bad news?"

Rolly went on. "Whoever is responsible for all this sent a message and photos, including photos of the yellow pages stabbed into these people, to the *New York Times*, the *Washington Post*, the *Boston Herald*, the three major networks and Fox News. The White House, the President himself, has asked them to withhold the story for a week. They've agreed to do it for a while, a few days. We don't know if they know about the RDD yet, but they might. It looks like we have a week here boys, maybe less. If these assholes don't see a story break soon who knows if they'll leak it on social media or in the Middle East somewhere. We just don't know. But we gotta move like hell, guys."

Rolly shifted gears, "Aiden, you gotta get up to that site and do your space man shit. Figure out what the hell happened there. We need a link from that site to something, anything. There's a plane waiting at Newark and that young analyst, Quigley, is coming with you. She's smart and she's been looking at this every waking hour since it happened. I have a hunch about this girl. I could see it in her eyes. She may know something she doesn't know she knows. Don't tell her anything. Whatever you say to her assume that fat fuck Capps will be listening.

Oh, and Aiden…We have no time for channels. Shoot anybody who doesn't cooperate in the face. Go."

Aiden looked at his watch, nodded to the pair, and hustled down the spiral staircase.

Rolly, turned his attention to his remaining partner, "Nesto, we can't afford to contact any authorities on this. I need Pokolov…tonight. I've arranged for a skiff to run us the forty minutes from the main island to Culebra and a car when we get there. It's you and me alone; maybe we can pull some help if it's in the region, but don't count on it. I don't know if Pokolov has anyone else there with him. He might have a bunch. But we have no choice. We'll go in heavy. We need this guy."

Nesto needed no such cajoling. "Do you have a plan about what to do to grab him and what to do after we grab him? Where we're taking him?"

A visibly exasperated Rolly, "Nesto, I don't know. I only found out about this guy within the past hour. We're winging it. My idea is that if he's alone, which I doubt, we squeeze him in his house. If he has help, which I assume he does, we neutralize the help and get him to a remote place. We'll drown the prick if we have to. We gotta do everything we can to keep a lid on this and still get our hands on this guy. We'll try our best not to make a mess. If we do, hopefully we can get a clean-up crew there before anyone's the wiser come the morning. It's the best I got right now given the options and circumstances."

Nesto, looking at his watch was all in, "Puerto Rico you say…Alright then… Vamonos."

Chapter 12

San Juan, Puerto Rico

It's known by a number of names. The locals call it Isla Culebra. The people on the mainland of Puerto Rico are more likely to call it "Snake Island," *Isla Chiquita* ("Little Island"), or *Última Virgen* ("Last Virgin" due to its position at the very edge of the end of the Virgin Island Archipelago). Whatever the locals or visitors chose to call it, it was stunningly beautiful.

The tiny serene tropical island sits twenty miles east of the Puerto Rican mainland and a little over ten miles west of St. Thomas of the Virgin Islands. The sleepy green island's total population of less than two thousand makes it an ideal place to get away from life's charges or for an assassin to go and unwind out of sight.

Incredibly the luscious paradise of an island had been left abandoned for centuries. During the era of Spanish commerce through the Americas, it was used as a refuge for pirates, degenerates, and scalawags. As far as Constantin Pokolov was concerned, it still was.

In the late 1930's in preparation for America's entry into WWII, the U.S. Navy began using the Culebra Archipelago as a practice theater for naval gunnery and bombing. War ships pummeled the landscape mercilessly. The result left a magnificently unusual topography which leaves first time visitors scratching their heads and snapping their photos.

The diminutive island measures a mere seven miles by five miles. The coast is marked by bombed out cliffs, sandy coral beaches and mangrove forests, making it easy to arrive after dark undetected and stay that way. Getting around the island unnoticed could be another story altogether.

Inland, the tallest point on the island is Mount Resaca, with an elevation of 650 feet. The second highest point on the island is Balcón Hill, with an elevation of 541 feet and where Pokolov's gated Spanish stucco and stone cottage stood surrounded by gardens and fences everywhere.

Entering and exiting the house safely was going to be a tough get. Nesto and Rolly, having no idea other than a satellite photo, would learn the hard way.

They arrived in San Juan, each man carrying a golf bag and fishing poles and both wearing the most obvious cruise wear they had purchased the previous day at the Target in Newark, New Jersey on their way to the airport. The process was made more difficult because finding summer beach clothing in November, in the northeastern part of the United States, meant very few options were available.

The flight from Newark to San Juan Puerto Rico hit the tarmac at 3:50 pm. The hungry assassin hunters went straight to the innocuous forty-two foot 1975 Bertam fishing vessel waiting for them.

The boat was substantial, powered by twin 325 Horsepower Detroit Diesel 6V71TI engines. The spacious fly bridge and ample lower helm gave it plenty of space aboard for what they needed while at sea. With a fully equipped galley and two separate staterooms, it was enough to carry several men aboard and much equipment. There would be five men going to their destination, but an unknown number coming back. Rolly was quite pleased when first he saw it.

As the men climbed aboard the vessel they were met by two young and eager Navy Seals dressed in civilian fishing gear. The deck of the boat was outfitted with every piece of fishing equipment one might want to own were they out to catch the largest fish in the ocean. Below deck was strategically stocked with every piece of equipment one might wish to bring along were they intent on starting a war.

"Boys," Nesto greeted the awe struck, newly minted Seals.

When Rolly climbed aboard the Bertram, one of the boys, to the shock of all aboard, saluted. Rolly was a mythical legend in the Seal community and being so proximal to the near deity, respectfulness overtook the young Seal's training. His salute betrayed his awareness of the clandestine mission afoot. Rolly's eyes bulged at the young man. The neophyte Seal immediately felt the rebuke.

"Oh, shit. I'm sorry, Sir." The quivering, deferential apology made the mistake worse. Again Rolly's facial expression tore into the young man.

Rolly was a hard ass and as rigid as they come, but he was also a young Seal once and while he hadn't experienced "jitters" in a long while, he remembered their affects vividly. He turned away from the young man without saying a word and moved quickly in the event anyone of consequence had been watching. He reached into a bench cooler and pulled out four beer bottles, then saluted both Seals aboard improperly. Then he demonstrably hugged each as if he hadn't seen them in a long while and started barking greetings to his long lost buddies as if he was already a little drunk.

He plopped down on the cushioned seat and swigged the entire beer. Nesto, sensing Rolly's play acting, clapped his hands as if to be beckoning a beer. Rolly tossed him a beer. Twisting off the cap he began swilling it like a high school kid might during the early hours of his prom weekend.

The sales job was perfect. There was no way a casual onlooker would conclude they were looking at professional soldiers, let alone two of the earth's most dangerous soldiers. Had anyone been looking in their direction they would assume they were witnessing old friends who hadn't seen each other in quite some time, at least two of whom would likely be sea sick at sea before long.

Rolly wasn't in a frame of mind for scolding or educating. In a matter of hours he and his men would be walking into a professional hitman's house, not knowing what weaponry waited inside or how many bad guys would be using those weapons. He was going in blind with a mindset to take the assassin out alive and nothing was going to distract him, not now. However many men were in that house and on that property, men likely also trained killers, he needed to take Constantin Pokolov out of it alive. There was no second way.

"It's alright son, forget it. Let's move," Rolly whispered to the kid as the boat began to move away from the dock.

After a few knots out to sea, Rolly reflected upon what had happened with the young Seal with some consternation. He walked the five paces to where the young warriors were seated. He muscled between them and sat down.

"Boys you ready?"

"Yes, Sir."

"Good. Have you memorized the targets face?"

"Yes, Sir."

"Good."

Rolly let a few seconds pass then looked each in the eye. He put his right hand on the shoulder of the young Seal who had made the dual mistakes at the dock, "Fellas, it's absolutely critical that we take Pokolov alive. Whatever you do don't kill that man, understand?"

"Yes, Sir."

He repeated himself with a somewhat stronger emphasis, "Alive."

Rolly remembered his early deployments and how nerves occasionally trumped his training, but not his natural ability. He himself once shot and killed a guy he really didn't have to, a guy in possession of needed information. His trigger finger just ran ahead of his reasoning. Normally he wouldn't care if a dirty, rotten murderer got what was coming to him, but this particularly dirty, rotten murderer may just hold the key to preventing a world war. Given the weight, he felt he had to say it still again.

"Alive, gentlemen… Alive."

Chapter 13

Culebra Island, Puerto Rico

The F470 Combat Rubber Riding Craft, or black "Zodiac" as it was referred to by the Seals, dropped into the water from the starboard side of the innocuous Bertram and the lightly armed raiders, a group of four, immediately jumped from the fishing vessel into the raft.

The men moved like a water ballet, practiced and synchronized, immediately blending into the black night ocean horizon and disappearing. The four were in identical black rubber dive suits, black goggles, and black painted faces, each carrying a black M4A1 carbine rifle and with an HK USP SOCOM (Special Operations Command) semi-automatic pistol strapped to his side, both weapons modified with silencers. These lethal whispers of death were the latest Seal baddassery. The highly trained, highly motivated warriors were in the business of summarily ending things.

The nearly undetectable raft was equipped with removable aluminum deck plates, paddles, bow line for securing the docked boat, and a "righting" line used to flip the boat upright in the event of capsizing. Using the strength of its 55 horsepower, two-stroke engine and pump jet propulsion on the silent power of its shrouded impeller, the raft whisked its four professional warriors, hunched down and pointed to cut wind resistance, toward its beachfront goal.

The boat of bad intentions slid over the nighttime beachfront waves like a sled on ice into the sand, where it was quickly deflated and rolled up. The bundle, with all its equipment that could easily fit into a closet, was pulled by the four men the exact number of paces as planned, fifty, from the beach and then jammed into the concealing row of high sand grass and thicket. On quick observation Nesto conveyed to the team that they were one hundred and fifty yards from the house. That the property was much more significantly elevated from the Seals position than was thought caused angst in each of the four. If Pokolov had concealed security they could be walking into a firefight with an enemy in a far greater position.

After concealing the raft, the four Seals began to gather themselves as they heard a vehicle pull up to the house. Rolly, on the first sound, threw his fist in the air, the signal to freeze. It was less than a second until Rolly and the others assessed it was an approaching vehicle. Rolly jettisoned his hand out laterally away from his body with his palm facing downward, the signal to go prone and crouch. The men seamlessly reacted to the signal and in the dark of night made themselves invisible along the thirty-six inch tall grass line. The leader put his hand to his own ear, the signal for the men to listen. They each nodded, flashed the OK hand signal indicating they understood and remained motionless in their crouched, tight military formation waiting for Rolly to offer the signal to move. When it was plainly clear whoever drove up in the vehicle had exited and gone inside, Rolly began firing off hand signals and indicated he would be lead scout.

Even after studying the satellite photos and reviewing intelligence about the lay of the land and the targeted structure, there was no way they could know exactly how easy or difficult it would be to get in and out, or how many people they would be dealing with. They only knew they were going to take Pokolov out alive. They needed to. There was no second way.

Pokolov was a trained assassin and they assumed the other men on the premises were as well. They were going to be attacking an unknown force from a disadvantageous position well below their target and the element of surprise was paramount. Rolly needed to take measure of the terrain, the number of men inside and outside, any women or children, entry point into the house and egress from it.

Rolly indicated by hand signal he would advance the beach first, recon what it was they were up against and return. The three Seals simultaneously raised their hands indicating they were ready.

Hunched low, Rolly slinked up the beach toward the house and moved at a steady pace, he set his eyes on the window light coming from the house. He stopped his approach just outside of forty-five yards of the house and went supine on the ground. Through the opening in the hedgerow he could see two silhouettes in the front yard, both were carrying rifles and pacing aimlessly.

Feeling as assured of his stealth as humanly possible, given the trust in his training and experience and the covering darkness, but always with an air of rigid caution in remembrance for all his fallen companions who didn't see it coming, he moved his torso up on one knee. Before he could even pull himself up on both legs… a growl.

An internal whisper, 'Fuck."

Still on one knee, he turned his head ever so slowly left only to realize what he suspected. Eighteen inches from the vein in his exposed neck was a hundred and sixty pound Dogue de Bordeaux. The barrel-chested type of French mastiff, a feared animal the world over, which for centuries were fierce guardians of Eastern European elites and often used by Russian military today, and with many more pounds per square inch bite than the biggest pit bull, was also crouched in attack position. Another growl. Teeth.

Another internal whisper, "Shit."

The mastiff was in control of his intruder. Or so he thought.

Before the mastiff knew what happened to him, Rolly, without moving a single muscle other than his right arm, violently thrust his seven-inch, black-covered stainless steel Gideon Tanto blade deep into the dog's right eye. The dog gave a muffled screech but before it could make another sound Rolly jammed the knife a second time through the dog's ribcage killing the noble defender.

Rolly hated killing animals and felt a sadness come over him. He always felt killing animals was a crime against nature. It made him feel an awful guilt in the pit of his stomach but that lasted less than a second this night.

Rolly moved ever so carefully around to the back of the house.

The fight was on.

Chapter 14

Teterboro, New Jersey

Time was short, growing shorter. Aiden boarded his borrowed Cessna Citation 560XL Excel at Teterboro Airport just outside of Hackensack, New Jersey and prepped the cockpit controls as fast as he could without being careless enough to miss a step. The sleek plane belonged to a CIA shell company registered and based out of Fort Myers, Florida to give it cover. The plane actually spent almost all of its time on the ground in Miami, Florida where it tracked prolific drug activity coming in from South America.

Aiden, an accomplished flyer, would pilot the plane himself. As a young Navy flyer he had been so highly thought of by a superior that it was recommended Aiden think about the Navy Blue Angels and he once sat for an interview by officials at NASA's space program.

He generally enjoyed flying the agile and fast CIA aircraft powered by two 3804 pound Pratt and Whitney turbofans but today there was no such pleasure. The quick flight from New Jersey to Washington National Airport would take a little over an hour today. Katy Quigley would join him and the two would then fly on to Oscoda-Wurtsmith Airport, a tiny airport in Oscoda Michigan, formerly operated as the Wurtsmith Air Force but opened to the public in 1993. The airport would be a short forty-five minute drive to the grisly murder scene in gorgeous and innocent Huron National Forest.

'Jesus Christ,' Aiden thought as Kate Quigley boarded the Cessna in DC wearing a gray business jacket skirt and pumps.

"Sir," Katy nodded to Aiden as she stepped into the cockpit in her black Jimmy Choo two-inch heels.

"Do you have a change of clothes, sneakers, anything like that? We're going into a forest here," Aiden pressed Katy. He had no time for greetings or salutations.

"I have some street clothes, some sweats. I didn't think I'd need them other than at the hotel or something." Katy looked herself over. She was confused at Aiden's indicting question since her gray business attire had never been challenged before. "I always wear this type of attire when conducting business."

"Well sorry, you're not wearing that. Go back there and put on whatever you have…now. Right now. We're going into the trees as soon as we land and we're gonna be moving quickly."

"I'm going with you into the forest?" Katy asked incredulously. "I thought I was just going to brief you on the way to Michigan. I'm just an analyst."

"Of course you're going. You have seen all the photos and I have seen only what you put up on the wall. I may have some questions and I don't have time for relays. Anything I need to know, I need now. You're coming along."

Katy stood there like a deer in the headlights staring at Aiden.

"C'mon, c'mon, c'mon," demanded Aiden. "Let's go. Get changed. I need you to brief me on everything you know about those dead guys on the way. Go get changed. Hustle."

A few minutes later Katy reappeared in the cockpit wearing a spandex track suit and an embarrassed look on her face. Aiden looked her up and down.

"Sorry. It's all I brought."

Aiden, skipping the small talk, "Tell me what you know about the bodies. Who are they?"

"We don't know. None of them came up on any lists. We've put out calls to our friends in the Middle East. So far nothing there either."

Aiden paused in thought. "Do we know where they're from?"

"No."

"Any of them have any other identifying marks. Anything from their DNA which might give us something?"

"No, nothing definitive. It's as if they were nowhere before. The DNA is a mess. It'll be months before they can sort that out, even a little bit. It looks like a mix of blood which puts them from all over the map. But with borders falling everywhere and fighters coming from all over, back and forth between Syria, Iraq, and Afghanistan, there's nothing which could help direct us to any specific country."

Aiden's experience kicked in, "Well, it's a friggin' war zone over there. Kids come from all over to fight someone in the name of someone else. No one knows who they are. Alright, thanks. Keep looking. Maybe we'll have some luck at the scene."

"There was one thing," Katy surmised. "Two of the men may not have been Muslims. They had cross tattoos. Christian tattoos."

"I don't know if even that means anything," Aiden speculated. "There have been thousands of young zealots who have accepted Islam and got themselves into to the fight."

"Yeah, but these were pretty elaborate tattoos, very elaborate. They weren't just plain crosses. They're very ornate symbols of the cross and they look very religious. Almost too religious to abandon. Something doesn't feel right."

Aiden looked at her curiously. She wasn't sure of anything. The ornate nature of the crosses bothered her and that two of the men had them bugged her more. Aiden had an off-putting sense of disquiet about the pair as well. Neither of them could put a finger on it but something about it didn't fit.

Chapter 15

Culebra Island, Puerto Rico

Rolly made his way around the two-story house with the wrap-around lemonade porch, casing the perimeter for guards and taking a mental blueprint of doors, windows, second floor exit possibilities and, as best he could see, get a count on how many might be inside before slinking back down to Nesto and the two young Seals waiting in the beach grass some forty yards away. The news they were about to hear wasn't good.

"Alright," Rolly began in a low, almost inaudible whisper, "When we get up there Nesto and I will breech the house." Rolly turned his eyes to the young Seals. "Two outside guards with AK"s," his eyes then darted his eyes back to Nesto. "Nesto, there are at least seven total assholes. Two out and I counted five inside the house. Obviously there could be more. We gotta breech the front and the back doors simultaneously."

Rolly pointed at the two Seals, "When Nesto and I are in place we'll give you the breech ready signal. Each of you will take one of the guards… QUIETLY."

Rolly got real serious, "Boys, listen. We're not in a wartime situation. We don't know who these people are and they all might be innocent. We can't just kill 'em. We are obliged to consider that they are innocent and to take them down alive. Disarm them quietly and control them. We're after only one man. I'm sorry but that's the way it is. Signal when you have them immobilized and we'll go in. If shooting starts then all bets are off, but lacking that situation you are to immobilize, not kill. Understood?"

Both Seals nodded that they understood. They were ready.

All communication going forward would be done by hand signals and it was likely to be a lot to communicate all in the dark.

Rolly took one deep look at his young warriors for any outward signs of fear or trepidation. They looked strong and ready and he was satisfied. 'Why shouldn't they be?' Rolly concluded to himself, 'They are Navy Seals, for Christ's sake.'

In a quick snapping, a whispered, confident military man's order, "Go."

Chapter 16

Oscoda, Michigan

Aiden's borrowed twin turbofan Cessna approached the lighted runway that was constructed of grooved asphalt and oriented in a northeast-southwest alignment at Oscoda – Wurtsmith Airport from just beneath the Canadian border. It was a beautiful sight from the low altitude.

"Jesus," Aiden said aloud to himself and to his pretty analyst, who looked like she was on her way to a yoga class rather than a grisly crime scene. "Look at this place. You got water, air, and roads easily accessed from Canada. Not a soul in sight. I don't like this at all. I need to know more about this airport."

The plane landed and taxied to a stop fifty yards from the designated terminal. A car would be waiting for the pair to make the forty-minute drive to the Huron Forest and interviews had been arranged with local law enforcement officials who had been first on the scene at the mass murder of the Muslim men.

Aiden was one of the three most elite Seals for a reason. His specialty was innovation, instinct and adaptation. Navy Seals are taught much about discipline and endurance and their mantra is one of survival and success by adaptation. Seals are trained to adapt and Aiden's ability to adapt, even to the most difficult circumstances, was off the charts. His was as much art as it was science, training, and repetition. His sense of subtle things was remarkable and his confidence to move on his instincts was ironclad. Throughout the countless firefights, traversing unknown foreign terrains, and sorting out the good guys from the bad guys, many had challenged those instincts as perilous to their lives while moving on Aiden's decisions, only to laud them as saving their lives when it was all over.

"Alright, look, change of plans. I'm going alone. You need to stay here and collect everything you can about this airport. Go back through months of security footage and see if there was an influx of Muslim men arriving in groups. If those men came in here they probably didn't come all at once. Look for patterns, small groupings of four or five men coming through at a clip. They might have come in on recognizable intervals. There is no detail too small. Also, see if there is any maritime access nearby, say in a twenty-five mile radius. This lake bugs me. They might have come in by boat. Something about this place screams 'c'mon in.'"

"If you find anything unusual, call me."

Chapter 17

Pokolov Safe House

The four man assault team was in place. Hand signals from the young Seals were passed confirming they had acquired their respective targets and were ready to move.

Nesto would go in from the front door and Rolly from the rear door.

When they were near enough to their access points, hand signals were to be passed for the young Seals to do the thing they were trained for: to take the fight to the enemy. Rolly raised his left hand and made an open fist gesture, the signal for move.

The young Seals didn't disappoint. Each of the guards were violently struck simultaneously and knocked to the ground. One was rendered immediately unconscious and the other needed a second blow. Both Seals moved like lightning with plastic hand ties and duct tape for covering the mouth and securing the legs of the downed security.

Before the first security guard hit the ground, Nesto and Rolly burst in through their respective doors, both screaming at the top of their lungs to disturb, confuse, and disorient any occupants, "Don't move, don't fucking move." Rolly and Nesto felt pleased by the open concept living areas on the first floor affording each a nearly full view of the space. A bathroom and a hallway leading into another room were all they had to contend with as far as visibility was concerned.

Both men moved like a heavily armed ballet in black face, crisscrossing each other while taking turns pointing their rifles at their new prisoners, darting their rifle barrels towards any open spaces, doorways and hallways and then back again at the stunned men sitting in chairs and on couches with their hands in the air.

Rolly kicked over the dining room table and shoved it into the corner to open enough floor space for their prisoners to lay supine. "Over here… over here. Down… down on the fucking ground," Rolly demanded.

The prisoners complied. They had a look of professionalism about them and instinctively knew how good the men who had taken them by surprise really were.

"C'mon, c'mon," Nesto prodded them in feigned frustration. "Lets' go…on the ground…C'mon."

Rolly counted the prisoners and looked at their faces. Pokolov wasn't among them.

Rolly pointing to the upstairs area of the house, whispered "Pokolov."

There wasn't time to for Rolly and Nesto to tie the prisoners and continue the search. He knew he had to go up the stairs alone for the assassin. He went back to hand signals for communicating with Nesto.

Rolly pointed at Nesto and tapped his own head signaling, "You cover this area." He then pointed at himself and up the stairs signaling, "I'm going up."

Rolly carefully and methodically ascended the stairs with his back to the wall and his rifle pointing upstairs. Whoever was up there knew exactly what was happening by now. When he was three steps from the top, he got his chin to the floor of the landing and looked at the layout of the second floor. There were four closed doors, one to his left and three to his right.

"Shit," Rolly whispered. That was a lot of space and a lot of opportunity for a professional killer to get the drop on him. But Pokolov was up there and he had to take him, there was no second way.

Rolly assessed the best thing was to start at the far end and work his way back. If Pokolov was in there, he'd have him. If he tried to run, he'd run into Nesto at the bottom of the stairs. If he tried to go out the window, one of the Seals would grab him. It was a long thirty-foot gauntlet to that back bedroom. He inhaled to steady his nerves.

Rolly crept down the hall passing two rooms. He waited a second at the door and then kicked it in like he had a hundred times before. Once inside the master bedroom unscathed, he realized there were yet two more doors inside, a closet and a bathroom. Rolly worked his way around the far end towards the closet first, employing the same strategy of furthest door first. He got down on one knee in the event an armed man was inside knowing by the time they shifted the aim of their weapon Rolly could discharge his own. He ripped open the closet door and no one was inside.

He moved to the bathroom on-suite. Moving carefully, he repeated the maneuver, again nothing. Only three more rooms to go.

As Rolly moved to the doorway he heard the doorknob at the far end of the hall turn. He had to move quickly. He pressed his back against the bedroom wall, took a breath and swung around pointing the barrel of his rifle at whoever was exiting the room. As he swung around pointing his gun he saw Pokolov standing still with his hands in the air.

Again Rolly dropped to one knee. If anyone was with Pokolov who had bad intentions Rolly would be ready.

"I'm alone," Pokolov spoke with the calmness of the assassin he was.

Rolly waited a few seconds and then gestured for Pokolov to approach. As Pokolov took his first measured step Rolly whispered, "slowly."

After Pokolov took his third robotic step Rolly stood and approached him, fully expecting someone to emerge from behind, closing the gap between Pokolov and himself. With about ten feet between them Pokolov began to kneel down. Rolly did not want movement. "No don't kneel…"

Before he could finish his command, the two bedroom doors on either side of the hallway, now behind Rolly, flung open. Men with AK 47's thrust their aim at Rolly. Rolly knew he'd been had, bowed his head, and put his hands up, his gun still in his right hand. One of the men slammed his fist into Rolly's kidney and Rolly fell to his knees in agony.

"Nyet!"

Pokolov turned his attention to Rolly, "Gun, slide it behind you, please." Rolly slid the gun behind him along the wood floor. The man who punched Rolly quickly bent over to take possession of the weapon. "Stand." Rolly complied as told.

In a low voice, "How many are down stairs? I heard two voices. How many?"

"Two."

"What is his name, your friend?""Ernesto."

Before Rolly could finish saying Ernesto's name Pokolov called out to him in a loud controlling voice, "Ernesto." He got no response. By now Ernesto was taking stock of his situation and trying to think of a way to get him and Rolly out.

"Ernesto," Pokolov called again, "I have your man." He turned to Rolly and demanded his name. "Rolly."

"I have disarmed Rolly. He has two men with guns pointed at his head. We are coming down."

Nesto positioned himself for a shot at whoever came down those stairs. He knew they might not be getting out alive and he wasn't going to let that happen if he could help it.

Rolly appeared first with his hands over his head. He made eye contact with Nesto and signaled he was going to make a move at the bottom of the stairs. Nesto would provide covering fire and maybe, just maybe, he could dive out of the way of the shooters trained on him. While he knew it wasn't likely he would avoid being shot himself, it would save Nesto and alert the two Seals outside giving the three men a chance against the nine inside.

"Your man will be killed if you are foolish, Ernesto."

Next came the first armed man and then the second. The second man was carrying his own rifle and Rolly's as well. All three weapons were pointed directly at Rolly.

"Slowly Rolly," reminded Pokolov.

Three steps to go Rolly thought to himself. He apologized to God for any wrong doing he may have done as a warrior and asked God nothing for himself, but to spare the other three of his team. He cleared his head. He needed to be quick and strong. The afterlife was for God and apologies. Today was about survival…his men and his own.

Two steps to go before he would make his move. One…

Pop, pop …the sound navy Seals knew well, mixed with a small sound of fragmented glass from a window through which the bullets were travelling. The shots instantly killed Pokolov's men on the stairs. Not knowing what had happened, Rolly dove into the kitchen as he planned and scrambled to his feet.

Nesto swung around and pointed his weapon at Pokolov midway up the staircase.

In the front door, left ajar during Nesto's breech, stood the Seal who had just fired the shots killing the two men on the stairs. It was the same young man who made the mistake on the pier for which Rolly had forgiven only eight hours earlier.

"Are you alright Sir?" asked Rolly's savior.

"Yeah, yeah, nice work." Rolly wanted to hug the kid but there was no time and they were still outnumbered. "Help Nesto secure the prisoners."

Rolly turned his attention to Pokolov who was now down on the first floor landing with his hands still above his head. "Constantin Pokolov, we need to talk," Rolly said as he turned his gaze to Nesto.

"Tie this piece of shit up. I'm going upstairs to see if there are any computers, phones, and other shit that may help us. We're taking them all with us, including the two dead. We'll burn the house. I want it all out of here in five minutes. Five minutes. Let's move."

Chapter 18

Huron National Forest

Aiden had to walk the near two-mile trek from the road to the murder scene where the twenty Muslim men had been savagely killed. He was careful to measure every step of the terrain in his mind and diligently look for anything that investigators might have been missed, anything that might help put him on the right path.

About nine hundred feet from the coordinates to the crime scene he found the broken foliage and foot traffic pressed down weeds, all which indicated the directional route they took surmising they were marched two abreast to their final resting place. He felt a forlorn wave of empathy come over him just as he had felt when in Iraq. He could see in his mind what was about to happen to these men and wondered how it was men could be so cruel to one another and indifferent to life.

In lock step with the ghosts he made his way to the murder scene.

'What the fuck?' Aiden in stunned amazement asked himself rhetorically. 'Where the fuck is everybody? What happened to the fuckin' crime scene?'

It was gone, empty forest space was all the eye could see. It had been cleaned, wiped clean. 'It's been less than three days. Three friggin' days. How can this be?'

Aiden knew from experience that investigating the murder of a single individual in such a setting as the one where he stood took more than three days. The murder of twenty individuals would surely take much longer.

'No way, no fucking way.' Aiden didn't need his famed antenna. His dry cleaner could have told him something was amiss here…seriously amiss.

Aiden spent the next hour going over every inch of the ground in concentric circles out to fifty yard in every direction. He could tell it would be fruitless. He knew he wasn't going to find anything and whoever it was that cleaned the area were pros, real pros and consummate pros. But he was obligated to try to find something and if something was there he was determined to find it. Maybe, if life was kind and karma was on his side, he might find a needle in the haystack. The more he observed, the more certain he was that this was wishful thinking. His next wishful thinking was sickening. Something was amiss…seriously amiss.

"Shit!" Those were bullets flying around him. One nicked forearm and there was blood but Aiden knew it wasn't serious.

Aiden's experience at being shot at overtook him and he reacted in an instant. He threw himself on the ground and took measure of his circumstances. The forest was thick and he moved light speed away from the direction of the firing. He drew his pistol but knew it was not going to be enough to fight off multiple attackers with long guns. He heard those sounds before. They were AKM's, the most pervasive variant of the Russian AK series of firearms. These weapons are all over the world, produced in many countries around the globe and have become the busiest small arms weapon in the Middle East. Anyone who has had these rifles fired at them could never mistake the sound. Aiden was certain of three things. There were at least two assailants, he was outgunned and he needed to get the hell out of that forest.

Chapter 19

Twenty Nautical Miles outside San Juan, Puerto Rico

Constantin Pokolov was brought out onto the deck of the Bertram fishing boat, but he wished it hadn't been. He was duct taped from his shoulders to his feet with his hands pinned to his hips at the wrist. His body was lying face up on the deck, but his head was out over the bough of the boat. He could feel his heart beat, but all he could move were his lips.

Rolly was on one knee beside the supine, taped assassin. "I know everything there is to know about you. I know where you were born. I know you were Spetsnaz and I know what you did. I'm gonna call you Constantin, Mr. Pokolov. Is that OK?" Pokolov nodded approval. What else could he do? He was a professional killer and a former Spetsnaz soldier known for his brutality. He knew when to cooperate.

"Good. It's a pleasure dealing with professionals. There is no need for you to deny anything. We were following her, so we were following you after you killed her."

Pokolov couldn't believe his bad luck. After all these years Cuba and the United States relaxed hostilities. 'Fucking Castro,' he thought to himself.

"I'm going to ask you questions. You're going to answer me honestly." Rolly glanced and raised his chin at the two navy Seals standing mere inches from Pokolov, one at his shoulders and the other at his feet. They flipped Pokolov over eyes down and pushed him over the edge of the boat to his waist. He could clearly see the ocean cleaving underneath him but he guessed they wouldn't drop him into the water. If they did they'd learn nothing and besides they weren't Russian KGB. They have consciences and that just wasn't how America plays the game.

"Look to your right, Constantin," Rolly demanded.

Pokolov looked to his right as ordered. What he saw horrified him. Rolly and Nesto had a man tied on a rope upside down. His upper body had been dunked beneath the surface all the way to his knees. He was one of the men shot dead in his safe house but Pokolov didn't know that.

What Pokolov could see of the man bounced violently along the black white capped water and bobbed beneath the black ocean.

Rolly let Pokolov take in the spectacle for a bit.

It took Pokolov mere seconds to realize that just feet from where he was dangling a frenzy of sharks were tearing wildly at the torso of the dead man. Terror came over him the moment he realized his captors were not the kind of Americans he supposed them to be. The terror was heightened by the idea if one of those sharks breached the surface no amount of cooperating with the American would help him.

"Look to your left, Constantin." Pokolov complied immediately. Five yards from Pokolov one of the two young Seals was tossing chum over the side of the boat. When Rolly was sure Pokolov was thoroughly terrified he glanced again at the Seals, they turned him upright and pulled him back into the boat.

"Those are hungry ass sharks. We counted seven of them but I'm fairly certain the word is out and there will soon be dozens more hungry sharks circling. I asked your man the same questions I'm going to ask you. He refused to answer. He was stupid. He's fucking dinner now."

Pokolov was stunned by the cavalier attitude of the man who had his future in his hands.

Rolly let that notion sink in for a moment. "Listen, Constantin I don't have time. We have a few more of your men downstairs and I promise you,

I'm going go through the lot of you, one by stinking one, until someone tells me what I need to know. Do you understand?"

Pokolov didn't move. He was still wrestling with the idea that he may very well be shark food in a few moments. "Constantin, I won't ask a second time. Do you understand me?"

"Da."

Rolly knew Pokolov spoke English well by their exchange back at the house, but he was gratified that Pokolov was so in the grip of fear that he naturally defaulted to his native tongue.

"English, do you speak English?"

"Da." Pokolov once again fell back to his primal self as he listened to the sharks tear at the now partial body trailing behind the boat just inviting more sharks along.

"Da?" Rolly pressed, "English!"

"Yes."

"Look me in the eyes, Constantin. That guy on the end of the rope, he's dead. He had his chance to answer me truthfully. He chose badly. You need to worry about you. Hey, hey, on me. On me… Look me in the eyes."

Pokolov turned whatever of his attention he had left on Rolly as ordered, but the better part of his mind was on all that was left of the headless and torso less body of his comrade.

"Constantin…Constantin… focus. I told you I don't have time. You need to get with me here. I need information. If I think you're lying to me I go get the next guy and you're fish food like your buddy hangin' over the fuckin' side of the boat. Who hired you to kill Khan in Havana?"

"Ya ne znayu!"

"English dammit!" Rolly's voice rising.

"I don't know!"

Rolly wanted to look like he had already had enough. He tossed his forearm and backhand in disgusted dismissal towards his young Seals. He reached down onto the deck and lifted a twelve-foot-long cut piece of rope flipping it onto Pokolov's shins. "Drop this stubborn prick in the water. Get me the next guy."

Rolly stood and walked away from Pokolov. He turned to his men and hollered. "C'mon move, get me another murdering prick…Now!"

Pokolov suspected he might be being played but he wasn't going to risk it. The thought of the sharks ripping him apart alive overwhelmed him. The American may just be a nut job cowboy. "Wait, wait. I tell you, I tell you. I tell you."

Rolly turned back to Pokolov. "Ok, don't fuck with me. You won't get a second chance… Who hired you? I asked you now twice. There won't be a third time."

"Muhamad Ima Atta! Please, Muhamad Ima Atta hired me."

"Where is this Atta, Constantin? Where is Atta now? I won't ask again."

Rolly turned to Nesto, "Cut that guy loose. If this asshole doesn't answer me right now, tie a fucking rope around his fucking feet and drop him in the fucking water."

Nesto cut the ropes holding the half-a-man. What was left of him plunged into the water. Bubbles swelled up and surrounded the body as the sharks took turns ripping away at the flesh. Pokolov couldn't see him fall but he heard the splash and clearly heard the frenzied sharks swarm their fresh fleshy meal.

"Lansing. Lansing, Michigan. He's an attorney in Lansing, Michigan. He hired me!"

Chapter 20

Huron National Forest

Aiden took a circuitous route back to his car. There were men with guns out there and he wasn't going to give them a target they could shoot at. He was careful, as careful as he could be anyway, not to disturb the dead November foliage. He'd have felt much better if there were summer leaves and shrubs which could provide better cover, but he was an expert in the trees and he felt his experience would win the day. He always felt his experience would carry the day because it always had served him before.

He wanted to circle back around and take them, but he thought better of it. Time was more important. Katy was on his mind. She might be under threat and he wanted to get to her if she was.

Aiden knew everything there was about hunting human targets and being himself hunted. He had spent a lifetime either one or the other. He could avoid detection like a ghost and he could arrive with his knife to your throat the same way.

He half circled back at least twice. He was reasonably certain that he had lost his pursuers but he wasn't certain, and certainty was what he was after. If he hadn't lost them, he would have to kill the pair.

When he was finally convinced he hadn't been successfully followed, he zigged one more time and then zagged back to where he had hidden his ride. With one more glance over his shoulder he jumped into his car and spun the tires.

Aiden was flying over the empty one-lane road knowing he had to get back to Katy at the airport. She was just a child in Aiden's mind and he knew these people, they were the most ruthless kind. The life of another was as meaningless as pocket lint. If they went after him, they might go after her. Indeed, it was very likely.

By now the men who tried to kill him were clearly aware that they had missed and there was no doubt they would try again. He suspected they had someone at the airport who now knew they had been unsuccessful in the forest. They had exposed themselves. There was no way they could know how much of themselves they had exposed, but they would surely consider it imperative that they not allow him or Katy to get out of that airport alive.

Aiden was digging for his phone when it rang.

"Aiden, it's Rolly. Are you still in Michigan?"

"Yeah."

"We got a name. He's a lawyer in Lansing. Lansing, Michigan. His name is…"

Aiden cut him off, "Hold that thought Rolly. Somebody just tried to kill me in Huron Forrest. I couldn't make them but I know there were two. And I can tell you this…Capps was wrong, they ain't right-wing militia, terrorist assholes. At least I don't think so."

"How do you know?" Rolly knew not to doubt Aiden's instincts since they had saved his life many times; nonetheless, he was curious to hear Aiden's deductive reasoning.

"They had AKM's, Rolly, AKM's. A bullet nicked me in the arm. And get this; the fuckin' crime scene was wiped clean. Real trade-craft clean too. No one there, not a soul."

Aiden's mind and his mouth were in full stream of consciousness mode now. "No way some backwater Timothy McVeigh-type cleans their own murder scene. This is a scene that law enforcement should be combing over for weeks and with the dust particles they found, perhaps months… and then they return again to the scene to confront me, a clandestine black ghost and with Russian AKM's no less. No this is fucking deep, Rolly.

Someone ordered that scene cleaned and that same someone, or someone else, alerted them we would be here. And they think I need to be dead? I don't think so."

"Sorry dude. You OK?" Rolly asked.

"I'm OK."

Rolly's response said it all, "Shit."

"I gotta cut you off and get back to the airport. The kid is there. I gotta call her. She has no clue. If they came for me they might go for her. I gotta get off the line, I gotta call her. I'll get back to you when we're in the air."

Rolly knew every second was precious and didn't want to waste another one. "Don't bother, go. We'll meet you at the Capitol Regional Airport in Lansing. Good luck, Sailor." He hung up.

Immediately Aiden dialed Katy. "Where are you? I'm on my way back to the airport. Where are you right now?"

Aiden was in no mood for wasting time and danger was near her, he just knew it. Katy could hear the frustration and urgency in Aiden's voice. She didn't know Aiden other than by his military dossier and a few hours' flight from New Jersey to Michigan. Their flight together indicated to her he was not a man to be trifled with. His military history indicated he was really not a man to be trifled with.

"I'm at the far end of the terminal with the head of security in his office.

How'd it go in the forest?"

Other than discovering the directional path the murdered men in the forest had walked he had nothing, other than someone tried to kill him. But he had no time for briefing his neophyte partner.

"Get whatever you can. Take what can be carried physically. Anything that can be sent remotely, electronically, we'll have it sent on to New York. I'll be there in twenty mikes…

ugh…twenty minutes. Don't leave the security office until I get there. It's not safe. I…"

Katy interrupted, "Not safe? What do you mean, not safe?"

"Someone took a shot at me in the trees. Whoever it was, they know we're here."

"What?" Katy was shaken. "Who took a shot at you?"

Aiden sensed Katy's fear and didn't wish to alarm her into a bad choice. "It's likely you're being watched. I don't think they'd make a move on you in such a public place, but I don't want to chance it. Relax Katy, just stay inside that office."

Aiden was lying. He thought exactly the opposite. These guys were prepared to kill thousands, hundreds of thousands, and that airport was as remote as they come. Aiden knew they were pros. They could kill her and she'd never see them. They'd be gone before she hit the ground.

"Should I…"

"Listen Katy, I don't have time to give you instructions, just stay in the security office until I come for you. I'll be there in seventeen minutes."

He'd be there in ten minutes. He jammed his foot on the gas pedal with the entire weight of his six foot four inch athletic frame.

Chapter 21

Oscoda-Wurtsmith Airport

Aiden pulled his car into the trees one hundred and fifty yards from the northwest side of the Oscoda-Wurtsmith Airport fence. It would be another two hundred yards from there to the terminal at the far end but there was no other way he could he could make his way unseen to the terminal.

While he was aggravated by having to sprint his way the last two hundred yards, he was gratified by the thought that if he could be easily seen so could any potential bad guys. Aiden ran a four-seven-five forty-yard dash in college and if all went well it wouldn't take him little more than three minutes to get inside the terminal.

"Sir," Katy answered the phone trying to muster all her cool so as to sound anything at all less than the wickedly anxious she was.

"Listen to me carefully and do exactly what I say. I need…""

"What is going on?" Katy interrupted.

"Shut the fuck up and listen. We don't have time. You're going to leave the room you're in and head east towards the opposite end of the terminal. There's a group of about twelve or so tourist groups mulling around a terminal counter. They'll be fifteen yards on your left. I don't want you walking through those people. Behind them, along the outer exit glass doors, there are benches with newspapers that people left behind.

I want you to walk to those benches and pick up one of the discarded newspapers. Fold it and put it under your arm, then continue walking right down the middle of the terminal. Got it?"

"Got it. Am I alright?"

"You're fine. Don't worry. Don't say anything to the security officer. Just thank him for his help and move. I've got eyes on you in the event anyone follows you. It's a precaution; old habits. Remember avoid that crowd of tourists. Get the newspaper and stay in the middle, no deviations. No bathroom, nothing but the middle until you see me. When you see me, walk in a straight line directly toward me. Don't wave, don't speak. Just walk right at me. No deviations, now."

Aiden didn't know Katy and couldn't predict how she'd respond if he told her what he knew. She looked young enough to be a high school girl but she was proven smart and appeared to be mentally tough. As an agent she would have received duress situation training, but until someone's been in it, it's unknowable what one will do.

Aiden had made two Middle Eastern men, twenty-something, who were waiting for her and him presumably. One was mulling about with the group of tourists and one was sitting at a bistro table thirty yards from where the first man stood, but only six paces from the tarmac access door behind where Aiden was standing and watching. He hoped they were the only two, but he had to take his chances.

Katy emerged from the security office and did exactly as she was told. She moved gracefully towards the bench with the newspapers strewn across it. Aiden had one eye on her and one eye on the young Middle Eastern man in the crowd, who had both eyes also on Katy. She thumbed through the newspapers and chose one, folded it and moved into the center of the terminal. Aiden thought to himself that the extra three seconds Katy spent looking for a section of newspaper of interest, which one would naturally do, was a nice touch. It told Aiden she wasn't panicking. 'That'll help sell it,' he thought.

As she passed the group of tourists the young Middle Eastern man picked her up and began to follow. He was ten paces behind her. When

Katy moved past the terminal counters Aiden emerged through the door and walked directly past the second man sitting at the table. Aiden had the line he wanted.

Thirty paces between Aiden and Katy became fifteen, twelve, eight, seven, six.

The man who had been following Katy reached into his coat. At that moment, Aiden saw Katy's eyes go wide. Before she could say a word, Aiden spun around and fired a bullet into the man who had been following him. The bullet hit him in the chest and he collapsed. Before the first man even hit the ground, Aiden had fired two shots into the man who had been following Katy. He also collapsed. Katy wheeled around to see the young dead man with the twenty-three inch Mini-Uzi submachine gun still in his hand.

Aiden and Katy looked at the dead man's scaled down version of the Uzi gun. Aiden saw it for a potential clue but Katy only saw how close she came to no longer being of this earth. Without wasting a second Aiden bent down over the dead man to look at the weapon more closely. He quickly realized it was not the Israeli Mini-Uzi it appeared to be at first glance. Rather it was a nine-by-nineteen millimeter parabellum with a thirty round box magazine which told him it was a Mini Ero, an illegally manufactured death machine from Croatia.

Aiden needed to rifle through the two dead men's pockets before the airport police could descend on them. They were Middle Eastern alright, but the weaponry they both carried were more akin to criminal enterprises than to terrorists.

Pointing to the second dead body, Aiden urgently ordered Katy to look through the guys pockets. "Take anything you find. Don't stop to read it. We have less than a minute before the police will be pointing guns at us. Go!"

"Two guys in the damn forest with AKM's and two more here with Croatian Eros. Who the fuck are these guys? Who the fuck is who anymore in this fucking crazy world?" Aiden rambled to himself.

Aiden had heard the footsteps of the three police officers running at him. Katy heard no such thing. She looked up to see the three Michigan State police officers pointing their guns at her face.

"Don't move. Hands up. Don't you fucking move. Hands up. Both of you, put your fucking hands up."

Chapter 22

Capital Regional Airport
Lansing, Michigan

The flight from Oscoda-Wurtsmith Airport to Capital Regional International Airport would take a scant forty-five minutes. After a brief stay among the Michigan State Police and a quick exam from a doctor on the scene for the gunshot wound to his arm, Aiden and Katy were airborne for Lansing.

Katy, still a bit traumatized, had no idea why she was on board the plane.

Aiden had her on the plane so she wouldn't be subject to questioning at the airport or anywhere else. His famous instinctual antenna was raised and beeping like mad. He didn't want Katy out of his sight until he could get some clarity behind the events of the last four hours. Something wasn't right. He could just feel it.

"Where we heading?' she asked an introspective Aiden. "You're hurt. Are you OK?" Katy went on from the copilot seat.

"I'm alright. Nicked me, no big deal. We'll be on the ground in Lansing in less than an hour. Tell me about whatever you found out."

"Lansing?" Katy fumbled through her handwritten notes a moment trying to prioritize the information she had gathered. "There's something you should know. While there's not much to tell I'm afraid about the airport, with respect to the questions you asked." Turning the pages of her notes, "Um... first...there isn't a major port near Oscoda and no groups of Middle Eastern men came through that airport in a bunch or incrementally that anyone found suspicious. I spoke to the head of security and he said there was no unusual activity at that airport since he'd been there, which means since the year he was hired, 1999. The only thing he said could be related to Middle Eastern men and unusual was post 9/11. The homeland security folks were all over two Muslim men who had been taking flight lessons here just prior to 9/11 through a group called Phoenix Aviation Services. They followed it and determined that it turned out to be nothing. They were both American citizens, but what you should know is both were lawyers from Lansing, Michigan."

Aiden slammed his hand into the flight control handle. The plane hiccupped scaring Katy half out of her mind. "Shit. Rolly called me in the car on my way back to the airport. The Russian in Puerto Rico, the one who killed Khan in Havana, gave up the name of the guy who hired him. He's a fucking Muslim lawyer from Lansing, Michigan!"

"Do you think they're related?" Katy asked almost rhetorically.

"Ah, I don't know. Lansing is teaming with a Muslim population, it could be something or it could be nothing. I'll talk to Rolly as soon as we land. He and Nesto will be waiting for us there. Anything else?"

"Yes, there is something else. While I was waiting for you I accessed the records of the two lawyers on a spec. One of the lawyers currently owns a boat and a slip in Rogers City Boat Harbor. It's a town less than a two-hour drive from Oscoda."

"Thick getting thicker," was all he said. The two barely spoke for the remaining thirty minutes of the flight.

The borrowed Cessna touched down on the runway at Capitol Regional and taxied to the assigned hanger Aiden had been given in flight. He turned the aircraft according to the waving orange neon arms of the ground airport personnel. Waiting for the plane, as promised, was Rolly and Nesto. They looked both angry and frustrated together at once.

Aiden shut down the smooth Cessna Citation engine and the two deplaned.

"He's gone," Rolly called above the sounds of the airport noise. "The lawyers gone, vanished."

"Where to, any idea?" Aiden responded while walking on the tarmac towards Rolly and Nesto.

Nesto jumped in, "Who the fuck knows, the desert, the mountains, some city in Pakistan. Who knows?"

"What was the rabbit lawyer's name?" Aiden pressed.

Rolly had it on the tip of his tongue. "Salman al-Sabwai."

Aiden turned his eyes to Katy and she nodded in the affirmative. They were the same man.

"Maybe," Aiden nodding his chin towards Katy standing beside him, "we know how to find him."

"How?" Nesto asked.

Again Aiden turned to Katy, "Tell him what you found."

Katy cleared her throat. She was proud of her diligence but because she was talking with America's three foremost warriors, and because she knew what would happen next, she felt a peculiar anxiety come over her. She took a moment to gather herself. Her voice cracking, she explained, "Salman al-Sabwai was one of two men who were discovered to have been taking flying lessons at Oscoda airport just prior to 9/11. Homeland Security looked into it and cleared the pair. They were American citizens and lawyers."

"Fuck me," Rolly chimed in disbelief.

Katy continued, "The second lawyer taking the flight lessons was a man named Rustam Asidilov. He's retired now and we know he keeps a boat on Lake Huron harbor in Roger's City, Michigan."

In the interest of speeding up the briefing, Aiden interjected, "The harbor is two hours due north of Oscoda Airport and just over an hour from the forest. I think this Asidilov prick ferried those murdered men in from Canada. I think he knows where Al-Sabwai is. He may have a shitload of other things to tell us."

Rolly spoke but he really didn't have to. All four of the people on the tarmac knew exactly where they were going, "And I think we need to go visit this mutt. To the bat mobile Robin," pointing at the Cessna.

"Jesus Rolly," a chuckling Aiden chided, "You gotta bring your pop references ahead about forty years."

"Whatever dude. How's the arm?"

"Ahhh" Aiden said waving off the question. He was not going to allow any pain to enter his consciousness, "Whatever, dude. Is that gray in your beard, I see? You're getting closer. Bring it forward another fifteen years."

"Nice work. Katy," Nesto said, talking out of the side of his mouth as he passed in front of her, "We thought you might be just a dork in a dress. Well done."

Nesto called over to Katy, "What kind of boat?"

"What?" Katy returned, not sure what he was asking.

"The boat registered to the lawyer. What is it? Like a car…a Buick, Cadillac, BMW… What kind of boat are we looking for?"

"Oh, OK…I'll look it up"

The four boarded the plane for the trip back to Oscoda-Wurtsmith.

Chapter 23

Boat Harbor

Rogers City, Michigan

Rolly and Katy sat inside a dock side restaurant peering out the window at Rustam Asidilov moving around on his boat. Aiden and Nesto returned from using the restroom and sat down at the table.

Asidilov looked nothing like a retired lawyer nor did he look at all Middle Eastern. At five foot six, the weathered, stocky, fair-skinned, salt and pepper bearded man looked more Western European than Middle Eastern and more fisherman or garden gnome than attorney as he worked to ready his vessel.

"Whatya got?" Rolly inquired of Katy. Before she could begin to answer Rolly's phone rang. "Hold that thought," he said, "I gotta take this."

Rolly walked out of the restaurant to take the call and less than a minute later returned. "The damn just broke. We gotta pick up the pace. The *Washington Post* is releasing the story on the Myers and Turner murders."

Nesto jumped in, "And the Coons murder?"

Rolly rolled over the question "Probably the Coons and Khan murders will follow as well, if they haven't already. Apparently they're getting inquiries from everywhere and fear the whole story is about to break on its own. We'll know in an hour."

Aiden surmised, "As long as they don't tie it to the Huron forest massacre we'll have room to move. If they connect those murders to the others there will be riots all over the Muslim world."

Nesto picked it up, "It'll become a crazy shit show brew of borders falling in line, all coming back Islam and aiming its madness at the West."

Rolly stayed with the thought, "Add a newly-financed Iranian war machine now that sanctions are lifted and all of it conveniently blaming right-wing Americans, Christians. All westerners will be targets. It's the perfect way to start…" Rolly stopped a second to reflect on whether or not he should even speak of it.

A bell went off in Nesto's head. Rolly didn't have to say it, "The perfect way to start a war."

Aiden seconded, "The best way to light a match to start a war? Light two matches."

Rolly now fully following that train of thought said, "The only thing left after one side of nut jobs and fanatics is frothing for war, is to fanaticize the other side. Explode a dirty bomb in a major American city and you've got 9/11 frothing at the mouth all over the U.S. A powder keg, a match, and boom, you've got fighting the world over."

The four sat there silent for more than a minute, each speculating what that apocalyptic world war would look like.

The three men at the table, seasoned in death tolls and tired of war, needed a moment to block the melancholia which was pouring over them. They had a job to do. Maybe they could stop this madness. They certainly couldn't stop it from a café table on a lake in Michigan. They needed that lawyer.

Rolly was the first to break the ice, "Sorry Katy, you were about to tell us what you have on Asidilov."

Katy was frightened by what she just heard about the prospect of a world at war. She wanted to cry. She wanted to go home and see her parents. She wished she had become a nurse like her mother recommended. She hadn't even fallen in love yet. She couldn't believe she was in the middle of it. She hoped none of it was readable on her face.

Her voice made a bit of a gurgling noise as she began. "Rustam Asidilov; Chechen by birth, moved to the U.S. in 1989 shortly after Perestroika. Devout Muslim. Became a lawyer and has represented primarily Muslim clients in Michigan, New York, and Washington, D.C. He retired in 2014. He's actually pretty well known among American Muslims. He's a founding member of the Organization of Islamic Conference, a group some at the CIA accuse of being a propaganda arm of The Muslim Brotherhood and the Iranians. He's been on all the political shows arguing Muslim positions. He's been to the White House at least three times as an active public advocate for Muslim issues. He met privately with Senior White House Adviser Hannah Gafar, Homeland Security Secretary Janet Napolitano, and Attorney General Eric H. Holder to discuss civil liberties concerns and counterterrorism strategies in the U.S."

"This guy is filthy," Nesto concluded what everyone listening at the table had surmised.

"Ugh, he's been sitting in on counter terrorism strategy meetings?" Rolly couldn't contain himself. "These fucking people… Why don't they just give these bastards our launch codes. Fucking morons. Alright, let's get this guy and see what he knows."

"Wait, there's one more thing," Katy said with a tinge of urgency. "Asidilov is married to the sister of a guy named Kamal Al Halbavea, senior member of the Muslim Brotherhood. Al Halbavea, on behalf of the brotherhood, just gave a speech approving of the Iranian government for its role in consolidating unity among the Muslim countries throughout the world. He specifically singled out Mahmoud Ahmadinejad for his stance on destroying Israel, being able to recruit hundreds of suicide bombers a day and his belief that Islam's intent is to rule the world."

"OK, enough. We'll take him and shake him. Let's…" Rolly started to say.

A hail of bullets shattered the restaurant window. The Three Ravens hit the ground. Aiden pulled Katy to the ground as Nesto threw two tables up in front and the four serpentined along the floor.

There were three men approaching from the front of the bistro having come on two motorcycles. Each of The Ravens had a pistol but the three men had those Croatian Mers AKM knockoffs that the men in the airport were carrying. It wasn't going to be a fair fight. The Ravens and Katy had to get out of there.

Nesto was the first into the kitchen. It would be several seconds of crawling before the others could make it as far as the kitchen. Chances were they didn't have several seconds.

The three assailants were cautious. They had missed their man in the forest and they had lost two at the airport. They knew the men they were up against were pros, likely Seals or Rangers. In any event they weren't going to go running in.

They were fanatics, but fanatics with some military training. They were arranged in standard two by one attack formation as they made their final steps outside the restaurant. They were anxious for a kill.

Rolly, at twenty feet, was the furthest from the kitchen. Aiden was half that distance, and he had Katy with him. Both knew they wouldn't make it on the run.

Rolly took charge using hand signals and a soft voice, "I'll provide covering fire. You make the kitchen."

Aiden knew Rolly was right. The probability was that he and Katy might make it but the likelihood that all three could was nil. Rolly's covering fire would be their only hope for him and Katy, but Aiden also knew Rolly's fire would pinpoint his position. The three men with AKM's would most certainly obliterate his position. Aiden knew Rolly was sacrificing his life for the hope of theirs. He loved Rolly for it and would have gladly traded places with him. He was closer to the kitchen, he had Katy with him and the math is the math, orders are orders. Aiden nodded. He was ready to move.

Rolly rose above the downed restaurant table and began to empty the clip of his P226 Blackwater hand gun. The updated SIG P226 killing machine had a twenty round 9mm magazine. He needed to fire enough rounds for Aiden and Katy to make into the kitchen. With Nesto already in there and the local police surely notified of the restaurant's gunfire by now, they would have a chance.

Once Rolly commenced firing into the front wall of the restaurant suppressing the advance of the three assailants outside, Aiden grabbed Katy by the arm and made for the kitchen.

Rolly tried to count as best he could the number of bullets being fired but lost count. He had two, three, or four bullets left. He needed at least three and a miracle.

The assailants outside in black face-covering caps, hearing Rolly's firing stop, began their assault. The first whipped around pointing the barrel in various directions and then concentrated his aim at Rolly's direction. A second man ran past the first man and began circling, stalking Rolly's covered position. The third man would come between them and all three would triangulate Rolly's position, keep him pinned down with machine gun suppressing fire from their Mers, and finally overwhelming him.

Just as the last assailant was about to make his move into the restaurant he went down with a grunt. As he fell he whipped his head around to see what it was that caused such intense pain to his neck and shoulder. Next to him stood Nesto, who had just thrust a nine-inch carving knife downward into the very top of the man's spinal cord. In an instant the pain was gone, so too was the man.

Nesto had made his way out of the back of the restaurant and had flanked the assailants. He chose to eliminate the first man with a blade so as to not make the other two aware of his superior position. Upon killing the man, Nesto aimed and fired his Glock 19 weapon at the second attacker just as he was ready to fire on Rolly. Being an expert marksman, he fired only one bullet into the temple of the second man killing him instantly, but before Nesto could let another bullet loose on the third man, now the lone survivor, he was discovered. The third man dropped to one knee and raised his weapon. He had him. Nesto was defenseless.

A shot. Down went the third man, falling without two-thirds of his skull, dead before his body went limp. Standing in the kitchen door was Aiden with his P226 drawn, exhaling.

The whole thing lasted less than thirty seconds.

Rolly leapt to his feet, thrilled to be alive, thrilled more to be in the company of such men as were his, but because their target was most certainly on the run and without a second to spare in which to express his gratitude, he shouted, "Let's go… Asidilov's on the move! Grab that Mers and let's go."

In one motion, Nesto bent down and picked up the dead man's machine gun and headed to the docks.

Chapter 24

Katy - Rogers City Marina

"That's his fucking boat," Aiden barked, pointing from outside the shot up, once quaint, restaurant at the boat heading out on the lake, now one hundred yards from the dock.

"Get a damn boat, Nesto" Rolly ordered.

Rolly turned to Katy, "Listen to me, we're gonna get this mutt. You stay here. The police will be here in minutes. Take care of them. Tell them as little as you can and then get the hell out of here. There's a bed and breakfast a few blocks from here that I saw when we drove in here. Go there. Don't check in. Tell the desk your husband is expected soon. Wait there. Don't check in and don't use your phone. In fact leave it on the ground. It's now twice we've been ambushed. Whoever it is, they know where we are. Assume they're tracking your friggin' phone… remember don't check in."

"My phone?" Katy asked incredulously.

Aiden, sensing that Rolly had spooked Katy and assessing that all the violence she had seen in such a short period of time might cause an overwhelming and potentially debilitating reaction, spoke in a soft and reassuring voice, "Katy, don't sweat it. We don't know anything about your phone or ours. But Rolly's right. They're on us. We've got to get to Asidilov and then we'll assess where we are and what to do. Until then, all of us have to assume we're being tracked. Do you understand?"

Katy nodded in the affirmative.

Sixty feet from the dockside conversation Nesto was starting the engine of a Baja 320. The cough, then roar of 430 horsepower 502 EPI MerCruiser engines in the slip was all the beckoning Nesto needed. Rolly and Aiden took off for the boat. The Baja was built for speed, topping out at 80 mph and it was perfect for running down Asidilov in his cumbersome fishing trawler. It wouldn't take long, maybe ten minutes to bridge the gap.

Less than four minutes had elapsed in the pursuit when Katy, still standing outside the empty restaurant, noticed Asidilov moving quickly along the dock. She hid herself out of sight next to the frame of the shot out window.

"Shit. He's not on that boat."

Katy froze for a second not knowing what to do. Something had to be done, and it had to be done right now, or he'd be gone. She bent down and pulled the kitchen knife out of the assailant Nesto had first killed and followed Asidilov from across the road of the docks.

He's heading for the parking lot, Katy thought to herself. I've got to get to the parking lot first. Why didn't I grab a damn gun? She hustled ahead making sure to remain out of Asidilov's view.

The Baja was now within five hundred yards from Asidilov's trawler and closing fast. Four hundred yards, three hundred, two, one, fifty yards, twenty. A man with a rifle appeared at the rear of the boat and fired a single shot. Rolly returned fire with one of the dead men's knock- off AKM's for an instant kill. A second man exited the cockpit and took aim. He didn't even get off a shot before plunging into the water after being hit.

The boat slowed and whoever was at the helm knew resistance was futile. He could only drag The Ravens out away from the dock in an effort to prolong the time before they realized Asidilov was not on aboard.

Asidilov made his way past the fifteen or so slips. A right turn would take him along the side of the boathouse towards the parking lot and his escape. As he made his final step along the boathouse into the parking lot Katy stepped behind him and poked him with the point of the knife.

"Don't move." Asidilov was motionless.

Something told Katy that the approaching police siren would not be good for what they needed. She knew The Ravens would soon find out they had been hoodwinked and would return as fast as hell. It wouldn't be long. She had to secure Asidilov out of sight.

"Move over to the house...slowly." Asidilov did as he was told. "Around the back...slowly."

Once Katy had Asidilov around the house and they were out of sight, she was sure to stand directly behind him.

"On your knees...on the fucking ground...NOW!" Asidilov complied.

"Hands up." Again Asidilov did as he was told.

As Asidilov dropped to the ground his eyeglasses fell from his face. Reaching down to pick them up, he cleverly and quietly snapped one of the temple supports from the glasses and put the remaining piece of his broken glasses in his shirt pocket.

"Hands up," ordered Katy with a sort of new found confidence. Her captive was out of sight and facing the boathouse and had nowhere to run.

As Asidilov began to raise his hands he whipped his right hand around and drove the temple piece into her thigh. Katy let out a yell and dropped to one knee in pain.

Asidilov was an older, out of shape man but he had big, strong, calloused hands that had been in many fights in his life. While still on his knees, he turned and punched Katy on the right side of her face, dazing her badly. She fell onto her side and the knife in her hand flew several feet into the parking lot gravel.

Asidilov took a look at the near unconscious Katy. There was no time to finish her off with the police on the scene at the restaurant less than hundred and thirty yards away. Any unnecessary movements or sounds that might bring police attention upon him would be catastrophic. He made his way towards his car.

Asidilov put the keys into the door of his 2011 Lincoln but before he could pull the handle he felt an excruciating pain in back of his right leg just behind the knee. He fell to the ground writhing in pain. Looking up at the female silhouette between him and the blue sky was Katy with a bloody blade dripping from her right hand.

"You fucking move and I'll kill you, you fucking piece of shit."

Katy was hurt badly. Her eye socket was throbbing from Asidilov's punch and she couldn't see a thing. Her thigh was also agonizingly painful.

"You lay right there, Mr. Asidilov. Don't move a muscle," Katy said hunching down herself, out of sight between the cars.

Aiden boarded Asidilov's boat first, then Nesto. Rolly secured the Baja to the trawler and boarded himself. They would grab Asidilov and get the hell out of there in the speedboat.

"Fuck," Nesto hollered, "He's not on the damn boat. Asidilov isn't here."

"Get into the Baja…go, go, go!" snapped Rolly as all three moved in unison.

Aiden's phone rang as they flew over the waves. Aiden saw it was Katy.

"I thought we told you not to use the phone!"

"Aiden, I've got Asidilov!"

"What?"

"I've got Asidilov. He didn't get on that boat."

"We know. We're heading back."

"OK, but hurry. I've got him on the ground between two cars in the parking lot just outside the boathouse. The police are up by the restaurant now, Asidilov is losing blood and I'm hurt."

Immediately Aiden's training in high stress situations kicked in.

"What do you mean, hurt?"

"I don't know. He punched me in the eye and stabbed me in the leg with something. I feel lightheaded and my eye is swelling. I'm having trouble seeing."

"OK, hang on. We'll be there in minutes. Hang on."

Chapter 25

Aiden - Rogers City, Michigan

Aiden didn't wait until Rolly docked the boat in the transient slip but leaped from the stern onto the Rogers City dock taking off for Katy.

When Katy saw Aiden approaching an instant sense of relief overtook her. She had been running on pure adrenaline. Suddenly she could feel the sharp pain of her wounds and a peculiar peacefulness of her security together at once. Aiden felt a similar feeling when he saw her standing upright. He could see she was hurt and his first instinct was to make sure she wasn't losing blood or in any danger of being too concussed to go on without getting to a hospital.

Aiden barely glanced at Asidilov lying on the ground as he writhed in pain from the knife wound in the back of his thigh. In addition to a significant amount of bleeding, it was apparent that his tendon had been severely cut.

"Look at me!" demanded Aiden while gently removing the knife from her trembling right hand. He steadied her face so he could study her eyes for confusion, dizziness, or signs of sensitivity to light. "Do you feel like vomiting or anything like that?"

"No, but I feel a little light-headed" she returned with a comforting lucidity.

"Any ringing in your ears?"

"No"

Aiden satisfied she wasn't highly concussed, moved his attention to her leg wound. ""OK, sit down on the ground. I need to look at that wound."

Katy complied immediately with the full confidence she was in good hands…and safe. Aiden ripped a seven-inch hole in her pant leg.

"It doesn't look too bad," she rationalized as she tried to appear tough, but hoping and praying Aiden wouldn't tell her otherwise.

"You'll live. Whatever it was nicked your bone. You're gonna feel it for a good long while, though."

A smile came to her face. A smile came to his.

Seconds passed before Nesto and Rolly came upon the three people lying, sitting, or kneeling on the ground between Asidilov's Lincoln and the car parked in the spot next to it.

Rolly had grabbed a rope, gaff hook, and some cloths from the deck of the boat. Nesto coming up from behind carried on his shoulder a large nylon first responder's bag which included a full EMS first aid kit. As they walked up on the three they took a lightening quick peek at Katy's face and without even acknowledging Asidilov's presence, looked directly at Aiden without saying a word. Aiden gave them quick answers to their unasked questions.

"She's OK. A little concussed and she has a stab wound just above her knee."

Nesto dropped to one knee and began working on Katy's reparation. He snapped an ice pack and handed it to her. "Hold this on your eye. It'll keep the swelling down some." Without stopping he moved to her leg with a wipe, bandage, and tape. Clearly he had done this a thousand times Katy thought to herself.

"Here take these Advils."

Rolly, satisfied Katy would fully recover over time, turned his attention to Asidilov on the ground. Asidilov, a lawyer long used to gaming the system, assumed he would be accorded his Miranda and medical attention. He assumed wrong. Rolly propped him up against his own car and slapped his face first with the palm of his hand then with the back of his hand.

"Did you punch a woman in the face and stab her in the leg, you fucking mutt? Gimme the keys to your car." Asidilov complied and Rolly flipped the keys to Aiden. "Now your phone. Gimme your phone."

"I'm an attorney. I have rights," Asidilov contested.

Rolly slapped him twice again, only harder. "Gimme your phone."

Asidilov knowing now his knowledge of criminal law was worthless, reached into his pocket and gave it to Rolly. Rolly looked at the phone and tried to unlock the screen. The screen prompted Rolly for a four digit code. Rolly looked at Asidilov with a determination which could not be mistaken. "The code?"

"No. I'm an attorney and you can't…"

Before Asidilov could finish his protest in legalese, Rolly shoved him to the ground and shoved a cloth in his mouth. He then thrust the gaff hook into the stab wound in the back of Asidilov's hind leg. Asidilov recoiled with almost enough rigidity to snap the gaff. Katy winced and turned away. Rolly reached down and ripped the cloth from Asidilov's throat.

"I'm not going to ask you again."

"7755"

Rolly coded the phone and it opened. Handing it to Katy he said, "You're the analyst, look at everything in it. Photos, contacts, recent calls …everything. We'll take this bum and his car someplace where we can talk between here and the airport."

"Stop at the rental," Katy busted in. "I need to grab my laptop. And my phone is up by the restaurant."

"We'll grab the computer but the phone is history. Leave it. They've been tracking us and I'm almost positive it's your phone," Aiden reminded her.

"We'll give you one of ours when we get back to New York," assured Nesto.

"OK, Mr. Asidilov," Rolly spoke while aggressively hoisting up the beat up and dazed lawyer, "Up you go."

Aiden jumped into the driver's seat and started the car. Rolly threw Asidilov into the back seat and climbed in while simultaneously asking of Nesto, "Nesto, tourniquet the bleeding." Asidilov bleeding out would be bad for their cause. Nesto ran around to the passenger side, climbed in, and went to work on the lawyer's leg.

Chapter 26

Asidilov - Rogers City, Michigan

"Alright Aiden, pull in there…eighty yards," Rolly said, pointing to a dirt road. "Keep the car running. Mr. Asidilov and I won't be long."

Asidilov closed his eyes and dropped his head knowing he was about to be in a position where he'd have to decide what level of pain he could endure. He looked at Rolly to see if Rolly's face might offer any sign of compassion or if there was doubt.

"OK, Mr. Asidilov. Out. It's time. Nesto, help Mr. Asidilov."

Nesto guided Asidilov out of the car and the pair followed Rolly to a small opening in the trees. "Hold on," Rolly said as he jogged back to the car.

"Open the trunk." Aiden popped the trunk and Rolly reached grabbing the fishing gaff which had become the symbol of pain. To Rolly it was the arbiter of truth.

Asidilov turned his head to see Rolly jogging back towards him with the gaff in his hand. The question about Rolly's potential for compassion had been answered. There would be none. Asidilov had seconds to determine for himself exactly how much he could take for his cause. He braced himself.

"OK, here." Nesto and Asidilov stopped as ordered. For a brief second Asidilov felt a sense of relief. Every step was an agonizing reminder of

Katy's stab wound and Rolly's revisits to the wound. He gasped for air, half for the air and half as an attempt to pry whatever empathy he could from the man with the gaff. Asidilov tried his best but he couldn't stop his eyes from being drawn to the gaff, that damned gaff.

"Mr. Asidilov, sit down," Rolly began. "I have no time…no…time. Nesto, take the tourniquet off his leg." Nesto complied.

"I'm going to ask you questions. You're gonna answer them… honestly. If I even suspect you are lying to me I'm going to rip a piece of your thigh off, bone and all. There's no second way. I won't challenge you to tell the truth. I will only do what I said. If you die here, you'll die because you're a fucking liar. Let me assure you, I don't give a shit if you live or die. Is that clear?"

Asidilov knew he was powerless but tried one last time to call Rolly's bluff. "If you kill me you'll get nothing."

With lightning quickness Rolly drove the gaff into Asidilov's open wound and yanked it back towards himself ripping through skin and muscle. Asidilov let out a scream, but it didn't matter here. They were miles and miles from any human ears that might be inclined to help him.

"Don't confuse me with the apology tour shit you see on Al Jazeera coming out of the White House. I will kill you here, now and sleep well tonight. I have your phone. I know where your family is. You have to ask yourself one question: Am I willing to die here and let my family die later today? I promise you this gaff will be plenty sharp enough later today to rip away at them too. Look in my eyes so you know I'm telling you the truth. I will kill them too. And it will be brutal, just as bloody as when you murdered those men in the trees."

Asidilov was confused and in unfathomable pain, frightened to death and out of time. 'OK, OK , OK, no more, no more. I tell you, I tell you."

Rolly could see he had him, but he knew he wouldn't be long for consciousness. Asidilov was a hardened terrorist, but he was not a young man and the last several years had made him a much softer terrorist. "Nesto, tourniquet that wound."

As Nesto went to work on stopping Asidilov's bleeding, Rolly went quick to work on getting the information he needed.

"Who came after us? Who is trying to kill us?"

"The Iranians."

"The Iranians? Why?"

"They know you are engaged."

"How do they know? Who told them about us?"

"This I don't know."

Rolly knew Asidilov was telling the truth, but he made one more pass at it. "How do they know about us?"

"I don't know. Someone in your government, someone near the President. I don't know."

Rolly thinking about the million possibilities got off his line a bit. "Someone in my government? My fucking barber could have told me that. Who?"

"I told you I don't know."

Asidilov started to appear heavy-eyed, almost sleepy. Rolly knew he had mere seconds before he'd lose consciousness and if he went under it was almost certain he'd never wake.

"Ok, you brought those men in on your boat. The men who were murdered, yes?"

Asidilov looked up at Rolly caught off guard. How did he know? He was frozen. He was grappling for a plausible deniability. Rolly loaded the gaff and aimed it again at Asidilov's leg. He didn't want to use it, as it would have surely put Asidilov under and perhaps for the last time. Asidilov thought similarly, but for entirely different reasons.

"You brought those men in on your boat from Canada. Yes?"

Asidilov nodded yes.

"Who are they? Where are they from?"

Rolly waited a second and then sensed Asidilov was wavering. Rolly hit him with the gaff.

"Ahhhhh," Asidilov cried as he grabbed for his leg. "Yes, I brought them in. They were prisoners. They were brought from Syria. They were prisoners."

"Prisoners? Prisoners of what?"

Asidilov went quiet. He looked up at Rolly with a sudden sense of power. "The caliphate."

Rolly looked down at Asidilov and wanted to kill him in the worst way.

"These men were Christians, weren't they? You rounded them up and brought them here to be sacrificed for your stupid fucking cause. Where is Muhamad Ima Atta?"

Asidilov was fading but Rolly had only two questions left.

"Where is Muhamad Ima Atta?"

"America will submit to Islam. The world will submit or die. Allah Akbar…Allah Akbar."

Asidilov was gone.

Chapter 27

Teterboro Airport, New Jersey

Aiden landed the borrowed Cessna on the tarmac at Teterboro Airport in Bergen County, New Jersey and rolled it to a stop at its appointed hanger. He shut the engine and sat at the controls motionless exhausted in every way a human can be exhausted. He needed some sleep.

Peeling himself out of the pilot's seat, he looked around at his passengers who were all fast asleep. "Hey…hey…wake up. We're here. C'mon, let's go… Get up," as he poked each.

Nesto looked up from his one squinting eye, "You OK?"

"Yeah…yeah…I'm good. I just need a few hours."

As Rolly began to hoist himself out of a dead sleep his phone rang, "Byrnes."

"Mr. Byrnes, Capps here."

Right away Rolly's asshole detector antenna rose up, "Yeah."

"We've lost touch with our Agent Quigley. Can you tell me anything about her whereabouts?"

"No," was all Rolly said. After two attempts on their lives and absolute certainty that someone in the chain was a traitor and a spy, Rolly wasn't about to disclose anything to anyone. He trusted no one, least of all a bureaucratic political operative like Capps.

"When did you last see her?" Capps pried.

Rolly didn't like it, and he didn't like Capps. "We left her at the airport in Oscoda."

Capps quickly changed gears. "The President is looking for an update. Now that the story has broken in the press, he's concerned about a response."

"Broken in the press?" Rolly responded. Something wasn't right. Rolly could just feel it.

Capps went on, "You haven't seen? The murders of Myers, Berpa, Khan in Havana, and Lerner were covered in both the *Times* and the *Post*. It's all over the television. They connected the murders by the yellow notes. It's a feeding frenzy."

"And the murder of the Muslim men?" Rolly knew the murdered men weren't Muslim at all, but he wasn't going to divulge a thing to Capps.

"They haven't released it. They know of it and have told the White House that they would withhold that piece for a while…a short while. The White house is looking for a narrative."

'A fucking narrative,' Rolly angrily thought to himself, 'The fucking world is going to shit and they want a friggin' narrative.'

Rolly dismissed Capps, "Fuck that. I don't have a God damn narrative. That shit is for the scrapes and if the fucking White House or the fucking President wants an update they talk to me directly."

"Mr. Byrnes, I am authorized…"

Rolly disconnected the call and turned to the other three standing beside him in the hanger, "Something smells. Capps just called looking for Katy and digging into where we are. He said the story broke and then says he's asking for a sit-rep at the request of the White House."

"The President never includes staff," seconded Nesto incredulously.

"Exactly," Rolly nodded, "somebody else is digging."

Nesto began spit balling, "Could be Capps just being a typical bureaucrat."

Rolly would have none of it. "No, I'm not buying it. Capps doesn't have the wood to go outside of protocol. He's either dirty or he's being used as a puppet. Whatever it is, it stinks."

Aiden, ever the strategist, ordered, "Alright then nobody uses their phone, nobody. Turn 'em off…now, right now. We stop on the way and get four prepaid phones. Until we can figure out who has us zeroed we can't take any chances. And don't call anyone on them but each other."

"Good call," Rolly said approvingly. If they didn't see his reasoning no one ever questioned Aiden anyway.

"The story broke?" Nesto asked moving on to the next issue.

Rolly answered, "Yeah, it's a fuck fest. But they haven't broken the guys in the forest. They will soon. We're running out of time."

"Rolly, I may have something here," Katy said with a level of uncertainty. "Look."

Katy handed the phone they had taken from Asidilov to Rolly. The phone screen had a picture of Asidilov sitting at his desk at his law firm.

"So?" Whatever she was getting at Rolly wasn't following. Katy looked over Rolly's shoulder at the phone screen.

"Sorry, the screen went small." Katy took the phone from Rolly and placed her thumb and forefinger on the screen to expand it to its fullest and cropped the full photo just left of Asidilov's right shoulder. On the credenza just behind Asidilov was a picture in a frame. The picture had three smiling people in it: Asidilov, his law partner and disappeared terrorist, Muhamad Atta, and White House Advisor to the president, Hannah Gafar.

"Fuck me," was all a clearly stunned Rolly could think of to say.

"I'm not finished," Katy said with a sense of authority. "Asidilov may have other ties to Hannah Gafar. I'm pretty sure he does."

"What?" Rolly asked, knowing full well Katy had further pertinent information.

"Gafar's father, a pathologist named Dr. Jonah Malic, had extensive ties to Communist associations and individuals; I accessed his files on my computer on our way here. The files at the FBI show that in 1950 Malic was in communication with a paid Soviet agent named Marcus Stein, who fled to Prague after getting charged with espionage. The Malic family Communist ties also include a business partnership between Malic's maternal grandfather, Rashid Zaid, this Marcus Stein character and...." Katy looked up from her notes into Rolly's eyes, "you guessed it, a guy named Asidilov, our Asidilov's father."

"Holy shit!" Rolly said with almost panic in his voice, "this is filthy."

"What the fuck do we do?" asked Nesto.

Aiden went right away to his natural proclivity for analyzing, "I'll tell you what we don't do. We don't speak a word of this in any of our channels or chains of command. We don't even access normal databases or research engines. The fucking President and this asshole have been friends for decades. He may very well be in on it if that's the case."

"No," responded Nesto, half asserting and half questioning.

"Aiden's right, this stays here," Rolly ordered. "One whiff of this and the game could be over. Until we figure out who's who and what's what… only us…"

"We gotta find this second lawyer." Rolly could think of little else.

Chapter 28

Fifty Two and a Half Barrow Street
New York City, New York

"Aiden, wake up. Aiden," Katy pressed as she shook Aiden's shoulder somewhat delicately, but just enough that it was a little more than delicate. "Aiden…"

Aiden, who hadn't slept in more than forty hours, ripped awake and grabbed Katy's arm while simultaneously springing from the couch, throwing his offhand forearm to her neck, pinning her against the equipment in Fifty Two and a Half Barrow Street. Warriors with a clear conscience may sleep deeply but they often wake up already in the fight.

"Jesus, Katy are you alright?" Aiden said releasing her with a tinge of guilt.

Katy brushed it off "Yeah, yeah, I'm OK. I know where he is. At least I think I know where he is."

"Where who is?" Aiden queried now wide awake.

"Atta. The other lawyer."

"And…?"

"Brussels," Katy asserted with enough of a level of confidence to inspire Aiden

"How?"

"I went over Asidilov's phone. There were tons of calls to numbers in Brussels. I did some digging. Turns out that several years ago, up until 2011, Asidilov and Atta owned a florist shop in Brussels together!"

Aiden knew she had him but pressed her anyway. "So what's that mean?"

"It means it was obviously a front. Fast forward…three times in the past fifteen days Asidilov got a call from somewhere in Brussels. I cross-checked the number against the florist; it's the same number!"

Aiden looked at Katy like a schoolboy looks at his first crush. "Katy, you magnificent bloodhound, I think you got him."

Katy looked at Aiden like a schoolgirl looks at her first crush. She shook it off and got deadly serious.

An antsy Aiden started to move about the room with a purpose. "Where's Rolly and Nesto? How long have I been out?"

"You were sleeping for about six hours. They went to buy more prepaid phones. Rolly is convinced we should throw out any phone we might use to contact anyone outside us. He said he was going to trap Capps and Gafar with one of them."

Aiden began packing his things. "Hey Katy, sorry about the hound dog thing. How's your face?"

Katy smiling from the flirting, and suddenly aware of her bruised disfigurement, had no opportunity to advance the lure of seduction. The front door opened and they were all back to being strictly business.

"Katy found the lawyer. He's in Brussels," Aiden greeted them.

Nesto looked at Katy, "Percentage?"

"Percentage?" Katy responded.

"How sure are you he's there?"

"I don't know…m…um…"

"Eighty-five," Aiden assured. No one ever challenged Aiden's instincts. If he was at eighty-five, they were at eighty-five.

"OK," was all Rolly needed to say.

Aiden satisfied they were on the move changed the subject, "You said something about trapping Capps and Gafar earlier?"

"I'm working on it. First, the lawyer," Rolly said not quite assuring them of anything.

He turned to Nesto as naturally as breathing, "Nesto, let the Embassy know we're coming for the lawyer. Make sure they know we have the ball and we have it at the guarantee of the White House. Let them know we're taking this asshole tonight and that's that. These new diplomatic appointees all have God damn reset buttons and no sense of anything real. We don't want some community activist with a sociology degree and a Master's in Scooby doo-ing screwing it up."

Lastly he directed his attention to Katy, pointing at her thigh and tapping his own temple where hers had been punched, "Are you good?"

Katy would not have these men worrying about her "Don't worry about me. I'm fine."

"OK, good. Stay here. Do your thing. Follow your instincts on Gafar. I want to know wherever Capps goes. Get us anything you can think of that will help us with the lawyer, connections, proclivities, history…anything. If we need to talk use only the pre-paid."

Rolly handed Katy a piece of paper, "I've written the numbers down for the phones. There are five unopened phones on the desk. Try not to leave the house."

"Let's go…" Rolly said to the room. And they were gone.

Chapter 29

Brussels Airport, Belgium

The jet carrying The Three Ravens to Brussels touched down on the wet runway in the mid-morning mist. The Ravens deplaned and quickly hustled to the two black VW Golfs waiting for them in the short term parking lots. Aiden and Nesto in one, Rolly taking the lead in the other.

The ride to the flower shop and apartment occupied by the florist's owner would take, according to the GPS, forty-one minutes. The drive was a pretty straight route. They would be there in less than an hour without traffic, giving them a few hours to get a lay of the land and plan the extraction which would take place immediately after dark.

A few minutes into the drive the GPS took the two VW's onto the three-lane freeway which would make up the bulk of the travel. The freeway was empty of travelers with open road ahead.

As they passed the town of Grimbergen, Flanders, a small hilly town in the countryside of Belgium, the road opened and the traffic picked up pace. Rolly couldn't help but notice the lovely hillside to his left, which the freeway had been carved into, and the deep ravine to his right, which dropped precipitously beneath the freeway. It really was a pretty ride he thought.

Rolly's phone rang, "Yeah, Aiden."

Aiden, calmly, "We got company behind us."

"Whataya got?"

"Sedan,.. green... Looks like three. Middle Eastern. They're not being shy."

"Shit!" Rolly screamed to no one particular.

In front of Rolly a fourteen-foot box truck suddenly yanked up its' back door. A Middle Eastern man threw the head of a grenade launcher directly at Rolly's VW which was blocked from changing lanes to his right and the concrete divider to his left. He fired the grenade.

Rolly hit the brakes and threw himself from the car as it was moving. The grenade hit and immediately detonated, flipping the car as it exploded. The heat from the explosion burned Rolly's pant leg. Not wasting an instant, Rolly threw himself over the concrete divider for protection. He took stock of his pant leg, and well as the rest of himself, now aching head to toe from bouncing and spinning on the asphalt.

Meanwhile the sedan in the rear opened fire on the second VW. Bullets were flying but, shockingly, nothing hit the abruptly swerving VW. That wouldn't last very long.

The VW quickly passed Rolly's position and came to a stop fifty feet in front of the burning VW. The box truck was sixty yards to their front and the sedan with the three men were about the same distance behind. They were pinned in.

"Gotta get to the trees. You first and I'll provide suppressing fire from here. When you get to the tree line you do the same and I'll make a run at them," Aiden said to Nesto as they hunched between the VW and the concrete divider.

It would be a three-lane run across the road and twenty more feet to the tree line. Nesto knew his chance of making it to the trees un-hit was slim; Aiden's chance was almost nil. Trying to provide covering fire from the trees sixty feet away, coupled with shooters closing rapidly in from two sides at once, was not going to be near good enough for Aiden.

There was no time to argue and Nesto was faster than Aiden. He knew Aiden made the right call, but he couldn't bear to see Aiden in such a position. "You go first. I'll cover you." Nesto offered selflessly.

"On three...ready?" Aiden ignored the offer. "One, two, three!"

Nesto made his break as Aiden leaped to his feet and began firing his semiautomatic feverishly at the men approaching from the rear. Nesto took off for the tree line. About half way through Nesto's' run, Aiden dropped to a knee, rested his assault rifle on the concrete divider and began firing at the truck in front. Once Nesto made it to the trees, Aiden dropped beneath the divider for cover. Nesto was alive. He had that much going for him.

'OK, my boy…your turn,' Aiden said to himself as he breathed in to calm his nerves for his own sprint.

However, while he had been firing at the truck in front, the men in the rear had advanced in attack formation along the concrete divider, closing the distance between them and Aiden's position. They were a mere twenty paces from him and separated only by an eight-inch thick concrete divider.

The two men in the truck in front of Aiden's position had both exited the vehicle and were completely shielded, one by the truck and one by the same divider, forty yards in Aiden's front. They had him and Nesto couldn't do a damn thing to save the man who had just saved him. The second he stood up and took a step he was a dead man.

Aiden got himself up on one knee and was preparing to run the gauntlet once Nesto began his suppressing fire. "C'mon Nesto," Aiden begged impatiently.

Pop, pop, pop.

'What the….a hand gun?' Aiden thought to himself.

Confused, he peeked over the divider to his rear.

"Fucking Rolly. Way to go!" He said with a renewed energy and joy, the profundity of which only a dead man who discovers hope could fathom.

Rolly had allowed the three men from the trailing green sedan to pass in front of his position. As they passed between him and Aiden, he stood up and fired three bullets, killing each with a single shot to the head. The world's finest sniper proved his worth once again in less than two seconds. Once he had killed the three he scurried along divider and connected with his more than grateful partner.

"Shit, Rolly, thanks," Aiden said as he patted Rolly on the shoulder.

"We gotta move. There's at least two left and they have an RPG. We gotta move."

Pop…a second passes…pop.

Once again Aiden peeked over the divider. This time his heart overflowed. Hope for survival had turned to certainty.

Once Nesto made it to the tree line he had a panoramic view of the situation and could see Rolly would soon have tactical position on the three approaching Aiden from the rear. He sprinted along the trees passing the position of the two who had exited the truck and ran as fast as the great athlete he was would allow, cutting across the three-lane freeway. The terrorists had their attention directed at Aiden's position and never saw him coming with his pistol drawn. He leaped over the divider and in mid-stride fired a bullet into the back of the man's head, killing him instantly. He dropped to the ground harmless forever to the world.

Nesto kept running. He still had to clear the front of the box truck where the second terrorist was shielding himself and readying his RPG. The terrorist would never get the chance. Nesto whipped around the front bumper of the box truck and fired a second shot into the back of the grenade launcher's head. The RPG and the man fell to the ground. The world's second best sniper proved it in a second and a half.

It was over.

No time for congratulatory handshakes or hugs. "Let's go!" Rolly called up to Nesto as he and Aiden leaped into the front seats of the remaining black VW. Nesto sprinted to the small German made VW leaping into the rear seat.

The car sped off.

"That's the third fucking time. Rolly they knew we were coming. Each time they knew we were coming." Aiden said with both confusion in his voice and anger.

"Maybe Katy spoke to Capps," Nesto said, brainstorming what might have happened to give them away.

Aiden was already calling Katy, "Katy, did you call anyone? Capps? Anyone? Your family? Anyone at all?"

"Alright, we'll call you later tonight or if we need you. In the meantime don't call anyone, OK? OK." Aiden disconnected the phone.

"It wasn't her. She said she hasn't used her phone. I believe her," Aiden offered confidently. No one ever questioned Aiden's famous instincts.

"Then what the hell is going on here?" Nesto asked to no one in particular.

"It doesn't matter right now. It'll be a few hours before they figure out what just happened. We've got to find this prick before he realizes we weren't among the dead back there. He might be scrambling as we speak. We'll worry about the leak after." Rolly always had a keen sense of moving forward.

"How long do you think it'll be before they're on to us?" Nesto asked, trying to mentally prepare for a busy night.

"It'll be a good while. There weren't any witnesses and the crossfire between the guys in the back and the guys in the front will make it look like they were shooting at each other," Aiden answered.

"Well, I guess that's a break," Rolly chimed in. "Do you think we'll have the night?"

"Hard to tell," Aiden went on. "They're Middle Eastern and that means they'll put their best forensics on it. If they're good, they'll be pretty quick to figure out that all five of them were shot in the head, pretty much point blank, in the back of the head from behind. That'll debunk the notion that they were firing at each other."

"Thanks, Einstein. How long before they figure it out and come looking for us?" Rolly pushed Aiden.

"Figure three hours, four…six max, if we're lucky."

Nesto summarized the groups' collective uncomfortableness, "Damn!"

"We're gonna run out of luck. We gotta find this leak," Aiden said thoughtfully.

"We gotta find this fucking lawyer," Rolly said matter-of-factly.

Chapter 30

Molenbeek-Saint-Jean, Brussels

Aiden studied every detail of traffic movements, number of apartment doorways, window egresses, shops, and the people on the street surrounding the house where they were near-certain Muhammad Atta kept his safe house.

"It ain't Bagdad," Nesto said to Aiden as they sat in the small black VW across the street and up the block from the house at Rue de la Carpe, in the Molenbeek-Saint-Jean section of Brussels.

"No, it's not," Aiden concurred, "but given how stupid these governments have been with refugees they might have as many bad guys."

The Molenbeek-Saint-Jean section of Brussels has been described by its own mayor as a "breeding ground for violence." Molenbeek sits just north and west of the Brussels city center. Beginning in the late 1960's the neighborhood saw large migrations largely from Turkey and Morocco. Now these few square blocks were more well-known for housing of Islamist terrorists, bomb makers, and bad guys needing to hide.

The neighborhood is a lovely collection of three, four, and five story walkups with seemingly symmetrically spaced window boxes which blaze the facades with all the color of a Monet spring. Despite the beauty, the area has become a hotbed of radicalization. The causes are many. Radicalization in prisons has drawn much attention, behind the burgeoning Muslim population. It is thought in Belgium that more than one in four of

Belgium's incarcerated are Muslim, while counting for far less than ten percent of the overall population.

None of the Three Ravens could care less about the math of it all or why so many bad guys had convened in so small a space. They only knew that their man was here, likely not alone, and they were nearly out of time before a devastating device would be exploded somewhere in another country, theirs, half way around the world. They didn't have time to build a plan for a safe extraction. It was a blitz. They were going in tonight. There was no second way.

Rolly appeared at the driver's side and Nesto rolled down the window. "Ok, nothing out of the ordinary. People coming and going. Nightfall is in an hour and we'll going in as soon as it's dark. I know it's not best but we may not have seven hours to spare. I'll make my way along the roof. At twenty-twenty we go. You guys go in night attack formation. I'll press from the roof. Don't shoot me."

Aiden leaned over the console between himself and Nesto "Shoot you? I don't think so. You still owe me thirty bucks." All three chuckled.

Rolly got deadly serious. You get deadly serious when you're about to do deadly things. "Split up for the hour. These people have been jaded by the recent police raids. No communication unless it's absolutely urgent. Remember boys, we need this prick alive. Twenty- twenty. Good luck." Rolly placed his hand on Nesto's shoulder then disappeared.

Aiden and Nesto sat for another minute, giving Rolly a chance to go unnoticed. "Alright my friend," Aiden said while offering his hand to one of the two men he considered his nearest relatives. "Once more into the breach. See you in an hour."

Nesto reached for the car door handle as his phone rang. Rolly was on the other end trying to sound as urgent as he could without raising his voice. "The fucker is on the move. There are five of them getting into two cars, a silver Mercedes and blue Mitsubishi van. Move, move, move. Do you see the van at the end of the street pulling out?

"I've got it. I've got it," Nesto responded.

"I'm going to take the Mercedes. Get the van. Get the van. Get out in front of the Mercedes before he pulls out. Three men inside. Go, go, go!" Rolly instructed before hanging up.

"Go, go, go. We gotta get that blue van. Go!" Nesto said as Aiden threw the key into the ignition and started the engine simultaneously putting the transmission in gear.

"Go Aiden. Get out in front of that Mercedes, the one with the guy getting in. Get in front of it. Rolly is going to take them. We need that fuckin' van."

Aiden did as he was told. The small black VW blew passed the Mercedes. The chase was on for the blue van.

Muhamad Atta knew he was made. He felt lucky that the men in the black VW had missed him. He punched the glove box in the passenger seat of the silver Mercedes. "Get out of here," he barked at his driver. Get out of …"

Before Atta could finish the order Rolly had put two bullets into the head of the driver. Atta recoiled in shock.

Rolly didn't waste a moment. With the butt of his pistol he smashed through the already shattered driver's side window. Opening the door he fired a bullet into Atta's knee, pulled the dead man from the seat onto the sidewalk and climbed into the already running Mercedes. He took a glancing look at the terrorist and threw the car into gear and went off after the VW which was in wild pursuit of the blue van.

"Mr. Atta. My name is Roland Byrnes. I'm an American and you're my prisoner of war, you fucking murdering scumbag. Sit the fuck still and I won't kill you."

"Fuck you. I'm an American too. You can't…" Rolly fired a second bullet into Atta's wound and then pistol whipped him in the forehead. Atta's head shot back into the headrest of the Mercedes passenger seat.

"I said sit the fuck still. If you wanna live another hour you'll do as you are told. Understand?"

Atta was a murdering terrorist, but right now he was a dazed and bleeding pile of everyday humanity. No amount of fanaticism could help him climb out of his suffering.

"Stay on him, Aiden!" Nesto called out as a rally to his partner.

"I've got him. The van is too cumbersome. He can't lose me. He's gotta do something else."

The van passenger window rolled down. The head of a Middle Eastern man leaned out and began firing his AKM. Aiden thought to himself it was the same repeating machine gun sound he had heard in the Michigan forest and again at the harbor side restaurant. A second later the back window of the van got blown out, shattered with bullet holes from the same unrelenting staccato machine gun.

"Ya mean something like that...Jesus?" Bullets too numerous to count were hitting the black VW, more than a few piercing the windshield.

Aiden calmly drew his side arm and fired two bullets directly into the back of the van window where the shots were coming from, hitting the terrorist in the face, thus negating at least that threat. The man in the passenger seat was not deterred and continued firing.

Aiden did his best to stay on the driver's side of the van to reduce the gunman's angle of fire, but with the curved roads and the drivers' serpentine moves he could only do so much. The Golf was getting hit and often.

Weaving in and out of oncoming cars and caring not for avoiding pedestrians, the van kept its top speed.

Brussels was an old city built long before city planners gave any thought to cars, let alone traffic. The streets of the Molenbeek-Saint-Jean, which were built for foot traffic and maybe the occasional mule or horse, were narrow, curved, and triangulated where two roads often converged into one. It would be the antiquity of the city's layout which would prove the undoing of the van driver.

The van slammed into a delivery truck and careened into a collection of cars lining the narrow road before coming to a smoking stop. The driver was injured badly. The passenger, bloodied but alive, jumped out of the van and began running towards the black VW trying to fire a weapon which had no bullets left to deliver. Nesto exited the car and fired a single shot into the chest of the daft terrorist, killing him instantly.

Aiden and Nesto moved ever so carefully up on either side of the disabled van. The driver, barely alive, looked at Aiden through the side view mirror, in his hand a grenade. Aiden moved carefully with his pistol drawn and pointed. Inch by inch he moved knowing there was a potential problem awaiting him. Just as Aiden was about to swing around and point his gun at the driver, the man reached with his left hand for the grenade pin in his right hand. Pop, pop, he was dead.

Standing in the passenger window was Nesto, who had been just a hair quicker to the door, just a hair less careful than Aiden. In war it's sometimes a hair that separates who lives and who dies. This time that hair benefited Aiden and passed a final judgment against the terrorist slumped over the steering wheel gripping an unarmed grenade.

It was the second time in as many days that Nesto had saved Aiden. It wasn't lost on Aiden but, just as it was a day earlier, there was no time for a thank you.

"Grab the computers and phones," Aiden called to Nesto.

Nesto jumped into the van and collected two computers and the pocketed phone on the dead man in the back of the van. Aiden removed the phone from the dead driver.

Just as they were about to make a getaway on foot, the silver Mercedes pulled up beside them. "Get in!" Rolly blistered. "Nesto, grab this piece of shit and put him in the back seat. Tie a tourniquet on that leg."

Nesto complied and Aiden helped load the near unconscious Atta into the back seat before jumping into the passenger seat of the Mercedes. Rolly hit the gas.

"Jesus, Rolly! What is it with you shooting people in the knee?" Aiden asked.

Rolly answered, "We gotta get rid of this car. We gotta get outta here and get somewhere safe where we can talk to Mr. Atta. We're blown. We're fucking blown. Someone told these pricks we were coming. That's three fucking times."

Aiden called Katy back in New York. "Katy, we got the lawyer. Nice work. Within the hour I'm sending you files from two computers. Do whatever you do. We need whatever info you can extract from these two boxes...any connections, indicators about where they plan to open that suitcase. Anything at all. Don't over analyze. These guys were on the run. They had broken down their equipment and cleared house. They knew we were coming. More than likely they've accelerated the timetable. Start with the suitcase and work your way from there"

"Aiden, the story broke about the men in the forest," Katy didn't know why she needed to get that in before Aiden disconnected. She just knew.

"Hold on. I'm putting you on speaker so we can all hear you," Aiden interjected.

Katy continued, "It's all over the TV. Apparently its inspired attacks on our embassies in Cairo and Tripoli and there have been two Christian church burnings in Michigan. The pundits are connecting the murders in the forest to the others and blaming right wing American Christians. Someone is posting pictures of the dead online, really graphic stuff. Overseas they're filling the streets and blaming Americans for the slaughter. They've fired over a thousand rockets into Israel from Gaza and Iran has called for an Intifada. A Muslim mob in Stuttgart rushed an U.S. Army base and killed two soldiers."

"Damn it!" Aiden responded. "Go to work on the files!"

Rolly cut him off to ask Katy a question. "Has the State Department put out a statement about the killing in Huron? Has the president said anything official?"

"No, not yet. The White House spokesman said something about calming the rhetoric and called for an end to religious violence."

Rolly was incensed. "Those friggin' people. The world is literally on fire and they want to keep trying to put it out with fluff. Jesus, I hate those people."

Nesto summed up what all three were thinking, "Shit, that bomb goes off and they'll consider it retaliation. Americans are gonna go nuts. We'll have no choice. There'll be fighting worldwide. It's gonna make the post 9/11 seem tame. And it won't be contained to Iraq and Afghanistan."

While everyone was listening intently to Nesto, Rolly had his ear on the radio. "We got another problem, boys. They know about the shootout earlier. It's on the radio that they're looking for men who may have fled the scene. They'll put two and two together, this scene and that one. We gotta get out of Brussels."

The Mercedes moved three blocks from the crash and made right turn. They were winging it now in a foreign country, a country they had to get out of carrying with them a wounded man. There was no embassy to go to, no safe house, and no one to trust but themselves.

All they were as a team would be tested now like never before.

Chapter 31

Omar
Molenbeek-Saint-Jean, Brussels

"We gotta get another car," Rolly said to no one in particular.

Three miles from the crashed Mitsubishi van, Rolly turned onto Boulevard Louis Mettewie and hit the gas. Halfway to the next traffic light he saw a bread truck operator in front of the Brico City market unloading a rack of bread loaves. Just past the Brico City market store Rolly pulled the silver Mercedes into an underground parking garage. "Stay here. I'll be right back," he said as he jumped out of his driver's side seat and took off running.

A few moments had passed when the bread truck driver loaded his handcart into the back of the van. He climbed into the front seat and turned the ignition to the truck.

"Ne bouge pas."

The truck driver jumped an inch in his seat when he turned to see Rolly kneeling on the floor behind him. He settled back into his chair. A look of terror came over him.

"Je ne suis pas un voleur. Parlez-vous Anglais?"

"A little," the trembling driver responded to Rolly's assurance that he wasn't a thief and to his question as to whether the driver spoke English.

"Good. I'm not a thief and I won't hurt you if you do as I say. Understand?"

"Oui…ugh…yes."

"Your name. What is your name?" Rolly asked in a calm manner.

"My name is Omar"

"Where are you from Omar?"

"I am from Armardeh, Kurdistan."

"Northern Iraq. You are a Kurd?" Omar nodded. "Good. Relax. I won't hurt you. Make a right and stop there in front of the garage… There," Rolly said pointing to the parking garage entry. As soon as the driver rolled just past the entry, Rolly ordered him to stop.

"OK. Leave the engine running and come with me."

The two men exited the van. The driver walked in front of Rolly. He put his hands in the air like they do in the thousand movies the truck driver had watched over the years.

"No, no, no…hands down, Omar. Keep your hands down." Rolly snapped in French in the event Omar didn't understand, "Baisse les mains... Down!"

The confused driver looked back at Rolly who was feverishly pushing his palms towards the ground so the clown wouldn't draw attention to the pair and the two entered the garage. As soon as they were visually picked up by Aiden, Rolly frantically waved them up. Aiden and Nesto exited the Mercedes and both carried the injured Muhammad Atta.

Rolly and the driver entered the truck. Rolly pointed the man to the driver's seat and he moved to the back of the truck and opened the rear door. Aiden and Nesto laid Atta's near limp body onto the cold, black floor of the van and climbed in pulling the rear door closed.

Rolly jumped into the passenger seat and pointed the gun again at the driver. "Drive! Conduire! Brussels Airport…now!"

The frightened driver pulled the gear shift, which screeched from the off-timed, aggressive hand of the nervous driver and they were off. A few seconds passed and the truck driver, sensing he was indeed not the victim of a robbery, turned his head to peek at Atta lying in pain on the floor. He turned and pointed to Rolly, "CIA?" Rolly, not wanting to explain simply nodded yes.

The truck driver pointed to Atta, "Terroriste?"

Rolly looked at the approving face of the driver, "Oui." The chauffer mock spit towards the terrorist and waved his hand forward indicating his willingness to be part of the extraction. In broken English and partial French he ranted, "This pieces shit is why I am here, why I am alone and my wife hides at home, afraid to go outside. Terroriste, terroriste attacked my city, burned my city. So many killed. Tant de morts. Shit! They ruin my family, my country. No way for a man to feed his family. I have nothing, so I must come here, where people hate me, because I am Muslim, because of this animals and their crazy shit, killing in the name of Allah, burning for Allah." Tears began to stream down his face as he drove. Twenty-two months away from my family, he thought. First begging for food, then by the kindness of a stranger, this meager job. He thought about eating the same leftover bread from his route, every day without fail, so he could save enough money to get his family out. Anger swelled. He spoke through his choked up, quivering lips, "I pray to Allah. I pray. Please, I ask him, please, I ask he burn them, all burn in hell."

The driver spit at the bound Atta one more time. Omar wiped the tears as he couldn't help recall all the terrible days he had been through in his homeland. "Quinze kilometer...um...five, five, five minutes."

"OK, Omar... Thank you. You are a good man." Rolly responded to the reflective driver, now considering himself fully a member of the extraction team. All three felt a sense of relief, but there was no time to rest for Rolly or the others. They had to organize their exit.

"Nesto, call the pilot and tell them we're out. Tell him we'll be there in fifteen and we're intending to be wheels up immediately. Do whatever he has to do to make sure no one stops us. Tell him to call the president if they say a fucking word. We don't want to be waiting a friggin' second on the ground. And tell him we're going to Lansing Michigan, not New York. We're gonna pick up any and all of Atta's family members."

Rolly turned his eyes to Aiden. "Call Katy, by now she should have everything there is on Atta's family."

Rolly wanted the terrorist to know that he was going to use whatever was at his disposal, do whatever necessary, including to his wife and children, to get what he needed from him.

Atta, having seen Rolly's commitment to the moment and his cause first hand in the form of two dispassionately placed bullet holes in his right knee, duly noted the horrifying implications.

Chapter 32

Fifty Two and a Half Barrow Street
New York City, New York

"Put him in the back room," Rolly whispered his instructions to Nesto "and make sure it's blacked out completely in there. I want this mutt to think we dragged him all the way to Lansing. I'll get the doc up here to patch this asshole so he doesn't check out before I can squeeze him."

Aiden and Nesto dragged an unconscious Atta into the back bedroom. They tied his hands and feet to the bedpost and footboard, shut all the blinds and curtains and covered Atta's mouth with silver duct tape.

All three reconvened in the operation room. Each man locked their eyes onto Katy's obviously concerned, busted-up face with one cheek now fully swollen, one eye fully black and blue nearly shut and all the other cuts and bruises sustained in her struggle with Asidilov.

"What?" Aiden sheepishly queried.

"You're not going to believe this," Katy responded as she ran her hand through her hair.

"What?" Aiden asked again without a hint of sheepishness.

"Atta's computer has all of the Secretary of State's emails, her personal stuff and her official stuff, including top secret stuff. And her staff's as well."

Rolly couldn't believe what she had just told them, "What the fuck? Are you serious?"

Katy explained, "Yes, I'm serious and it's the reason they knew you were coming for Atta in Brussels. They picked it off the cable we sent through to the State Department. The email we sent to the embassy alerting her that we were conducting the operation. When we alerted State we were coming, it being a 'high priority' extraction, and potentially a disavowed one at that, the Secretary was brought into it. She alerted the Ambassador at the embassy that we were coming. When she alerted him, she alerted Atta. Moron. She has no idea the damage she's doing."

"Are you fucking serious? How?" Rolly demanded.

"The Secretary and her band of yes men use personal non-encrypted email accounts, outside of State's secured servers. All her communications emanate from a non-encrypted server. Any high school kid with a laptop could get in there and see everything."

Aiden was flabbergasted, "Jesus Christ. Don't they give a shit about security, about fucking protecting secrets?"

Katy was rolling, "Apparently not. And, get this. Half of these idiots use non-encrypted phones. My dry cleaner could have hacked this stuff. She's got thousands and thousands of sensitive emails out in the open. All they have to do, Atta and anyone else, is just read her emails."

Nesto was having a world of trouble getting his head around the disregard for state secrets or the safety of operatives in the field. "Oh my fucking God!"

Katy kept talking, "Luckily, there wasn't time for us to plan the extraction in advance or Atta would have been gone. That you were winging it meant you got there so quickly they didn't have time to break down the house and move it down the street. But that's how they knew you were coming. That's how they knew where to cut you off. I've hacked into the Secretary's email account myself. It took less than a minute. That's how they knew. I'm sure of it."

The doorbell interrupted what was going to be a cursing and swearing session. "It's the doc," Nesto said as he looked out the window at the man below standing at the door.

Rolly nodded to Nesto. "Let him in. I don't want this prick dying on us. We've got a whole lot of talking to do."

Nesto depressed the security buzzer opening the door two stories below. A few seconds later a middle-aged, balding, bespectacled man walked into the room. He didn't say a word. Nesto pointed towards the bedroom. The doctor looked straight ahead and walked through the room without speaking or even nodding to anyone. He had clearly done this before and disappeared into the backroom.

Aiden picked back up on the Secretary's email account. "That selfish bitch!" he barked. "Our fucking lives are at stake and she's sitting at home floating national security secrets into the atmosphere for all to read so she can avoid FOIA disclosures? What a self-serving... Why the fuck would anyone do that?"

Rolly had one ear on Aiden and one ear on the backroom. He wanted to get at Atta. "To hide her shit from the American public, that's why."

The veins in Aiden's neck and forehead bulged in anger, "That bitch! That fucking bitch!"

Rolly and Nesto could remember Aiden getting furious only twice before. He was the most calculating man either had ever known. In both instances his fury turned into action and his action turned into the death of more than ten Taliban fighters, two by hand.

"You said that already, Aiden," Nesto said trying a bit of humor in an attempt to get Aiden off the road he was fast heading onto.

Rolly saw what Nesto was doing and got in it. He immediately moved to interrupt Aiden's mushrooming diatribe. "Alright, alright, fuck that for now. We'll deal with the stupid skank in a minute." Rolly needed another thing from Katy first.

"Katy, did you get the stuff on Atta's family?"

"I did."

"Put the pics up on screen one," Rolly said pointing to a large TV screen hanging on the wall surrounded by several smaller screens.

"He has a few wives around the world, only one in the U.S. Her name is Marina Nemat. Here she is." A Michigan driver's license appeared with the face of a Middle Eastern woman opened on the screen.

"He has twelve children, three American born, all sons; they currently live in the U.S. They are natural born citizens. The oldest is Nader, a professor of Systems Engineering at Eastern Michigan, forty-nine. Haleh is an attorney in Detroit, forty-six. Nariman is a code communication engineer, thirty-nine and employed by Intel in Santa Clara, California."

"Any of them on any lists?" Aiden asked of Katy.

"No. From all appearances they've led clean lives."

"Bullshit. A systems engineer, a code communication expert, and an attorney? No way they're clean," Rolly overwrote Katy.

"Well, they're clean with respect to any lists."

The doctor appeared from the backroom. He walked into the middle of the group. "Nice work on the wound. Is this your work, Aiden?"

Aiden nodded that indeed it was.

"Are you sure you have no medical training?"

Aiden could only offer a courtesy smile. He was trying to suppress his anger at the Secretary of State and bring himself back into focus. He was in no mood for compliments, less for levity. The doctor sensed the urgency and the unwillingness of the room for banter. "He'll be fine. Well, not fine. He won't die on you tonight. He'll never walk right again. But I removed the bone fragments, cleaned the wound as best I could under the circumstances, and rewrapped it. He's in a shitload of pain but he'll be able to talk."

"Doc, stay close and ready an extraction team. We're gonna put some pressure on this guy and then we're on the move. We're going to need you to come pick this guy up quickly and get him out of here. We're going to be on the move. Understand?" asked Rolly.

The doctor nodded, clasped his medical bag shut and left without saying another word.

Rolly picked up a laptop from one of the desks in the room. "OK Katy, I need you to put all four of those faces on this laptop screen for me. Aiden, is the Secretary in on this?"

Rolly was perfectly confident in Aiden's gut and it had never failed them before. They were going to move the game forward entirely on Aiden's instincts. They trusted him that much.

"No, she's an asshole and should be in jail, but she's not in on it. Gafar on the other hand is. We've got to expose her… safely. Katy use your dirty talents on this. We need to know the extent of the problem. How it is that they got her emails? Who it is that has them? We need to know the size of the holes and who else might be in danger because of this. Hack the shit out of this. We need to know."

Katy was stunned. Could it be that she was actually going to hack the Secretary of State's email? Could it be that others were out in the field in danger because of this? She grew angry. Nesto snapped her out of it when he prioritized it all, "We've got to find that friggin' suitcase first. If that thing goes off its World War Three. The selfish moron's email will be the last of our concerns then." The room went silent.

Katy's hands kept moving. She broke the introspected silence, "OK, there," she said pointing to the laptop.

"Aiden, put your phone on vibrate. I may call you from inside." Rolly picked it up, tilted his head, "Alright… Here we go." He and the laptop headed to the back bedroom.

Chapter 33

Barrow Street,
New York City, New York

Rolly and his men had dealt with all manners of fanatic. Mostly they were young uneducated men, from very poor backgrounds, who had been lied to and manipulated into thinking death for the cause in this life meant wonderful things in the next life. Rolly rarely gave much thought to why fanatics do what they do. Mostly, as they lie dead at Rolly's hand, he felt sorry for them having been screwed by people who knew better, the scum who were feeding the poor saps the nonsense that led to their grizzly deaths. But then he would chase away the sentiment and grow even harder because of the misery they intended to inflict. The man lying tied up in the next room was that scum. Rolly had to call on every bit of his control not to hurt the bastard before he could get what he needed.

The door opened to the blackened bedroom. The light from the outer room made Muhamad Atta's pupils contract and eyes squint. Rolly entered the room slowly and closed the door behind him. He let the light from the computer screen act as a flashlight until he got to the bedside.

He placed the laptop and a phone on the table and stood there looking at the bound terrorist. Atta could see his family members on the screen and his heart sank, it wasn't supposed to go this way. It was supposed to be the glory of the caliphate for Islam and its billions; instead, it was a moment of fate for one man and his family. Rolly gave Atta a few seconds to lay in the dark and contemplate his dilemma.

Rolly leaned down and turned on the bedside lamp. He bent over and pulled the tape from Atta's mouth. Atta tried to speak, "I'm an American. I have…." Rolly smashed his fist into Atta's face dazing the prisoner.

"You're not an American. You're a fucking scumbag."

Rolly had to remind himself again that, despite his hatred for the pain Atta was trying cast over the nations of the world, not to hurt the man too much.

"Please, I want a lawyer."

Rolly's self-control and his self-admonishments fell short. He smashed Atta's face again with his fist shattering the skin connecting his ear.

"Shut the fuck up."

Atta dazed, in pain, and confused, laid still and quiet.

"Remember what I did to you in Brussels? You should know I killed Asidilov because he was stupid. He didn't answer me honestly. You know now I don't negotiate and I have no time to waste."

Rolly stared blankly at Atta. If he was unafraid of death for himself as fanatics often are, perhaps he would alter his fanaticism for someone else, someone close. Rolly was betting that the many years of living in the United States would have given Atta a different perspective regarding the value of human life, more specifically his own family's human lives.

"Muhamad, look closely at the computer." Atta stared straight ahead at the ceiling not realizing the cards Rolly was holding. Rolly was having none of it. He grabbed Atta's hair and yanked his head so Atta would have no choice but to see the screen.

When he was convinced he had Atta's full attention, he spoke softly but firmly. "Your youngest son, Nariman, will be the first since he's in California." Placing his finger over Nariman's face on the computer screen, he continued. "The rest of your family is here in Michigan with us. Look in my eyes so you know I'm serious."

Atta now could not look away from his son on his enemy's computer screen. Rolly slapped him hard. "Look at me!"

Atta looked into Rolly's eyes with a deep hatred and an extreme contempt. Rolly was only concerned that Atta knew his predicament.

"I'm going to ask you questions. You're gonna answer them truthfully or I'm going to kill them one by one. I'm going to get what I want or I'm going to kill those boys. If you lie to me, I pick up that phone and Nariman picks up his seventy virgins and whatever else is promised to the dead asshole. Then Nader, then Haleh, then your wife too. Yes, your wife."

Atta was about to say something, but thought better of it. He closed his eyes and prayed. Prayers were not going to help him. Nothing was going to help him.

"You have two choices. One, you can go to Gitmo if you answer me honestly. There are meals and sunshine, TV, and soccer matches. Hey, this weak-ass president's been letting terrorists out of there by the week. You may even have a chance to be set free and get back in the fight someday. Or two, I'm going to kill you here and now. But know this. I'm gonna get what I want. Look at me. I'm going…to get what I need. You have to ask yourself if you're willing to sacrifice your family."

Rolly gave Atta a moment to think.

"Ready?"

Atta nodded.

"Remember. I will not revisit my questions. If I pick up that phone, Nariman gets put down. Look at me….ready?"

Atta nodded again.

"Where is the bomb going to be exploded?"

"Somewhere in Arizona," Atta answered.

Rolly looked into Atta's face, "Where in Arizona?"

"I don't know"

Rolly reached for the phone.

"I don't know. I swear. My job was to smuggle the men into the U.S., into Michigan, and kill them. That's it. The bomb is someone else. I swear!"

"Where in Arizona?'

"I told you I don't know."

Rolly shoved the tape back over Atta's mouth and picked up the phone. He dialed Aiden's phone. Aiden Answered.

"Kill the tech," Rolly spoke softly, but firmly into the phone. "When I call you again kill the one they call Nader. When you kill that one leave his body in the gutter for the rats to feed on."

Atta's eyes bulged and his face immediately went to sheer panic. Rolly ripped the tape off Atta's lips, "Nariman is dead because you lied. Nader is next."

"Please...I'll tell you what you want to know. Please..."

"Where in Arizona?"

"Downtown Phoenix"

"When?"

"This week. Thursday or Friday during business hours. They are waiting for a signal."

"A signal? From whom?"

Atta looked up at Rolly, "The Mullahs in Iran."

Rolly tried his best to hide how he felt about the magnitude and the ramifications of what Atta had just told him. He swallowed hard. "Who is carrying it?"

"I don't know. This is true."

Rolly reached for the phone on the nightstand.

"I don't know who. There is a handler."

"Who is the handler for the suitcase?" Rolly calmly asked. "I won't ask as second time."

"I don't know. I just know a person in the government, your government. A person who can… " Atta was calculating and Rolly didn't like it.

"Who can what? You tell me right now or I pick up that phone." Rolly was close. He knew Atta was trying to give him enough not to get his son killed, but not enough to wreck the plot. He grabbed the phone and the screen lit up.

"To convince your president to negotiate for peace with Iran after their missiles destroy Tel Aviv and Haifa."

Atta's fanaticism took hold. His pain all but disappeared. His eyes widened. You could see he wanted to scream it out loud. "The Arab world is demonstrating now all over the world. They want blood, your blood. When the bomb goes off in your streets, America will not know what to do. The Arab world will rise up. The American president is a coward. The Mullahs tell us he will seek diplomatic solutions while the West crumbles."

Rolly thrust his face closer, "Who's the contact in the White House?"

The terrorist, in a frothing trance, continued on his rant, "He will call for calm all over the world."

"Who's the contact in the White House?"

"Allahu Akbar, Allahu Akbar."

Rolly grabbed the phone. "Kill the lawyer and then bring me this prick's wife. I want him to watch me kill her."

Atta's eyes contracted and his own personal situation came quickly back into view, "No, please. I will tell you. I will tell you."

Rolly had him. He could tell. "I won't ask you again. Who's the contact in the White House?"

"I swear I don't know. I just know a person in the government, a woman, a woman close to the president. She is the handler. She is close enough to keep Teheran informed about American and Israeli actions."

"You stupid caliphate fucks. The Israelis won't ask permission," Rolly argued.

"Your president hates Israel. Israel will die without the support of the U.S. All the Arab nations will descend on them from the north, south, east, and west. This will end them."

Rolly leaped to his feet and sprinted from the room. Everyone in the war room was waiting for instructions. When the door blasted open and Rolly came in they knew it was go time.

"Nesto, get the Doc back. Tell him to bring a team to take this piece of shit. Aiden, take Katy through the Holland Tunnel and call Capps."

Rolly turned to Katy. "Katy, when Aiden gets you over to New Jersey he'll drive towards Newark airport. When you get just south of Jersey City call Capps and tell him we're on our way to Syria. Tell him we've got a lead on the dead Muslims in the forest. Make sure you use the word Muslims. Keep him on the phone for a minute or two, long enough to triangulate your phone. Then ditch the phone."

"Aiden, more than likely Capps will pass it on to his contact, which I'm certain is Hannah Gafar or someone once removed from her. After Katy makes the call, get back here as fast as you can. But make sure you aren't followed. If I'm right, they'll be on that phone in a heartbeat. Hustle, we meet back here in an hour."

Nesto asked Rolly, "Where are you going?"

"I'm going to put my foot up a sitting president's ass."

Chapter 34

Oval Office

Washington, D.C.

Rolly hated this president. All the way up from the West Village to 96th Street on the IRT number one train, he reflected on how much he hated the guy. He hated him to the core. But he had something bigger going on in his core. He dialed his phone.

A woman answered the phone. "Three Ravens for the president" was all he said. She disconnected the call.

Rolly walked away from the subway entrance seeking a place where he could talk away from any ears.

His phone rang. A woman's voice, "Three Ravens. Twenty minutes."

Rolly could care less about the president's current engagement. "Tell that fuck he doesn't have twenty minutes. I want to talk to him now." He disconnected the call without a response.

A minute passed, "Rolly, this is the president. What is the urgency?"

"Are you alone?" Rolly quickly pushed.

"No."

"Get alone and call me back…alone," Rolly hung up the phone on the president.

A minute passed. Rolly's phone rang.

"Are you fucking kidding? I'm the president of the United States. How dare you hang up on me!"

Rolly could care less that the President was annoyed. "Are you alone?"

"Yes."

"I need to see you. Today…alone."

"I can't do that." The president wasn't going to allow Rolly to dictate the conversation.

"Mr. President, you have a spy in your inner circle. A spy who is in a plot to start World War III."

"What? Who? What the fuck are you saying, Rolly? I don't believe you. What's this about?"

"I need to see you…today…alone. And you can't tell anyone. Anyone."

"You'll tell me now!"

"No."

The phone went dead for five seconds.

The president was furious, "Mister, you'll tell me now or I'll have you thrown in jail for the rest of your life. You hear me?"

Rolly could never be intimidated. "Mister, you can do as you wish, but only after we meet. You have a spy, at least one, very near you, conspiring to detonate a dirty bomb among your citizens so to create a war. You're pissed and I don't give a shit. I have a plan to stop it, but I need your help. You need to meet me. Today...alone."

The president, still angry, capitulated, "OK, where?"

"You meet us behind the Hotel Lombardy at 6:30. It'll be dark by then. We'll be in a white unmarked van. Come alone and tell no one…no one. Not even your wife." The President disconnected the call.

Chapter 35

Hotel Lombardy

Washington, D.C.

The president's driver pulled a black Ford Five Hundred around the back of the Hotel Lombardy and saddled up next to the unmarked white van resting in a parking spot nearest to the garbage dumpster as Rolly had instructed. The side door of the van opened. Rolly exited the van and climbed into the back seat of the Ford.

"This better be good, Byrnes. I had a heap of trouble rearranging things so I could get here," the president curtly said to Rolly.

Rolly didn't like being called by his last name. Instead of engaging in a wasteful argument he went right into it. "You have a spy, Mr. President. Worse, she's part of the plot to detonate that suitcase. She's part of a conspiracy to start World War III. It's about the caliphate".

"Who?" the President demanded.

"Hannah Gafar."

"You're crazy."

"Look, I don't have time to go into it. I'm telling you she's filthy and she's planning to do serious harm to this country, to the world, serious harm. I wouldn't tell you any of this until it was all over but I need your help and I need it now."

The president's facial expressions went from confusion to denial to sadness and back again. "Rolly, I don't believe this. I've known her for twenty years. I can't imagine this is so."

Rolly dismissed the president, "It's so."

"How?" the President asked in a low, fatalistic voice.

Rolly had no sympathy, "How? I'll tell you how. Because she saw how idealistic you were, how naïve, how gullible you were, and how utopian your shithead hopes were. She's been planning this for a long time. "

The President went incensed. "How dare you? How dare you talk to me that way? I'm the president of the United States. "

Rolly snapped back, "I don't give a shit, you stupid fuck. The caliphate's been planned for seven hundred years." Rolly turned sarcastic, "You've known her for twenty years," he said mimicking and mocking the president. "These bastards have been at this for centuries. They've been waiting for a schmuck like you. She played you. I don't give a shit if you're pissed. You should be embarrassed. The truth authenticates itself… and it will vindicate itself. She's in on it. And she alone can lead us to the suitcase. The fucking clock is ticking so save it."

The president was about to challenge Rolly once more but the reality of the situation, and his faith that while Rolly was clearly an insubordinate he was also as honorable as they come, overrode the challenge. He decided to hear Rolly out. "OK, OK, enough. What do you want me to do?"

Rolly didn't wait. "We need you to find a reason to go to Phoenix this weekend: Thursday, Friday, Saturday. We know the suitcase is in Phoenix and Gafar knows when they're gonna let it go. They need you to be alive to call for calm after it goes off and after the Iranian attacks on Israel."

The President interrupted, "What? Attack on Israel?"

Rolly didn't miss a beat. "Not attack, attacks. They're planning on attacking Israel on several fronts. They need you to call for calm after the bomb goes off and riots erupt around the Middle East."

The president felt a sickness he had never felt before, "I don't understand. What about the other murders? Turner, Myers, Coons, and the others. How is this connected?"

Rolly felt bad for the poor guy. The world was about to explode into a million pieces, leaving him with the stain of it on his legacy for all time. "Those murders were contract hits. They brought in radical Muslim Chechen mercenaries to commit those crimes to establish the perception in the Muslim world that the Christian Right was rising up. They needed to place the needle squarely on the right, the Christian Right. What better way is there to do that than to murder people conservative Americans hate?"

"Damn it," was all the president could think of to say.

Rolly went further, "It was a set up to springboard the idea that the Muslim world was certain to soon be under assault. The Muslims murdered in Michigan were the final piece. The sad part is they weren't even Muslims at all. They were Christian prisoners brought here from Iraq. They dressed those poor bastards in Muslim traditional garb and murdered them. Sheep to the slaughter, poor bastards."

"And Garfar? How did you discover?"

"Mr. President its best if you didn't ask in the event you are ever asked under oath. Let's just say we connected the dots. Suffice it to say we're certain she's in on it. We believe once she hears you're planning to go to Phoenix she will make a call to the carriers and postpone it until after you have departed Phoenix. We should have three or four days to find it. Hopefully we can cut them off and stop it."

The President looked stunned, "You want me go there, to be there in Phoenix where the suitcase is?"

Rolly couldn't believe the President didn't get it, but he didn't want to diminish the man any further.

"No, you're not going anywhere near Phoenix. Go to Camp David. Go to Palm Springs and play golf. We need you to say you're going to be spending the weekend in Phoenix. We'll do the rest."

"Oh, I see."

"Where is Gafar right now?"

"I don't know."

Rolly handed the president a prepaid phone. "Well find out where she is ASAP and let me know as soon as you can."

The president was still a little foggy but determined to move the game forward. He called the White House secretary on his phone, "Martha, where is Hannah right now? No, sweetheart, I don't want to talk to her. I just want to know where she is. No, I'll hold."

While waiting for the information and palming his phone, he whispered to Rolly, "This is breaking my heart." Rolly sympathetically tilted his head as authentically as he could but actually had not a smidgeon of such feeling for the man.

The woman on the phone returned. "OK, hold on"

The president again placed his palm over is phone and turned to Rolly. "She's in her office at the White House. Whatya wanna do?"

Rolly whispered, "Tell her to stay there. Its 6:40 now, tell her to meet you at 10:30."

The president lifted his palm from the phone, "Thanks Martha. Please let Hannah know that I'd like to see her at 10:30, please. I have a change of plans."

The secretary asked for clarity about the time. The president responded abruptly, "No not tomorrow, tonight." The president disconnected the call and turned to Rolly, "What now?"

"Figure out a reason to go to Phoenix before you talk to her. Make sure you're alone with her when you speak. Don't tell her about your plans until I call you. I need to get a lock on her phone. Call me using this phone…this phone only. As soon as you tell her of your travel plans, dismiss her and call me. We'll have a team in Phoenix by then and a team on her. There is only one number in the contacts on this phone, it's me."

The president clearly had a massive doubt about it all and was fighting hard not to reflect on how history would recall him were Rolly and his team unsuccessful. "This is very unusual. She may get a sniff that I'm on to her."

Sensing the president's disquiet, Rolly felt he needed to give the president some encouragement and get him off his doubt. Maybe some jocularity would do the trick, "You'll be fine. You've been lying to three hundred million Americans for well over a decade. I'm sure lying to one more will be a breeze."

As soon as he said it Rolly, knowing he may have overstepped his bounds, regretted it. To his surprise the president took it well.

He smiled a bit and said, "Jesus, Rolly, that doesn't help at all."

"Sorry, sir. I need one more thing."

The president, by now, was prepared to give Rolly anything he wanted. "What?"

"I need to get in direct touch with the head of the NSA. I need to be locked into Gafar's phone when she leaves your office. Most importantly, I need to triangulate the location of, listen into better still if possible, any connecting phone calls thereafter. If they're smart, they'll have her insulated by layers and layers of depth in chain."

The president was trying to follow along.

"And with respect to the NSA Director, even he has to be on a need to know basis. Gafar has connections everywhere and a ton of pull at the highest levels of government. People will help her naturally and I can't have a breach. I can't have accidentals. She may even have someone inside the NSA. I won't have time to debrief him. This has to stay between you and me. You must make that a demand if we are to be successful."

"You'll have it. I'll call him and have him call you ASAP."

"OK. The phone I just gave you is the only one you and I will communicate on. Always be alone when you use it, go into the bathroom if you have to. It's imperative no one see you using it. It's on vibrate. Once I have a lock on her phone I'll text you the word, 'clarity,' after which you can alert her of your intention to go to Phoenix. Make it a good reason."

"OK, I'll come up with something completely believable. I'm always changing plans," the contemplative co-conspirator assured Rolly.

Rolly felt, for the first time, the cooperation of the man he had derided for so long. He felt as if the president was putting politics aside for the first time, 'Thank you, sir. Good luck".

The president reached out his hand to his antagonist. Rolly gave him his hand.

"No. Thank you, Rolly. God speed."

Chapter 36

Washington, D.C.

*I*n his accustomed curt style, Rolly answered his phone, "Byrnes." Immediately Rolly grew rigid in his demeanor, "Yes, sir. Thank you, sir."

The CIA/NSA director offered Rolly any and all cooperation with the agency. Rolly didn't wait and went right into it.

"Sir, I need access, rather my associate, one of yours, Katy Quigley, needs full access to Hannah Gafar's phone. I also need any phones Garfar calls in the coming days and then I need all phones those phones call. It's a matter of national security. How soon can I get it?" Rolly listened intently to the director's answer.

"Great, thank you. I'm going to have Quigley call you in ten minutes from our facility in NYC. She'll be calling you using a prepaid phone and she'll say the say the word 'clarity' so you can be sure it's her. The phone she uses will be discarded, so she'll only call you once."

Again the director promised the full weight of his capabilities for which Rolly was grateful.

"Thank you. If we need anything else I'll call you on this number; also using another phone."

The director interrupted Rolly to ask about why the prepaid phones were necessary.

"We have a mole, at least one, maybe more. On three separate occasions our whereabouts and/or our plans have been compromised. One of my men got hit behind the breach. We can't settle this matter until the more pressing issue is put to bed. Sorry for the inconvenience, but that's where we are. "

Rolly listened as the Director guaranteed his services once more.

"Thanks." Rolly disconnected the phone and immediately dialed Aiden, who was already back at Fifty Two and a Half Barrow Street.

"Aiden Palmer." Aiden answered the ring tone.

"Aiden, are you with Katy?"

"Yes, Nesto, Katy, and I are here at the house."

"Great, put me on speaker."

"OK, hold on," Aiden pressed the phone screen allowing the phone to go on speaker, "Go ahead Rolly."

"Katy as soon as I hang up I'm going to text you the CIA director's telephone number, call him immediately. When he answers say the word clarity, that's your code in. He's setting up a war room at CIA. He's going to coordinate with you to get you access to Hannah Gafar's phone and any phone her phone calls, and any those phones call, and so on. Anybody that talks to that phone! Aiden, can you hear me?"

Aiden was short, "Yeah Rolly, go ahead."

"OK, we need that Cessna and we need to get heavy," Rolly said asking for as much firepower as they could muster. Rolly continued, "You and Nesto pick me up at Dulles as soon as you can. The lawyer said the suitcase was in Phoenix and we need to be there now. Katy you got the ball. Take all the pre-paid phones we have left, use one and throw it aside. Don't use it twice. You can't get zeroed."

Nesto interrupted, "Rolly, the president?"

"What about the president?"

"Can he be trusted? I was thinking about his stand on radical Islam these past seven years. How he couldn't even say the words. The apology tour business. His friendship with Will Myers. Lying about the Iran deal. His closeness with Gafar all these years. Should we be trusting this guy?"

Rolly was silent. He was thinking about Nesto's points and a deep sense of worry came over him.

"Aiden?" Rolly turned to the only instincts he trusted as solidly as his own. He just couldn't reconcile his inherent distrust of the president with the notion that he would so summarily betray the country, but Nesto was right. All appearances suggested he might be in on it. Maybe Aiden would bail them out.

"I don't know. I think if he was really in on it we wouldn't have been called at all. He would have let it play out in pieces. Does it really matter now? We gotta get that bag. If he's in on it so be it. It's the bag…the bag's the thing. We gotta see it through."

As usual, Aiden nailed it. Rolly got his mind off the incredible notion that a sitting United States president could be in a plot to detonate a dirty bomb on his own people.

"Well, let's hope he's just the stupid liberal that we believe he is and not something worse."

"Is there anything worse?" Aiden chimed.

Rolly smiled at the levity but the smile didn't last long and he quickly readdressed Katy.

"Katy, we need all your skills, the illegal ones too. Whatever you got, we need it, the best you've got. Nothing is too small. We need you to follow the calls, all of them, relay them on to us the moment you find something. We need to know locations first. If you have an opinion we want it. Whatever else you can find out about Gafar's movements too. In an hour or so the president is going to put these in motion. It's on people, go."

As soon as Rolly hung up the phone, Nesto and Aiden, as exhausted as they were, scrambled about the place collecting their weapons and travel gear.

Katy for her part, sat motionlessly. The weight of what was about to happen seemed a million miles away from hacking into the three major credit bureaus, changing post financial crisis damaged credit scores for the better, and high-fiving her cohorts. This was a pivotal moment in history and the outcome of her actions would send the world in one direction or another one quite different. One altogether horrifying.

She didn't ever fear authority; she had a kind of natural disdain for it. But now she would be directing the head of the NSA and making demands of people many years and many security levels her senior.

She had always felt like she was living on the edge and she had a sort of attraction to the rush, but she didn't recognize the kind of trembling she was experiencing. She knew she was central to the largest world event since Hitler invaded Poland and she was chasing ghosts. She was scared to death.

Rolly thought similarly. He knew his capabilities and the capabilities of the other Ravens. He was supremely confident in their collective skill sets, they moved like a machine. It was more than a little unsettling however to contemplate that their first mover, indeed the future of world peace or world war, rested in the hands of a girl he hardly knew, barely old enough to buy a drink in a bar.

The world hinged on the talent of a young girl all alone at a computer screen.

Chapter 37

Phoenix, Arizona

Aiden put the wheels down on the runway of Phoenix Sky Harbor International Airport at 1:14 am and taxied to the hanger. When he shut off the jet engine he sat for a second rubbing his exhausted eyes. Rolly and Nesto, beaten down from effects of having spent the last few days in fits of anxiety and fights for life or death, slept virtually the entire flight.

Nesto noticed Aiden sitting in the slightly hunched unaccustomed stillness, "You OK?"

"Yeah, I'm fine. Good to go."

Nesto was keen to notice Aiden's stillness. What he couldn't have seen was the fact that Aiden had been sitting at the controls for the final two hours of the flight praying to God, at times frantically beseeching him, for the strength to stay awake and the steadiness of mind to land the plane safely. He was that tired.

A large, black Chevy SUV loaded to the teeth with long guns, explosives, hand guns, and scopes was waiting for The Ravens in the terminal. The three men loaded more firepower into the truck and sped off for the Renaissance Phoenix Downtown Hotel. The hotel was a mere four miles drive from the airport.

The three men had no idea who they were looking for or what the explosive device looked like, but they knew the device would do the most damage in the most densely populated part of the city.

The Renaissance Phoenix was the nearest hotel to the center of the city. Rolly checked in at the hotel lobby while Nesto and a punch drunk Aiden waited in the car. One room. One room with two queen beds on the ground floor nearest the street was all Rolly needed. As far as the hotel desk was concerned. He was alone.

The three men piled into the room, each with their duffle bags of guns and underwear.

As soon as the men dropped their bags on the floor, Rolly went straight into organizing the watch. "OK, two beds, three-hour sleep rotation. The minute Katy can finger the suitcase, we move. Aiden, you take first watch."

Aiden whipped his head around in disbelief. He had just flown the plane from Washington, D.C. to Phoenix while Rolly snored and Nesto nervously twitched in his slumber the whole way. "Are you friggin' serious?"

As soon as his eyes could focus on Rolly he knew he had been played. Rolly, staring back smiling at Aiden, pointed his finger at Aiden as if to say, 'Gotcha!'

Aiden, with a minor bit of embarrassment, smiled and lovingly said, "Asshole."

Aiden, wasting not a single second, collapsed onto the bed, fully clothed but for his shoes. He was dead asleep before Nesto could finish brushing his teeth.

"Lights out," Rolly said as if speaking to a pair of Cub Scouts. He threw the switch on the lights and plopped down into a small barrel chair by the door with his black AR-15 semi- automatic resting in his lap.

'C'mon Katy, c'mon,' he whispered to himself. The room went quiet.

"Rolly, Rolly, wake up," Nesto quietly urged. It was 5:05 am but the room, with curtains drawn, was still pitch black. "Rolly, get up. Katy's got something."

Rolly thrashed around in the restraint of the chair. "What...what, what?" he said not yet fully in command of his freshly-jolted wits.

Nesto handed him the phone. "Katy. Its' Katy. She thinks she may have them."

Rolly now fully alert grabbed the phone. "Whatya' got Katy?"

Katy tried to be succinct. "I followed Gafar after she left the White House. Around midnight she called a man in New York. I'm following that guy now and he immediately called a second man in Flagstaff and gave him orders to move. Rolly, the plan wasn't delayed because of the president's visit as we'd hoped. It was accelerated!"

"Fuck," Rolly didn't see that coming. He was certain the attack would have been delayed and they would have days to find the suitcase. Now they had only a few hours.

Katy kept going, "I triangulated the call to a hotel in Flagstaff. I hacked the hotel computer and found the guy's name. His name is Hamid Dabashi and he's out of Lansing. He checked into the room with another guest. They checked out of the hotel a half hour ago."

"Shit," Rolly was trying to get his mind around the circumstances but knew they were behind the clock and they had far too little to go on.

Again Katy kept going, "I traced Dabashi to a rental car out of Flagstaff. He's rented a gold Ford Fusion."

"Great work. Keep at it," Rolly said in congratulatory tone.

Katy knew she couldn't let Rolly keep talking. "There's more. I made an educated guess and took it upon myself to look into where the most crowded part of the city was on a Thursday morning. In the heart of the most populated area is the Phoenix Convention Center. Gathering there today, in that building, is something called the Progressive National Baptist Convention Center. They're having their 2016 meeting there."

"Katy, you're beautiful! It has to be that. Eighty percent anyway."

Katy responded with the firm confidence of someone who knew for certain, "It's more than eighty percent. It's a hundred percent. I hacked the list of attendees. A group, called the Arab American Organization for Peace bought two tickets online late last night. The names set aside are a guy named Ahmed Aborz and one Hamid Dabashi. He's gonna be there this morning. I think he'll have that case with him."

"Aw, Katy. I'm going to buy you a drink when we get back. Anything else?" Rolly asked, not expecting there to be anything else.

"Yeah, I hacked into the Michigan Department of Motor vehicles. I'm texting you the DMV photos of both men."

"You're a genius! I'm definitely buying you a big…big…drink."

Katy's voice went real serious, real matter of fact. "Before you start buying me drinks, there's something else."

Rolly did not like Katy's tone. He didn't like it at all, "What?"

"Rolly, I stayed with Gafar like you asked and the first man she called, the guy who called Dabashi, his name is Salar Elahian. Rolly, there's a second case, a second bomb. There wasn't one bomb in the Huron forest, there were two."

"Oh my God! When are they planning to let it go? Do you know?"

"Monday I think. I'm not sure about anything. Somewhere in New York City, I believe. I don't know for sure. Elahian said something about the original plan, something about Monday and New York City. That's all I have. I'm listening to four phones and combing the emails that I've gotten into. I'm digging, but everything is vague and it's moving so fast. I'll keep trying to find any connection or plans Elahian may have. I haven't slept in two days." Katy's voice trailed off.

Rolly felt a deep concern for Katy's ability to stay focused. Sleep deprivation in battle has a cruel way of liberating the mind from reality, supplanting it with ghosts and goblins, poor eyesight and 'I can't do its.'

"Stay on it Katy. You're doing great work here, really great work. I know you're tired. We need you to stay on it. Stay on it. We'll get back to you. I'm out."

All the while Nesto and Aiden, fully awake and dressed, stood silently listening to the one side of a conversation. They knew there were new details and those details were not good, not good at all. They waited for Rolly to feed them the news.

Rolly handed his phone to Nesto. He had no reference to go on which would have given him confidence in Katy's staying power, but he couldn't think about that now. "I'm worried about her. She's tired."

He quickly got back on task. "Here's pictures of two men, commit them to memory. They're the ones. One of them will be carrying the case. They plan to let it go in or around the Phoenix Convention Center. Katy found them on the list of attendees there today. It starts at 8:30 am and my guess is somewhere just after that they'll place it somewhere and get the hell out of there. Gentlemen, we have two hours to figure it out, find them, and stop it. Take a good look at those faces. Dead or alive. Alive preferably, but the case is the thing. Kill the guy with the case on sight. Make sure he isn't rigged to it first. My guess is he won't be and this will be a drop and escape thing. The drama is in the aftermath, the nuclear component. But use your judgment. I was wrong about them delaying this thing, way wrong. They accelerated it. We'll try to take the guy without the case. But kill the case as soon as you see him."

Aiden's famed instincts told him there was more. "What about the other business?"

Rolly dropped his head for a moment. He lifted it and looked Aiden in the eyes.

"Katy thinks there's a second case, a second dirty fucking bomb. She's following another piece of shit in New York. She thinks they have a plan to let that one go in New York somewhere on Monday."

"Holy shit," Nesto plowed into the conversation, "These bastards really are trying to start a world war aren't they? Two nuclear explosions on U.S. soil in three days?"

"She thinks there's a second case?" Aiden softy asked.

"Yes, thinks. She's doing the best she can. She's got Gafar and Gafar's contact in New York. There's something planned in New York City for Monday. She thinks it's a second case. I don't have time right now to interrogate her. We got this…here…now. There's nothing we can do about New York right now. We got two hours to kill this suitcase, let's focus on that. If we live we'll address New York City."

Nesto and Aiden both knew Rolly was right and hoped Katy was wrong. But whoever was right, and whatever it was that would follow, they needed to get their minds right so they could attack it.

"Let's go, boys," Rolly extolled his partners as he patted both Nesto and Aiden on the shoulder as each hustled past him and out of the hotel room.

"Aiden," he called, "Get Katy on the phone. See if she can get the CCTV's in and around the convention center."

"On it," Aiden responded and before he was securely seated he started dialing. Katy answered on the first ring.

Aiden could hear the exhaustion in her greeting. "You OK, Katy?" he asked.

"Yeah, just tired. You guys are the ones in a problem. Are you guys OK?"

"We're fine. Listen we need to know if you can get us the CCTV's."

"CCTV's?" She didn't even know what the acronym was.

"Yes, CCTV's; closed circuit televisions."

"Oh my God," Nesto quipped realizing she didn't even know what it was they wanted.

Katy may not have known what they were but she had hacked many a camera to please her high school girlfriends and many more since. "Oh, the cameras inside the convention center?"

"Yes, those and outside ones if they have them as well."

"OK. I don't think it will be that hard; however, I won't be able to relay the streams." she advised.

Aiden was pleased by her confidence. "You'll have to talk us through what you're seeing. Anything that you see, anything out of the ordinary, we need you to convey. Good luck."

"Good luck to you…to Phoenix…to everybody."

In two hours either the world would be careening into World War III or World War III would be put on hold for another seventy-two hours.

Chapter 38

Downtown Phoenix

The large, black Chevy Suburban carrying The Ravens would only have to travel a quarter of a mile to the Downtown Convention Center, a mere five blocks.

They could very well walk the distance, but carrying all their weaponry would be absurdly less than concealable. If they made a mistake or if they were put in a position where they had to pursue Dabashi, they would be disadvantaged on foot. They had no choice but to drive the five blocks and park it somewhere out of sight. The truck set out due west towards the convention center.

Three blocks from the convention center Rolly pulled the truck to the curb and Nesto exited. Rolly then drove the truck directly past the front entrance, careful to drive slow enough to get a good look at the entrances and egresses or anything suspicious, but not too slow so as to be obviously casing it. It was only 6:30 am and the road was desolate. You would hear a pin drop at this hour on this downtown city street.

Rolly drove the suburban three blocks further west beyond the convention center and turned right at the corner. Aiden exited the vehicle and Rolly continued to the next corner, making another right turn he made his way back towards the target.

Less than a minute later Rolly pulled into the underground parking lot and parked the truck. He looked at his watch and time seemed to be standing still. He wasn't itching for a fight but whenever he found himself approaching one, time just couldn't move fast enough for his liking.

Rolly decided he would wait a total of fifteen minutes in the truck. In the underground parking lot he had no phone signal and no phone signal was akin to blindness. On the other hand, if Dabashi was coming by car he'd more than likely come real early. He decided to wait fifteen minutes then make his way to the lobby to check in with Aiden and Nesto, and then repeat the process every ten minutes thereafter.

On some level Rolly wished for the days when detonating a bomb of any capacity for mass casualties meant loading a truck with dynamite and driving it beneath the targeted structure. It is far easier to identify a sixteen-foot box truck full of explosives in need of a parking spot than to find a solitary man with a bag or suitcase on foot in a crowded city. He didn't know who he was looking for, what he was looking for, or even if they were in the right place. The nature of war sure had changed, he thought to himself. Today the world was at war with a single man, and they didn't even know it.

Rolly never felt he had to justify his warfare and he rarely felt the weight of war while he was conducting it. The battle was between him, his men, and those guys. He was arguably the world's best warrior and always thought he'd prevail because of his training and his skills. He put what he was doing in a box. Bad guys were out there, an ocean away, planning to kill Americans and he was determined to get them first. He'd go across the ocean and if he failed, if he was killed, there'd be another American defender sent in his place.

But this time was different and he was a different kind of antsy because of it. If he failed here, this morning, there would be no follow on defender, no retreat and try again. There'd be only death and dying.

He thought of September 11, 2001 and how many people had died behind that attack, millions more had been displaced...millions. If he failed this morning, millions would die behind the miss. It was a heavy thought and it frightened him. He had to shake it off...and quick.

Three blocks to the east, Aiden slowly made his way towards the convention center; three blocks west, Nesto did the same. The two men were converging on the targeted building. Both men felt the same overweighted quality to what they were doing that Rolly was feeling inside the building. Nesto's mind drifted to his wife, Aiden's mind gravitated to the peacefulness of the lake in White Sulfur Springs. Both wondered if there'd be anything worth going back to.

Not knowing was the hardest part.

Not knowing makes for wandering focus. Wandering focus makes for missed signs.

They had to shake it off…and quick.

Chapter 39

Phoenix Convention Center

6:40 am turned slowly, snail slowly, into 7:40 am. The early morning gray turned into the early morning yellow. The sun was up. Where were the terrorists? Were they mistaken about it all? Was Katy right? Was Rolly unwise to trust her judgment? Would the damn bomb go off somewhere else in the city or in another city altogether? What the fuck was happening?

Rolly made five different trips, using three different routes, from the underground garage to the lobby and back again. He tried his best to slow his mind, to stop the questions attacking his nerve endings and his confidence. He couldn't do either. Though he had years of sniper training and years of engaging deadly enemies, he simply couldn't repose on demand. He was too agitated, too nervous. A phase of his life was pivoting this morning; a new phase was opening for humanity tomorrow. It was impossible to gather himself fully in the space between. He was standing still feverishly while waiting to play his part in the outcome.

Aiden and Nesto had each closed their respective gap between where they had been left off and the convention center. Time was not a friend to either of them and their nerves needed a break, not a reminder of how much trouble we were in. They couldn't prowl around, but couldn't stand still and be seen either. Each minute felt like a month and a month is a long time to be cursing one's own stretched skin.

Aiden began making his way towards a coffee shop, which he had approached twice in the last hour but hadn't gone into, when his phone vibrated in his pocket.

The excitable voice on the other end was Katy's, "Aiden, I'm in. I got the cameras. I tried to call Rolly as he ordered but I got no answer and these prepaid phones don't have voicemail."

"Rolly is circling to the lobby from the underground parking lot and he has no phone reception below ground. Do you see anything? I'm getting friggin' nervous here. The breakfast part of the convention starts in thirty-five minutes and these guys are nowhere to be found."

"I just got in. I haven't seen anything but I have two looks in the lobby and I have the front of the building."

"Alright, stay on it. If you see anything, call Rolly first. If he doesn't answer then call me. OK?"

"Wait!" Katy saw something on the CCTV. "Two men just entered the lobby. One of them is wheeling a black suitcase."

"Are they Middle Eastern men?"

"I can't tell. I can't see their faces. They're wearing floppy hats."

"Hats? Indoors? In Arizona? Fuck! Call Rolly and tell him!"

"Wait Aiden!" Katy screeched.

Aiden was still on the phone with her but getting angry that she wasn't doing what she had been told. Rolly needed to know about the men in the lobby and she needed to keep trying Rolly's phone. Aiden needed to get off the phone so he could let Nesto know he was breaking off surveillance. "What?" he barked as loud as he could without drawing attention to himself as he hustled towards the convention center.

"The guy with the suitcase just passed it off to another man and he went into the staircase. The fucking guy with the suitcase is in the stairwell and the two guys who gave it to him are walking towards the front door of the building. I think they're leaving."

Aiden's hustle turned into a full sprint. "Call Nesto and tell him which way the two men leaving go. Tell him I'm in the building going after the guy with the suitcase. He needs to get the other two men. Tell Nesto to get them!"

Aiden put the phone in his pocket, which was no easy task while running. As he approached the building he saw the two Middle Eastern men in hats approaching the automatic doors. He slowed himself to a walk. Nesto would have to deal with the men leaving, if at all. He had to get that suitcase…or die trying.

As he entered while they exited, Aiden in a desperate attempt to act naturally, despite his heart racing like an Indy car in May and his burning desire to shoot them both dead, looked straight to the ground and then to his watch as he passed. The Middle Eastern men took no notice as they were trying themselves to act naturally. Aiden had no idea what might be waiting in the lobby, if there might be a shooter or a bomb vest ready to go off if things went sideways, so he couldn't very well draw attention to himself by running frantically through the lobby.

While Aiden was making his way to through the building Kate tried again in vain to get Rolly. The phone rang only twice before she disconnected the call. If Rolly could hear the ring, or feel the vibration, he would've answered it after a single ring. She dialed Nesto.

"Katy?" Nesto answered.

"Nesto listen, the suitcase is in the stairs. I couldn't raise Rolly so Aiden went in after it. There are two men wearing floppy hats who just exited the building after they passed the case off to a third man. Aiden told me to tell you to get those guys, not to let them escape."

"Floppy hats?" Nesto asked rhetorically, talking more to himself than to Katy.

Nesto was nearly two city blocks away from the convention center, but the streets were still empty at the early hour so his vision was not impeded and he picked up the two guys easily. They were still wearing the hats to conceal their faces from any street cameras but stood out like a sore thumb.

"I got 'em. Call Rolly. Keep trying him until he answers." Nesto disconnected the phone and began stalking his prey.

Katy dialed Rolly's phone, all the while with her face trained laser like on her laptop screen watching as Aiden walked into the convention center lobby and stopped to get a layout of the land and who might be a danger. 'The stairs are on the left, up on the left,' Katy hollered at the screen as if Aiden might hear her telepathically, "On the left, Aiden."

Rolly didn't answer. Again she dialed and again no answer.

Aiden, satisfied that the lobby was free from danger, at least as far as he could tell anyway, picked up the stairwell. Moving quickly, but not frantically, he headed toward it while trying to control his breath in the expected event he had to sprint the stair. Steadying his wits so to be clearheaded about what to do when he located the suitcase, Aiden reached for the door handle.

"Oh," a startled Katy chirped at her phone when Rolly answered it. She couldn't count how many times she had unsuccessfully dialed Rolly in the past fifteen minutes, but it was more than a dozen. It threw her off when he answered it.

She quickly recovered. "Rolly, the suitcase is in the stairwell and Aiden just went in after it." Rolly was going the long way around to the lobby by exiting the underground parking lot from the outside of the building and this stopped in his tracks. "What?"

"I couldn't reach you so I called Aiden. He went after the case. He's in the stairs. He just went in."

Katy knew she had mere seconds to bring Rolly up to speed. The bomb was on the move and Aiden's life was in danger in a stairwell twelve hundred miles from where she sat but only eighty yards from where Rolly stood waiting for Intel.

"I tried to call you a hundred times in the last minutes. Dabashi, at least I think it was Dabashi, passed the case off to another guy who took it into the stairwell."

Rolly didn't mean to cut her off, but he cut her off. "The roof. The bomb's nuclear shit spreads in the open air. It's going to the fucking roof."

Katy sensed the end of Rolly's assessment and went right along.

"I got them on the cameras. The two passed it off and left the building. Nesto picked them up after they exited the center, and I don't know what's happening there. But Aiden's in the stairs and the case, and its carrier is in there too."

"Keep watching the cameras. I'm going after Aiden."

It was less than a hundred yard sprint from where Rolly was standing, a sprint he had run in less than twelve seconds as a young Navy Seal, but it seemed a mile and a quarter. He took off running.

Aiden opened the door to the stairwell and went into the gray, poorly-lit cinderblock vestibule. Like Rolly had, he figured the case was heading to the roof of the convention center where it would be detonated to infect the surrounding area and poison as many people as possible.

Before his second step landed inside the stairwell he felt a thunderous punch to his face, violently spinning Aiden and cutting off oxygen to his brain. He didn't fall but the blow threw him sideways into the railing of the stairs. The collision with the railing to his ribcage knocked the wind out of him. Before he could even catch some air back into his lungs, or get himself upright, a second blow to the back of his head came from another direction. This one rattled the inside of Aiden's skull, tossing his brain about against the inside of his cranium, stretching its thin connective tissues. He fell to the ground like as if a dropped sandbag.

Aiden was up on his knees as soon as he hit the cold ground unlike most men who would have been totally out. Aiden's height saved him from being put out by the first blow, as it had slightly less power having had to punch upwards. The second blow, more devastating to be sure, still didn't knock him unconscious. His athleticism and strength of character were responsible for that bit of fortune.

He wasn't fully out but he wasn't aware of anything much either and it was only his natural instinct which made him try to get up. Something in his training told him there were two different people attacking him and that one of them or both were about to kick him. Something in the sense of his enfeebled reality told him he was unable to defend himself but his makeup told him to try anyway.

Training is a peculiar teacher. It teaches an expertise that seemingly can act on its own when the mind is busy elsewhere. Aiden's training was all he had left and his mind was indeed elsewhere. While his mind was trying to locate itself, his instinct predicted his assailant's next move. Aiden knew his ribs were exposed and were begging to be assaulted. The attacker saw it too. He took a step with his left foot towards Aiden and fired his right foot as violently as he could at Aiden's midsection. It was a mistake.

Aiden's body rolled towards the attacker into the kick which caught him in the upper right arm. It hurt like hell but it threw the assailant's balance out of kilter just enough to cause him to stumble back a bit. Aiden whipped his left hand around the back of his attacker's left leg and pulled it towards him with all his might, flipping the man on his back. Then lunging at the man with the weight of his torso, he followed with a vicious punch to the man's groin.

Before Aiden could make a second move he felt a monstrous kick just beneath his extended arm which he had needed for leverage to throw his punch into the man's groin. Aiden's chest felt like it had collapsed. He was still trying to regain full consciousness from the initial blows to his face and head and now he couldn't breathe. He had no defense; no training could save him now.

With the first attacker gasping in a fetal position, the second man pulled a knife from his boot. Raising his arm above his head he looked for the perfect placement of the blade to thrust his knife into the tall American to kill him without the need for any more fighting. He chose a spot and saw an opening.

Pfft, pfft…two millisecond long wispy sounds introduced themselves. The man dropped the knife and grabbed his own chest. He looked at the silhouette in the doorway and fell, falling first to his knees and then collapsing face first into the back of Aiden's' shoulder.

Nesto stood in the doorway of an office building that was a little more than a city block and diagonally across the intersection from the approaching two Middle Eastern men. Though empty handed, he pretended to be lighting a cigarette outside of the building.

The two men reached the intersection and made a left turn, waking away from Nesto's position. Nesto waited for the men to get a third of the way down the street and began to follow from the other side of the street. The streets were not empty but they weren't busy either. The men were now walking down a side street where there was almost no foot traffic. Nesto felt exposed but what could he do? He couldn't let them get further from him than a distance he could close should they get into a vehicle and start the engine.

"Aiden...Aiden look at me. Are you alright?" Rolly asked as he kneeled next to his injured friend, with one eye on Aiden, one eye on Aiden's surviving attacker, one eye on a dead security guard, and both eyes on the stairs above that.

"Are you alright?" Rolly asked with great concern. The light was dim and Rolly couldn't tell the extent of Aiden's injuries. Aiden was coming to but he was still having trouble inhaling and he still wasn't sure what had happened.

"Are you alright?"

"I think so," a shaken and still unsure Aiden responded.

Rolly took that to mean he hadn't been shot or stabbed. To the warrior there is a profound difference between hurt and injured. Not shot and not bleeding meant Aiden was hurt, not injured.

Rolly leaped at the man hunched over both hands still cupping his genitals. Rolly landed his one knee on top of the man's chest. It was the move of professionals. It was the very same move the man beneath Rolly's body weight had used to control Will Myers in the lobby of his New York apartment only a few days earlier before they killed him.

"My name is Rolly Byrnes. I want you to know the name of the man who is going to kill you if you don't do exactly as I say. I'm going to ask you only once...once. How many are up there?"

"Fuck you," the obviously psychopathic murderer responded.

Rolly didn't have the time or the inclination to sort things out. Pfft... the wisp took less than a second. He fired a single, muffled bullet into the bridge of the man's nose.

Rolly looked at the dead man and said to no one in particular as he sprinted up the stairs two at a time, "He's not Middle Eastern. He's Eastern European. What the fuck is going on?"

When the Middle Eastern men reached the corner they made another left and headed back towards the convention center. Nesto couldn't let them out of his sight so he sprinted across the street and ran along the building as close to it as he could. When he got to the edge of the building he snapped his head out to pick up the whereabouts of the two men. He knew he had closed some distance between them and had to be careful not to expose himself too soon or they'd run. He needed to corner them before he could make a move. If he could corner them, he planned to kill one and disable the other. In any case he wasn't going to let them get back to the convention center.

The men as it turned out were not walking back to where they came from. They were making their way across the street and away from Nesto's position. Nesto took a second peek around the edge of the building to assess where they may be going. A few hundred feet from them, just behind the convention center, was an open public parking lot about a third full by now with parked cars.

'OK,' Nesto thought to himself, 'They're gonna get in their car and drive off. They'll be trapped. They'll be armed to the teeth, but they'll be off the street. I'll have the advantage. Worse comes to worse, I'll kill the driver and try to secure the other scumbag.'

Rolly busted out of the door on the roof of the convention center and with both hands on the butt of his pistol darted his eyes first left then right. Forty feet away, hunched over and unzipping a large black duffle bag, was Rolly's target with the suitcase.

Rolly had no idea about the bomb. All he knew was that it was near him and it hadn't yet been detonated. He wanted just to shoot the terrorist in the back but he was fearful it might automatically detonate the bag. He surmised the carrier was going to lay it out on the roof, get himself a few miles away and then detonate the explosives, but nothing was certain.

"Don't move. Don't you fucking m..." Before Rolly couldn't finish the command the burly, dark-eyed, dark-haired Slavic wheeled around, dove into a roll and started unloading a high-caliber magazine at Rolly.

Having the benefit of only a hand gun, Rolly took two large strides to his right and dove behind a refrigeration unit. He wasn't hit, but he knew he was dealing with a professional and he was severely outgunned. He had to get the terrorist's flank. If the guy was a pro, as Rolly assumed, it would be only seconds before he figured out he could use his superior weaponry for suppressing fire to control Rolly's movement and get an angle clear enough for a kill shot.

Rolly steadied his nerves. He remembered what he learned from reading about the great generals in history. "Initiative, always the initiative," he said to himself.

The Slavic was a pro. Rolly took safety behind the air conditioning unit and the Slavic moved to his left taking a crouching position, semi-protected behind an exhaust fan. He wasn't fully blocked but he was two full strides from where Rolly was expecting him to be.

Of his weapon, the Slavic figured he could get off several rounds and kill him. Rolly closed his eyes for a second and asked God for speed and courage. 'One... two ...go!' Rolly screamed at himself internally as he leapt to his feet and ran to his right attempting to create his own angle and maybe get a kill shot if the Slavic bomber wasn't ready for the boldness.

The quick move Rolly made to his right caught the Slavic off guard but the Slavic's change in location caught Rolly off guard too. Rolly didn't see him right away and the Slavic thought Rolly would fight it out from a protected position. Because Rolly made a sharp move to his right before advancing, the Slavic's gun barrel had become momentarily blocked.

The Slavic would have to rise up a hair to get the barrel of his gun past the edge of the curved exhaust hood. No problem he thought, he still had a protected position and Rolly had fired two shots in the wrong direction. The American was fully exposed, he had him. He rose up several inches, whipped the barrel over the top of the exhaust hood.

Then down went the Slavic, with half his head missing. The assault rifle fell and bounced on the roof as the Slavic landed a few inches from it. Rolly whipped his pistol around towards where the fire came from. Standing in the open doorway connecting the stairwell to the roof was Aiden, blood all over his face, clutching his ribs, still having difficulty breathing.

"Is that it?" Aiden said, pointing at the suitcase and dropping gently to one knee for rest.

"Yeah, that's it," Rolly responded. "That's only one of em though," Rolly lamented. "There's the other one on New York and we need some damn luck, maybe a miracle."

Rolly reached into his pocket and dialed Katy.

She answered, "Are you alright? Is everyone alright?"

Rolly knew there was more to be done and Nesto was out there somewhere. Maybe they could grab Dabashi and interrogate him.

"No time Katy. We're OK. Listen carefully. I need you to do three things. First, get four or five blocks away from where you are. Wear a hat and scarf or cover yourself with a sweater or something. Call it in. Call Capps and tell him we neutralized the carrier but we haven't disabled the bomb. Tell him it's on the roof of the convention center and he's to get a fire evacuation of this building and a crew here. He'll know what to do. Hang up on him immediately. Don't give him even a second to ask questions and then toss the phone. You'll be in danger so take another route back to the house. When you've finished, hustle back and follow the calls from Gafar and anyone they call and anyone they call all the way down the line. My guess is Capps will call the White House within seconds and she'll be putting the others in motion. Hustle…go!"

Katy got out immediately.

Nesto watched as the two Middle Eastern men entered the public parking lot as expected and knew exactly what to do. There was only one way out and he was going to cut them off. Once he was certain they couldn't see him he broke for the parking lot exit row.

What Nesto didn't expect was that they weren't going to their car. There was a plain van waiting for them. The driver of the van screeched to a stop and the two men climbed in.

"Damn it!" Nesto didn't see that coming and he hated to be exposed. They didn't see Nesto but it didn't mean Nesto was in a good place. He was going to have to run in front of the van while it was moving, not from a fixed position with some cover.

The van was sixty yards away from the exit barrier, a small thin wooden drop arm that the van could barrel right through, so Nesto was going to have to get inside of it. His run turned into a sprint.

The van driver saw Nesto coming across the lot and hit the gas hard. The back tires spun leaving a three-yard skid mark. The van revved, jumped in a jerky motion, and got traction which accelerated the van considerably.

With less than twenty yards to go to the drop arm, Nesto in full gallop ran across the face of the van. With less than seven feet separating him from the front windshield he fired a bullet into the van. The bullet pierced a small hole in the windshield on the drivers' side and a small hole in the forehead of the driver.

The van veered off to its left smashing into a pair of parked cars and causing the radiator to rupture dispensing steam from the hood of the caved in van.

Nesto leaped and rolled over the hood of a Honda Civic taking cover behind it, giving him time to take stock of his situation and it wasn't good.

From the van sprang three men carrying assault rifles. The men not yet fully aware of what they were up against ran backwards into the parking lot and split up. Nesto knew he was now at a huge tactical disadvantage with three men with assault weapons against a solitary man with a pistol. He was in big trouble.

The Middle Eastern men had seen only one man and were fairly certain he was alone. Since they didn't know the dirty bomb was no longer a threat they operated on the premise that they had to get out of there before it went off. Using a series of hand signals the men separated in tactical spread, each approaching Nesto's highly vulnerable position from a different angle.

It they were smart they'd use suppressing fire and flank him, perhaps even get directly behind him.

'Shit, Nesto, you can't sit here,' Nesto thought to himself. But three assault weapons against his pistol put him in the worst position. He only had two options. He could make a run for the street and let them escape or he could make a stand and fight. To a man like Nesto Suarez, whose honor and country were to him more valuable than oxygen in his lungs, this meant there really was only one option. He checked his watch to calculate the time he had to take the fight to the enemy.

On the roof Rolly was tending to Aiden and biding time to make sure no one would accidently stumble upon the bomb and detonate the thing when they heard a car crash. They knew Nesto had to be involved.

Both men ran to the roof's edge facing the noise at the back of the convention center. Rolly, in much better physical condition than Aiden, got to the roof's edge a few seconds before Aiden arrived saying, "It's' Nesto alright."

Rolly and Aiden could not see Nesto but they deduced where he was by the skulking men approaching his position from three different angles.

"He's fucked," Aiden surmised. "C'mon Nesto…get out of there."

Aiden and Rolly were a mere two hundred and fifty yards from their best friend in the world and knew they couldn't move fast enough to get to him. Even worse was having a birds-eye view of his killing and being powerless to save him, he was a dead man. They knew he was going to war for his country anyway. It broke their hearts.

"Holy shit!" Rolly spun around and took off running toward the dead Slavic. He hadn't moved that fast in years and adrenalin was racing through his bloodstream. He reached down and grabbed the dead man's high-powered rifle and ran back to the roof's edge.

Before Rolly could fully rest his rifle on the roof's edge and get his eye to the scope, Nesto rose up from behind the car taking three strides directly toward one of the terrorists as he fired his pistol. He knew he hadn't hit anything but the return gunfire told him where they were so he could reposition himself at a more advantages position. Making his way to a row of cars he was able to get better spacing and perhaps an angle that afforded he could pick one off and get on the move again.

While the terrorists were surprised by Nesto's aggressive move, they weren't dumb and they didn't panic. They immediately set themselves in a defensive position, expecting Nesto to follow his training and act aggressively.

The third man, the man who hadn't fired at Nesto, got himself to the front of the lot and quickly ran around behind Nesto's position. Nesto was trapped. The moment he poked his head up the man in the rear, the man Nesto could not know was there, would have a clear shot from close range.

Nesto kneeled on the ground trying to hear movement, any movement that would give away a terrorist.

The Middle Eastern man had the drop on the American and he knew it. What he didn't know, what he would never know, was that two hundred and fifty yards away, with a perfect line of sight and perfect firing position, was the world's perfect sniper, a sniper with a hundred and eleven confirmed kills, kills from over a thousand yard, a man with a purpose, had him in his crosshairs.

Rolly calmed himself and in between heartbeats fired a single thirty caliber bullet from the dead terrorist's weapon into the back of another terrorist's head killing him instantly.

The two remaining terrorists heard the shot. They didn't know who fired it or at who, but they were determined to get the hell out of there. Both men began unloading their magazines in Nesto's general direction so to keep him pinned down. They figured if they could make it to the street they could hijack a car and make a run for it. They figured badly. Their movements were restricted by the rows of cars and firing as they moved only slowed them down.

Rolly fired only two more shots. Under the conditions it was an easy shot for an accomplished shooter. For the world's foremost sniper, it was a lay-up. From a little over two hundred and fifty yards, with no wind at all, and the sun at his back, Rolly killed them both by placing a single bullet in the forehead of each man, each three quarters of an inch above the bridge of their noses. To the casual observer it would look as if they had been marked between the eyes with a red felt pen.

Chapter 40

Phoenix Sky Harbor International Airport

A minute at war is more exhausting than a year of toiling in the field, a lifetime more exhausting than sitting at a desk. Rolly, Aiden, and Ernesto were more than exhausted as they boarded the Cessna for the flight back to Teterboro Airport in New Jersey. They were experiencing a new type of war, one they could never have before envisioned. It was in and among them, in American hotel lobbies, in American parking lots and concert halls. It was being fought with box cutters and nuclear charged isotopes from lighthouses. It was being fought by men in masks, unaffiliated men representing no country. It was an intangible war, waged in intangible terms, using intangible words.

To the men, who were battered and spent yet climbing the steps of a single engine plane one exhausting step at a time, it appeared that such a war having no tangible concepts against which warriors have made their stands for thousands of years, and having no single thing they could call a beginning, may indeed have no end. It was a new kind of tired and a terrible one at that.

Aiden was the first to board the plane and merely bending to get into the pilot seat of the cockpit was excruciating for the six foot-four inch quiet man. His ribs weren't broken but the violent kick he received under the stairs of the convention center had given his ribcage a shock. The force of the kick separated the rib and stretched the connecting tissue very near the tearing point. He winced as he sat. He didn't want to wince, it wasn't a macho thing. He didn't want his team, his friends, his family really, to see him in pain and to worry. They had also been under fire, at risk of death. It was his turn in the barrel and he didn't want to shrink from it for their sake.

Nesto climbed aboard next. He didn't say anything to Aiden. He looked at his swollen shut right eye and the golf ball-sized knot on the back of his head and wished it had been himself with those pains. He didn't stop as he passed his hurting partner. He simply placed his right hand on Aiden's shoulder, gently, corporeal, without inflection, as if to say I wish it were mine to take away the pain.

Rolly was last to climb into the plane. Rolly was older than his two buddies but on some level knew both men he led were more mature than he was. He believed certainly that both were smarter men. But there was a thing about Roland Byrnes that made him the perfect leader. He had it all: empathy, courage, boldness, he was tactical and strategic, he could read men, and his determination was legendary. But there was something more that ratified his leadership in the minds, and hearts, of the men he led. He was paternal. He was safety. He was the straight line. If you were confused, he was wisdom itself.

Rolly plopped down in the copilot seat thumbing through pages, not actually reading them, just to have time to collect his thoughts. He knew the complications of the killing they had just concluded had a new ugliness to it. A warrior, any warrior with a conscience that is, after a battle of any kind, has to fight off the pangs of guilt, the rationalizations of worthiness, the what-ifs had it gone wrong, and countless other things indigenous to each man's character. Rolly knew there were so many more contemplations racing through his two brothers' minds and so many more apparitions flying around in their souls behind what they had been engaged in and what still lay before them.

Rolly laid the pages on his lap, lowered his head slowly, his chin very near touching his chest. He closed his eyes for just a second and slowly reopened them looking straight ahead as he spoke.

"I've never been more proud of any men in my life. This country is lucky to have you both."

Nobody said a thing as several seconds passed. They loved one another truly and if they were to survive the next few days it would be that love which would become the reason for it.

Several more seconds passed. Rolly turned and looked at his beaten pilot. "You OK?"

Aiden glanced back over at Rolly. "Yeah, I'll be alright."

"You know how to start this thing?"

Aiden looked at Rolly and tossed him the smile of a man who knew he had been kidded, "Yeah, I know how to start this thing."

"Well, let's go sailor. It's not gonna fly itself."

Aiden engaged the engine. He gave his endeared leader one more wry smile.

Rolly gently slapped Aiden's thigh and chuckled. Aiden felt safe again.

Nesto was already asleep.

The plane rose into the azure Arizona sky. They were on their way again to fight, on to the next war front.

They called it home.

Chapter 41

Barrow Street, NYC

The front door at Fifty Two and a Half Barrow Street pushed open slowly.

Rolly entered the front room first, looking like hell. Dropping his bag and going straight past Katy to the kitchen where a beer was ready to surprise him with a new and never before so feverish a fervor. He opened the door of fridge and reached in.

By now Nesto was limping into the room looking like a younger version of hell. He nodded at Katy, who by now was turned around in her desk chair watching the slow parade of wounded warriors. "Hey," he said as he lumbered into a side room.

"Hi," she said with a hint of surprise at how bad the men looked and with more than a little curiosity as to how they'd come to look so poorly.

A few seconds later Aiden walked into the room. It took him a bit more time to scale the thirteen steps to where Katy sat staring at the open door waiting until the third man, her favorite among them, who had saved her life in the airport only a few days earlier.

When Aiden hobbled into the room Katy felt her stomach sink to the ground. The tall, handsome man looked anything but like himself. Rolly and Nesto, as exhausted as both men were, had at least grabbed a few winks on the plane ride back from Phoenix to New Jersey. And neither had been pummeled mercilessly in the stairwell by two different Russian terrorists.

Katy tried her best to conceal how flummoxed she was but her natural instincts grabbed her by the heart and thrust her at her friend. She leaped to her feet and took two bounding strides towards Aiden.

Aiden could see the glistening tears form in her eyes and feel the concern she had for him. Although he wanted to take her in his arms and feel human touch without the intent to harm him, but he was hurt, hurt bad. He didn't know how bad his injuries were and he had no intention of finding out. But he knew her touch would send him into spasms and pains.

He put his hand up to prevent her from touching him pointing slowly at his own ribcage as explanation for the unrequited display of affection. Leaning awkwardly to the left, he let his backpack slide from his shoulder to the ground and forced a smile out from under his bulbous, swollen cheekbone, "Sorry…ribs."

"Jesus, are you alright?" she asked with an urgency that made the question far less than perfunctory.

"I'm OK; ribs are a little sore though. Are you OK?"

"Yeah, I'm fine. My eye is feeling much better. What happened?"

"Later. What happened to you?" Aiden asked as he waved his hand about her head and body. "When did you last sleep?"

Katy's femininity kicked in and she immediately became aware that she hadn't changed her clothes or showered for three full days. She had sprinted a half mile to call Capps and after ditching the phone, ran, as hard as she could, another mile plus to get back to the house. To make matters worse, her healing eye socket had bruised to black and she looked like nobody's kid.

"What a pair we are," she said smiling a woman's smile while trying to hide her womanly charms in the camaraderie.

Aiden was in too much pain to get or receive any hidden messages. His eyes were too beaten up to read the signs or between her lines. He was concerned for her. She needed to be sharp and they may very well need her to survive the day.

"When did you last sleep?" he asked again.

"I don't know, two days ago maybe. I dozed in the chair a couple of times I guess."

"Upstairs. Go upstairs and take a shower and lay down." Aiden pushed with a little more vigor.

"But I'm following Gafar," Katy answered pointing at the desk where two laptops were flickering.

"Go do what you're told," Rolly interrupted and both chins snapped to where Rolly was standing in the kitchen doorway. "You're no damn good to us in the condition you're in."

"But…," Katy was about to begin to make her case for staying on the hunt.

"But nothing," Rolly jumped over her voice with his. "I'm not asking you, I'm telling you. Go."

Rolly turned his head towards Aiden, "You too."

"Four hour shifts. Me, Nest, then you two. That'll give you eight hours. Katy, was there anything new that moves the thing up from Monday?"

"No."

"OK, I don't think letting it go on the weekend makes any sense, Monday on a workday makes sense. That gives us today and tomorrow to find it. We'll be worthless if we can't get some sleep. Show me what you've got and then get some sleep."

Rolly turned to Aiden, "Are you sure you're OK? You want me to call the doc in to take a look?"

Aiden, cranky from the pain and the lack of sleep snapped back, 'I'm OK, no doc."

Aiden knew he should allow the doc to have a look but it was likely he'd find something and open up an argument Aiden was in no mood to have. He was going to see it through, as Rolly was fond of saying; there was no second way. He wasn't going to balk at Rolly's demand for sleep however. The human body and the human mind sometimes can make an argument too firm for the human will to refute.

Rolly and Aiden glanced at each other expressing their joint affirmation of the sleep rotation plan.

Rolly moved to the desk, plopping down as an overly tired man would and peered over the screens of two laptops as he waved Katy over. Moving behind him and hunching over, she first explained first what never to touch. Then what she had been following, who she was following and pointing to the yellow legal pad sitting to the laptops right, who called who and the new player's identification. There was a second pad, a smaller white notebook, with scribbled names, references to "pathways and corridors" and what looked like gibberish Rolly assumed was computer code.

"What's that?" he asked her.

"Don't mind that. It's stuff I'm following…hunches…nothing material. Please don't touch it."

The code and gibberish were far more than hunches. She had broken into computers, emails and phones of government officials, both foreign and domestic, and the many people they had communicated with. She had pushed, pulled, and kicked her way into some remarkable leads, but without anything concrete she didn't want to open up cans of worms or Pandora's box. Her order that Rolly not disturb it told Rolly she was onto something, maybe something deep.

Few people had ever spoken to Roland Byrnes like that without consequences, but Katy had been spot on in Phoenix, super cool under pressure, tough in a fight, and awake for nearly two full days. He wasn't going to press her, not yet anyway. He looked up at the disheveled blonde's heavy eyes, her blackened and bruised face admiring the maturity and toughness she displayed. He was amazed at the young girl's organizational skills and her savvy. Twenty year field operators had less on the ball than this chick, he thought.

"OK, is there anything specific you're looking at? Rolly asked.

"It's too long to explain. This is Gafar's number," she relied pointing to a yellow sticky pinned to the laptop screen. "Any calls going in or out of that phone we must have. Type it into the laptop here," she continued pointing to a second laptop. "This will either open up a new stream or add to an existing one. Secondly, it will drop into the CIA database and the calls from any number entered here will be recorded and then record any calls that phone makes and so on. Basically we'll have two things we can use. One, we will establish a link between any phone in the stream and any phone entering into that stream. We can then go back and listen into any call that was made by any of those phones. Understand?"

Rolly nodded, but with a sense of frustration. "It's still a bit of a needle in the hay stack," he lamented.

"Yes, but we have to start somewhere. Start with Gafar. She's the key. I've prioritized her calls on this laptop," she said pointing to a third open laptop.

"Any calls she makes will establish a center of influence notification. Theoretically, that is. These people are the likely conspirators. I'm following them more than I'm following her. Get it?"

"I think so," Rolly said trying to follow her as best he could.

Katy sensed he wasn't fully following. "Look by now Gafar knows the Phoenix thing failed to go off. She doesn't know we know about the second case though. More than that, she hasn't been arrested so I assume she believes she's OK, she's safe. She is going to call a bad guy to make sure the caliphate plan stays alive. They'll just have one event, not two.

"Yeah, I see," Rolly said, expressing that he had more clarity.

Katy was not done. "If Gafar knows Phoenix failed, every one of the bastards who are in on this thing, including the Iranian Mullahs, is also painfully aware and there must be panic among them. She's gonna communicate with somebody that it's still a go and when she does we'll be able to put the rope around the bitch's neck."

Rolly had been impressed with the skill and determination of his new team member before, but he was really impressed with her now.

"Remind me never to get you mad," he said to her only half kidding.

She smiled, "Oh you don't have to worry. You'll be alright."

"Still I'm sleeping with one eye open when you're around."

She smiled again and slapped Rolly's shoulder playfully.

"OK if something happens or the chatter picks up, I'll come get you. In the meantime get a shower and some z's. Something tells me we're all gonna need it."

Katy turned and began walking away but before she could get through the door Rolly called out, "Katy," she turned back, "Well done."

Chapter 42

Alexandria, Virginia

She had trouble falling asleep earlier but time and nature had finally put her under. The phone on her night stand woke Hannah Gafar from her sleep. She twitched and took a second to focus on exactly what the sound was. The phone ringing had never rung before. It had only been used for outgoing calls previously. She needed another second to figure out exactly where she was. Looking at the clock on her nightstand, it was nearly 2:00 am and she was agitated that she had only slept a little more than an hour. She had no choice but to answer it, she knew who it was.

"This phone was never to be called," she snapped at the caller.

A male voice with a heavy Middle Eastern accent rushed over her protest, "The bomb did not go off. What happened?" the voice asked in demanding tone.

"I don't know. I'm trying to find out."

"I cannot reach Dabashi, I cannot reach Atta, and I cannot reach Rastam. Have you heard from these men?"

"No," she answered.

"Something is wrong."

"Of course something is wrong if it didn't go off. I just don't know what happened yet," Gafar answered.

The male voice changed the subject, "We are going ahead with the plan for Monday."

"I know. We've come so far," Gafar said with a fading resolve in her voice.

Hearing the trepidation in her tone he spoke abruptly, "No law will conflict with Islam, we move Monday."

"Yes, Islam will destroy non-believers," Gafar followed with a cult like monotone incantation. Snapping out of her trance she went on, "However, if any one of them, Dabashi, Atta, or Asidilov, has been captured the Americans may be on to our intentions. I think it's too dangerous to go near the United Nations building."

"Those men would never talk," the male voice insisted.

Gafar knew the voice would say that and she responded quickly, "There is a second way, a second option in New York City."

"Go ahead," the obviously intrigued voice demanded.

"I don't think they know about our plans since I'm certain I would have heard by now. But if the CIA becomes aware of our plan by Monday the protections at the UN and in the area surrounding it will be massive, including drawing virtually all New York police to the area, making other areas vulnerable. There is a major event planned in New York on Monday."

"Go on," the mail voice pressed her.

"Monday is November first, three days until the election. The Republican nominee will be meeting with his potential transition team and a good part of his cabinet at one of his buildings in lower Manhattan. We can attack the infidels there and make Allah's will known for all the world to see."

"Yes. We will do this. My sons will carry the prophets' message to this place. Allahu Akbar."

Gafar responded "Allahu Akbar."

Chapter 43

Barrow Street, NYC

Warriors have a peculiar affinity for sleep, that is, sleep in a bed. It's the place for their un-remembering, its anesthesia, oblivion. Life awake always seems to be threatening them with death. Waking up for men in war is never accompanied by a sunrise of anticipation. Sunrises meant putting on combat boots. There's a moment in the act of tying ones boots before a fight that is worse that the fight itself. The field manuals never put a name on that moment.

The smell of coffee drew Aiden down the stairs. For exactly eight hours he had slept deeply, but not comfortably. His awaking brought on the familiar recall that bruises, particularly bruises of the bones and ligaments that have been stretched and twisted, heal slowly. Aiden walked into the situation room slowly, very slowly. Nesto and Rolly were already half way through their third cup of coffee.

"Jesus you look like shit," Nesto said to the poor wretch.

"I feel like shit."

"Sit, man, sit. Coffee?" Nesto asked as if he didn't already know how badly Aiden wanted a cup. Aiden nodded affirmatively as expected.

"How do you want it?"

"Black like my prospects," Aiden replied through his fattened lips.

While Nesto retired to the kitchen to fetch his friend his renewal, Rolly stared at Aiden's face. It was an awful sight. His left cheekbone was so swollen it forced his fat lips to appear as if they were pointing to the right. His eyes were so near swollen shut it looked as if he was squinting to repel the sting of an onion while looking directly into the noon day sun. He had an inch and a half raspberry on the right side of his forehead, the result of hitting the concrete floor. There were two long deep scratches of his face left by his assailant's ring as it got to the facial skin just before the blows arrived and his lips were split in several places. The poor man was hurting from head to toe. Rolly took it in. He smiled.

"Don't say anything," Aiden said to him threateningly.

Rolly couldn't help himself, "Man, oh man, did you defend yourself at all?" he teased through his chuckling.

"I saved your ass, didn't I?"

Nesto arrived with the coffee. His soul was willing but as he took a sip, he realized his lips were not, "Ugh."

"Too hot?" Nesto sympathetically asked.

"A little," Aiden put the cup down to cool. He wanted to drink it but thought perhaps when it became room temperature he could get it over his lips.

"What have we got?" Aiden asked Rolly.

"I don't know exactly. I recorded calls into missy pants computers here and I'm trying to keep up, but I can't say I've learned much, certainly not enough to take us anywhere. I'm gonna wake her up in a few, I just wanted to give her a full eight hours plus. The poor kid hadn't slept in days and looked terrible. Not near as bad as you, but… She's a tough little thing."

"She is," Aiden concurred as he flipped Rolly the bird and smiled. "When I shot those two bastards in the airport she was cool as a cucumber."

"And taking down Asidilov by herself was pretty badass too," Nesto chimed in.

"Who knew?" Rolly said so he might move on. "Anyway, I figured we'd have a coffee and wake her."

"I'm awake." All three heads turned to Katy in the doorway.

She was alert and ready and hadn't lost a sense of her appearance. She was showered, hair blown dry, and other than the remnants of a black eye she had received from Asidilov she looked pretty as hell.

Nesto, still standing asked, "Coffee?"

"Please," Katy replied as she moved towards her desk set up.

"How do you like it?" Nesto queried as he moved into the kitchen.

Katy couldn't hear him, already typing on her keyboard while flipping the pages of her notes. All three watched her intently with furrowed brows while exchanging shoulder shrugs. She was too focused to hear Nesto ask a second time. Rolly broke her concentration when he barked abruptly, "Katy!"

Her head jerked in surprise towards Rolly, who was sitting a mere ten inches from her right shoulder. "What?"

"Coffee, how do you want your coffee?" Rolly said pointing to Nesto standing in the kitchen doorway.

She was reading feverishly by now and didn't apologize. Something had clicked, "Um um um....I don't care."

All three looked at one another again with a bit of confusion. She reached to the laptop in front of Rolly's chair. Rolly was in the way.

"Move," she snapped as she pushed the arm of his chair forcing it to roll backwards away from the desk. Rolly helped it along so as to clear the area and not block her.

Nesto arrived with the coffee. "Milk and sugar," he said as he put the coffee down well to her left. She paid him no mind.

Katy began flipping through notes and typing more furiously. All three men stood behind her, praying she wasn't just thrashing about blind.

"What? What is it?" Rolly asked her.

Paying him no mind, she stood up, ran out of the room and up the stairs.

"What the..." Aiden said to no one.

Before they could say another word Katy returned with Asidilov's phone. She plopped down office chair so aggressively it rolled several inches left before she could catch it and bring it back into its proper place in front of her laptop. Powering on the phone she almost begged, "C'mon, c'mon," to get it to come to life.

When the phone powered up she stood up and began thumbing the phone screen, then sat down still thumbing and then stood up again. The men were concerned about the erratic nature of her movements but were sure she thought she had found something. Not wanting to be the one to disturb her train of thought, they backed off and collected tightly behind her.

"It's you!" She screamed at the phone. "It's you, you fucking prick!"

Katy had forgotten her place, even forgetting that others were in the room with her. She stood there silently for a second embarrassed by her language but it quickly passed. Sitting back down she started going through websites while her eyes darted to a second screen that had logged all the phones which had been directly linked to Gafar's phone logs and her notes.

"Whatya' got Katy?" Aiden asked her softly.

She paid him no mind and her movements intensified. Whipping her head around violently, she asked no one in particular, "Did you by chance get Dabashi's phone in Phoenix?"

"Yeah, I took all three from the guy's in the parking lot," Nesto responded.

"Well, where the hell is it?" she screamed not caring about anyone's feelings.

"It's there in the bag," Nesto said pointing to a blue bag at the end of the desk which looked much like a collapsible little nylon travel cooler.

Katy lunged at the bag. "Which one is Dabashi's?"

"All four phones are marked," Aiden explained, "but the screens are locked."

"No, they're not," Katy snapped backed as she sort through the phones and laid one down beside the other until she got to Dabashi's phone.

Katy threw herself back down into her desk chair and again the chairs wheels took her away from the desk so that she had to catch herself and drag the chair back to its rightful place.

"Whatya' got," Aiden asked again.

"Nothing, nothing, nothing, nothing," Katy responded not realizing that she was repeating the same word and so quickly.

"What?" Rolly called out, trying to be heard over her stammering.

"Nothing," she shot back quite loudly. "Shut up. All of you... Ugh ,ugh....shit!"

"OK, OK, OK..." she started again. "Where is that page?" she said as she began ripping pages away from her legal pad and tossing them on the floor. Picking up Dabashi's phone and she began keying in a code, hoping to unlock the screen.

"OK, OK, OK, OK, OK..." she went on, "Ugh, ugh... Shit!"

Again she began tearing pages out and throwing them on the floor, four, five, six, seven pages.

Aiden, Rolly and Nesto were powerless to help her, whatever it was she was doing, but none wished to be yelled at again so they sat down and watched her intently.

"OK, OK, OK, OK... Ha! Fuck you!" She whipped around hollering at the three men, "I got him. I got in. What an asshole. What an amateur!"

The three leaped from their chairs not exactly knowing what she had but each really impressed with her determination and hacking ability.

"The first letter of each of his four grandchildren? C'mon. What a clown!"

"What does it mean?" Rolly asked her.

"It doesn't mean a damn thing," she replied as she turned her back on the three men, "not yet anyway."

Again Katy returned to the computer screens, phone logs, and her notes, primarily focusing on the two phones.

"Give me a minute," she said while writing numbers and times on a yellow pad.

"OK, OK, OK, OK... Hold on."

The three hoped to be feeling more confident but only felt more confused by her hyper activity.

"OK, OK, OK, OK... Ha! Fuck you!" she screamed out again.

For the next several minutes she went back and forth between phones and computer screens. The three men felt like they were waiting for the birth of a child while the wife agonized in unending labor. They could do nothing but wait and pray for something which they did not know.

Six minutes passed when suddenly she jumped to her left and swept everything off the left side of the desk, giving her enough room to put her notes down. The chair shot across the room and banged into a file cabinet eight feet from where she had sat in it.

The three men hustled over for an explanation of what she had uncovered and hopefully something they could use. Hunching over her, Aiden and Rolly on her left, Nesto on her right, looked at her notes, but they were written in gibberish.

"OK, I think I got him," she began.

"Who?" Aiden asked hoping to get on board with her thought before it ran off again.

She pointed to a picture on one of her laptops. "Him!"

"Who the hell is he?" Rolly asked demanding something more.

"The second bomber, the second case. That's him."

"How?" Aiden followed in.

"On the way back from grabbing Asidilov I wrote down all the recent calls on his phone. I then started cross referencing any calls which touched both his phone and Atta's phone but came up empty." She pointed to the computer where Rolly had been sitting. "I programmed that computer there to recognize any such calls. When I came down this morning I noticed there were two calls made to Atta's phone and one call to Gafar's phone at 2:26 am. Now that's a late night call, don't you think?"

The men knew where this was going now and their adrenalin began to overtake their injuries and their pains.

Katy continued, "The closer was Dabashi's phone. Yesterday, on five separate occasions, this bastard's phone," again pointing to the picture on the computer screen, "called Dabashi's starting just after you killed him."

"Holy shit," Nesto said aloud.

Katy brought it home as she was scrolling through her laptop for a photo of the man she was describing.

"His phone touches all four phones: Atta, Asidilov, Dabashi, and Gafar's, the only number which does. I think when no news broke of the bomb going off this guy went searching for why not. When he couldn't get Dabashi or Atta, I think he panicked and called her for instructions as to whether to continue as planned or abort the thing altogether. Whatever they decided, that's your man. That's the guy. Find this piece of garbage, you'll find the case."

"Who is he?" Aiden asked.

Katy landed on the web page she sought.

"His name is Hadith Maududi, sixty-one-years old. He's a Muslim cleric in Jersey City, New Jersey. We've been tracking this guy for years. Real bad guy. He's the son of Abdul Maududi, the asshole that brought Sharia and a world of trouble to into Pakistan. Many give the father credit for what we now call Sharia Law."

Katy reading from the page on her laptop, "An Islamic State is a Muslim State, but a Muslim State may not be an Islamic State unless and until the Constitution of the state is based on the Qur'an and Sunnah." She turned around in her chair for a second, "The son is this guy on steroids."

Scrolling through webpages, she found what would give the men a sense of what she was saying.

"Here. He said this in 2009, ready? He said 'Islam is a revolutionary faith that comes to destroy any government made by man. ... Islam doesn't care about the land or who owns the land. The goal of Islam is to rule the entire world and submit all of mankind to the faith of Islam. Any nation or power that gets in the way of that goal, Islam will fight and destroy. In order to fulfill that goal, Islam can use every power available, every way it can be used, to bring worldwide revolution. This is Jihad.' He operates a mosque in Jersey City, its radicalization central. That's your man. He has five sons. Two live with him here in New Jersey. Three younger ones live in Iran."

Silence overtook the room for a second. They knew they were going to Jersey City. They were pleased the terrorist was only a twenty minute drive but they had been fighting for six straight days and needed to gather their emotional strength to make it seven.

Rolly broke the silence. "Great work, kid. Give Aiden and Nesto everything you can on the mosque, this cleric, and the two sons. I need pictures of the two sons, if they exist, and any bad guys running with him. We need his connections around the world and find any connections he has to Gafar if you can. I have a sense it'll take us where we need to go and if not it'll open up a path to some other scum. First get me the address of the mosque and the cleric's home. The pictures too."

Katy didn't wait to affirm Rolly's request. She jumped down into the desk chair, wrote the name **Hadith Maududi on a new page of her yellow legal pad,** and began typing.

Rolly turned his attention to Nesto and Aiden. "Aiden, you OK? Can you go?" The question was a cursory one. Rolly knew Aiden; he wasn't going to be denied. Aiden nodded he was ready.

"Nesto, you?"

Nesto nodded similarly.

"Alright then, we take two cars. Nesto, you have the house. Aiden and I will take the mosque. I'd like to take this Mook-dudi as he moves between the house and the mosque. Let's get these bastards. I want to be in Jersey City by lunch."

Chapter 44

Jersey City, New Jersey

The drive from Fifty Two and a Half Barrow Street in Lower Manhattan was a quick one on a Saturday morning and the Holland Tunnel was only three minutes away, making Hadith Maududi's home and the mosque less than a twenty minute drive from there.

Using Google Maps and Google's Street View, they now had full knowledge of the house and the street. Hadith Maududi's house was not at all remote. The row houses in Jersey City were tighter than tight next to one another. Getting in and out unseen would be impossible. If they had to break into the home they would but it wasn't an optimal scenario. If people were watching the house they would likely scrap their plans and the bomb would disappear. Rolly was willing to risk it as a last resort, but he was hoping it wouldn't come to that.

If they couldn't trap Maududi as he made his way in the streets between the mosque and his home, the plan was to be to break in to the home and secure him there. The variables as to where Maududi was and the possibilities was to what he might be doing were endless.

Whatever it was, they had to take him before Saturday turned into Sunday. It was decided if night fell and Maududi didn't show himself, they would take the house and, depending upon how many were in the house, either interrogate Maududi inside the home or extract him back to Fifty

Two and a Half Barrow. One thing was certain. They were taking Maududi this day.

Aiden and Nesto drove their cars through the exceedingly narrow Jersey City streets past Maududi's home. They were careful to keep a good space between their cars so to offer no appearance that they were together. They caught a break when they discovered the drive between the house and mosque was a straight line of three blocks. If they were lucky Maududi may just choose to walk between the two. If he drove a car from the home to the mosque they could easily trap him in the street between the two.

The two cars made their way the three blocks past the house and drove straight past the mosque. Aiden circled around and made a second pass of the two structures. Nesto followed a minute later.

Aiden drove his car several blocks away and pulled into the parking lot of a CVS drug store and waited for Nesto. A minute later Nesto and Rolly pulled into the same lot and all three exited the cars.

Nesto spoke first. "It's tough. It's so dense with row houses, apartments, and stores. If we take him off the street there's a high likelihood someone will see it. I say we take the house after dark."

Aiden spoke next. "I concur. Taking him off the streets is too high risk. If we're seen, it's over. That suitcase will be gone."

Rolly knew they were absolutely right. "OK, we take the house after dark. Until then we stay the course. Nesto you watch the house. Aiden and I will take the mosque. If this mutt leaves the area more than ten blocks out we'll take him off the street. Yes?"

Nesto and Aiden nodded that they understood.

"OK boys, study the pictures of these three assholes, eyes open, and be sharp. Good luck."

An hour and thirty-six minutes had passed since the men separated when Rolly's phone rang. On the other end was Nesto's voice, "I got one of the sons leaving the house. He's getting into his car with a small dog."

Rolly put his phone on speaker so Aiden could hear. "Go with him."

"Should I take him?" Nesto asked.

"Negative," Rolly snapped, "It's the father we want. If the kid is going for milk and doesn't come back, we're blown. Follow him and I'll take the house. Stay on him. He may lead us to the suitcase, who knows. Let us know if he does anything unusual. "

"Copy that," Nesto responded

Rolly turned to Aiden, "I'll take the house on foot."

Rolly exited the car and made his way down sidewalk of cracked concrete towards the cleric's house.

Twelve minutes later a second son emerged from the house and Rolly recognized from the photo Katy had provided. As he climbed into his blue BMW 328, Rolly called ahead to Aiden. "Aiden, the other son is heading your way in a blue BMW 3. See him?"

It took Aiden less than five seconds to identify the vehicle. "Got him."

Rolly went on but Aiden already knew what he was going to say, but Rolly said it anyway. "Follow him, I'll watch for the cleric."

"I'm on him," Aiden said as he disconnected the call.

The sun was shining but the crisp November wind whipping down the Hudson River was offsetting any warmth the noon day sun was providing. Rolly was on foot now and had no idea how long he would have to be outside. The distance between the mosques and the house was a mere three blocks. He could watch both the house and the mosque, but he'd have to keep moving. He'd have to keep moving without drawing any attention to himself; he'd have to be there and not be there together at once. He'd have to weather the cold wind and have some luck. Luck has a way of blowing away in the wind when you need it most sometimes.

It wasn't a minute after Rolly had exited the car when Maududi emerged from the house. At the curb a man with a white Dodge Journey was waiting for him and the cleric walked around the white truck to get in the passenger side.

Rolly was walking towards the truck that was nearly a block away. So many thoughts raced through his mind as he approached the vehicle and he wanted so badly just to stop the vehicle. He knew he could create a scene in the street but if he did the bomb plot might dissolve or move again. He couldn't risk it.

The white Dodge Journey drove right past him leaving Rolly to wonder if perhaps he was going over to the mosque. Rolly ducked into an apartment doorway and pretended to light a cigarette. If Maududi was indeed going over to the mosque, Rolly would stake it out until Nesto or Aiden, or both, returned. He was begging Maududi's driver to pull into the driveway of the mosque. The driver however, had other ideas and drove right past the mosque and disappeared. Luck had betrayed him.

Rolly, disappointed that Maududi had slipped past him while Aiden and Nesto were following his two sons called Katy. Before she could extend any kind of greeting, he started barking out orders. "Katy, I lost Maududi. I need you to stay with his phone. I…"

Katy interrupted Rolly, "You lost him?"

Rolly became immediately agitated by the perceived implication of his failure. "Never fuckin' mind. Stay with his phone. Aiden and Nesto are following the sons. He got past me. Stay with his phone."

Rolly disconnected and immediately felt bad about his tone with Katy. Rolly didn't expect Katy 'not' to be with Maududi's phone. He just felt somewhat helpless and had the need to do something. His people were excellent in every way and he thought to himself 'you need to calm down, bro.'

Across the street from the mosque Rolly found a pizza parlor where he could sit and wait out of the cold wind. He was also hungry.

"Two slices and a Coke, please," Rolly requested of the Armenian pizza man. The man tossed two slices into the pizza oven and poured him a Coke from the fountain behind the counter. He placed the Coke on the counter in front of Rolly, "Five seventy five," he said.

Rolly reached into his pocket and drew out a ten dollar bill. The pizza man gave Rolly his proper change. "Thanks," Rolly said to the man, "Not too hot, OK. Thanks."

The pizza man lifted the now sufficiently warmed pizza onto a large wooden tray and in one quick motion transferred the pizza onto a white paper plate and placed it on the counter in front of him. Rolly thanked the man again and took his meal to a counter facing the store window where he could keep an eye on the mosque while he ate his lunch. Rolly took a bite from the warm slice of pizza. He figured he could buy a half hour if he ate it slowly.

Half way through the first slice of pizza Rolly's phone rang and it was Aiden.

"He picked up two mutts from a house about three blocks from the mosque. We're in Manhattan and the two guys got dropped off very near the United Nations Building. They went in two different directions and the son is still in his car at the curb on the phone. They have backpacks Rolly. Do you want me to take one of them? I can't take both since they've separated."

Rolly outside of the pizza parlor now, thought for a second. "No, it's Saturday so there's nobody of consequence there and the streets will have three quarters fewer people in them than they will have on a workday morning. Go ahead and take a picture of the knapsacks and maybe we can circulate it with the NYPD. The carrier of the case is already where he needs to be and they'd never jeopardize moving it this late in the game. No, they're not likely to do anything today. Stay with the son and get a pic of the bag."

"Copy that."

Nearly an hour had gone by since Maududi had gone past Rolly and nearly fifteen minutes since he had finished his lunch. He was back out on the street watching, pacing, when Nesto drove by right by him. Several seconds later his phone rang.

It was Nesto, "I'm back in the drugstore lot and the kid is back at the house. Friggin' weird. He drove around for an hour, only stopping once to take his dog for a pee, selfish bastard. He just stopped the car on the shoulder and took the dog into the grass. So basically he made a big circle from here up to Hackensack and back again to the house."

Rolly interrupted Nesto, "Wait, the father, Maududi, just pulled up to the house. He's going inside with his driver as well. Keep an eye on the mosque."

"Copy that," Nesto responded.

Twenty-five minutes after the father returned to the house, a blue BMW pulled up in front of the house. Out climbed the second son, the one Aiden had followed to Manhattan, he went directly into the house. Seconds later Aiden drove past the house and Rolly pulling the car over to the side of the road two hundred yards away from where Rolly had been standing. A few seconds later, Rolly climbed into the passenger side of the car.

Aiden spoke, "So it's the UN?"

"Looks like it," replied Rolly blowing warmth into his cold hands. He went on.

"Everybody is in the house. Let's get Nesto over here. Assuming they all stay home, we take them tonight."

Five minutes after Aiden had called Nesto to join them he arrived and climbed into the car. "I put the car in a lot and told the attendant I didn't have an idea how long it'd be there but that I needed a spot I could move out of quickly. I told him my elderly mother was ill and I may have to take her to the hospital and couldn't have my car blocked in. He parked it right inside the gate. If we have to move I can get it out quick."

"Good thinking," Aiden said approvingly.

"Something is bothering the hell out of me though," Nesto said to no one in particular.

"The kid drove down the hill, got on NJ Turnpike, took the exit for Route 80 where he drove up to Hackensack and then out to the Garden State Parkway. Then he circles around back via Route 3 and back down the Turnpike from there. He made one big circle. That's it. He stopped once to take his dog to pee. That's not what bothered me though." Nesto paused to recall and slowed his speech, "Just after he got off the Turnpike and onto the eastern spur, you know that two and a half mile long connection spur from the end of the Turnpike to Route 80 there. You know which one I'm talking about? Where the marshes are? Where it smells like sulfur?"

Aiden knew it and nodded so, "Yeah."

"Well he slowed down and pulled off to the side of the road on the left lane shoulder to take the dog out of the car, the left lane shoulder, not the right lane. I mean of all the nerve."

"Maybe he thought someone was following him," Aiden offered. "Could he have made you?"

"I don't think so. That road is really sparsely traveled on a Saturday but I was way back. In fact, I was in the toll plaza at the time so he had enough time to take the dog out. If he thought I was following him wouldn't it be a stupid way to try to find out? "

"Maybe he got a text or call or something," Rolly hypothecated.

"Yeah, maybe," Nesto replied obviously deep in contemplation, "maybe."

"Alright, alright, put it out of your mind for now. Obviously he doesn't care about customs. There's no way for us to know what the prick was doing there. We can ask him tonight. We're taking the house tonight… preferably quietly. Let's get our plan together for that."

Chapter 45

The Incursion - Jersey City

They had taken turns watching the house and the mosque for better than eleven hours, not an easy stakeout up on The Heights section of Jersey City. Perched up on the Hudson River, The Heights allowed for stunning views of the Manhattan skyline and on a clear day views of the Verrazano Narrows Bridge leading into Staten Island, New York. When the wind blows down the river in November it has a tendency to whip straight up the hill and cut its way through the Heights. On this November night the men watching and waiting could attest to its sting.

Each man staked out the house or the mosque for forty-five minutes, fifteen minutes on foot, fifteen in the car and fifteen minutes again on foot. It was nearly 2:00 am and they had a good sense of the traffic patterns, foot traffic, and surrounding map. They knew every inch of the street, every inch of the mosque's perimeter, and every inch of the house exterior. What they didn't know, what they most wish they knew, was the interior of the house because that's where they needed to go, that's where their target was.

They were pleased that no one had left the house since Maududi, his driver, and his two sons had returned earlier in the afternoon and the two cars remained in the driveway.

The layout from the front of the house was perfectly set up for an incursion. The small, two-story house was set back ten paces from city sidewalk and the front yard was entirely paved. The driveway was secured the length of the property by an unlocked thirty-six-inch wrought iron fence badly in need of a paint job which opened and closed on rollers. The driveway was itself tight between a row of storefronts to its left leaving no path to the rear of the house and an apartment building to its right with a very narrow alley to the rear of the house.

They weren't at all pleased that the alley was entirely blocked by trash bins, broken furniture, and other items. Getting over the piles of trash and back behind the house for a breach from the rear of the house was determined to be unwise and unsafe. All three would go in from the front. It wasn't the optimal method but they were hoping the element of surprise would offset the disadvantage of not having rear access.

Aiden and Nesto were sitting in the car across from the mosque. It had been more than eleven hours since they had seen anyone going into or leaving the building and over an hour since they saw anyone walking the streets at all.

Nesto's phone rang and he put it on speaker.

"Alright boys here we go," Rolly said. "It's 1:45, fifteen minutes."

Nesto turned his phone off and tossed it on the floor in the passenger side of the vehicle. He wouldn't need it from here.

Aiden and Nesto glanced at their watches. Each grabbed an identical black bag from the backseat of the car, exited the vehicle, and walked off in different directions without saying a word.

Rolly was first to arrive at the house. He had blackened himself from head to toe and one could hardly see him as he casually walked along the darkened storefront windows left of the house. His all-black skullcap, tightly-fitted sweater, pants, and boots blended into the façade of the structures making him virtually invisible. When he made it to the edge of the stores he leaped over the wrought iron fence and hunched in front of the two parked cars. Scurrying to the far side of the driveway he squatted down between the apartment building and the car parked furthest from the front door of the house. He opened his black bag, removed an assault rifle, and slid the empty duffle bag under the vehicle.

Thirty seconds later Nesto repeated the exact same motions, followed thirty seconds later by Aiden.

When all three were present and armed, they nodded to each other that they were ready.

Rolly put three fingers up, two, one.

Chapter 46

Minus One - Jersey City

It started with a tap on the shoulder.

"Remember boys. We need him alive." Rolly whispered in Aiden's left ear just before he made his frontal assault on the wooden door.

Aiden had kicked in hundreds of doors over the years; it was specialty, albeit a dangerous one. Once he had kicked in a door in Fallujah rigged with explosives. Thankfully he noticed the wires wrapped around the lock before the explosion and was able to partially shield himself by spinning away from the blast. The blast burned him badly. The memory of it didn't deter him tonight.

The door flew open like it had been hit with cruise missile when Aiden kicked it.

Given his experience with doors and the tremendous torque he could generate with his frame, he suspected the door would give but he didn't think it would give in so easily. He was hoping the rest of the targets would surrender so meekly.

Aiden rushed into the house and spun to his right pointing his assault rifle first to the right and then to the left. Nesto and Rolly moved in synch behind Aiden. They had done this so many times before it looked choreographed, almost ballet-like.

A middle-aged bearded man who had been sleeping on a foul-smelling, maroon, velvet couch in his underwear had already sat up and was reaching for a pistol on the end table to his right when Aiden saw him.

It took less than a second for Aiden to put two nearly-silent bullets into the man. He never got a grip on the pistol as it fell to the floor. The bullets flipped the man straight back onto the couch into a sitting up position as if he might be watching television. Aiden took a step towards the man. He was dead alright. Pfft…Aiden shot him once more just to be certain, just to be safe.

"Clear," he whispered aloud and exited the room.

Nesto and Rolly had run down the hallway of the house leap-frogging each other as they passed the empty kitchen and an empty backroom. There was no one on the first floor, other than the dead man in the living room. Nesto looked out the back door to a very small, but disgusting, backyard filled to the rim with all manners of trash. No one had been back there in months, maybe years. Satisfied that no one was on the first floor or trying to escape from the back of the house, they returned quickly and carefully to the center hall at the base of the stairs leading up to the second floor. Aiden was waiting for them there.

Sounds could be heard coming both from the second floor and from below. Nesto heard the sounds below and whoever it was, they were behind a closed door adjacent to the kitchen leading down to the basement of the house.

Using only hand signals Rolly communicated that he and Aiden would move up the stairs and Nesto would stay there on the first floor guarding the door to the basement.

Aiden led the way as they moved slowly, carefully, until they were at the base of the stairs pointing their rifles upwards, pausing a moment to gather their timing.

The 1950's house was a small row-type home. They knew the relatively small size of the structure meant the bedroom or bedrooms, would butt up against the stairway having no room for a hallway. If there was to be any defense it would be at the top of the stairs.

Aiden and Rolly could be heard steadying their breath in exactly the same manner and at the exact same moment.

Rolly tapped Aiden on the shoulder and they instantly ran up the stairs. One step, two steps, three… When Aiden hit the third step he dove to the ground.

Once the man on the landing above heard Aiden hit the third step he wheeled around the wall and pointed his rifle at where he expected Aiden's torso to be. Before the shooter could pull his weapon down to where Aiden actually was, Rolly fired a single shot which hit the shooter in the forehead. He was dead before he hit the ground.

Rolly was on the move up the stairs faster than the dead man was falling down them, leaping past Aiden who was still lying on the top step with his weapon trained upwards in the event there was to appear a second shooter. As he reached the landing of the second floor Rolly signaled Aiden to move up.

Nesto kneeled down on one knee listening intently for what was happening to Aiden and Rolly as they made their way. When he heard the single round being discharged and the body hitting the floor he knew instantly it was one of theirs. He said to himself 'two down.'

At no time did Nesto stop aiming his rifle at the basement door, if anyone were to make the mistake of coming through the door it would be a fatal mistake. They'd make it no further than the top step.

The most successful warriors do more listening than shooting. While the enemy is thinking, the warrior is listening. While the enemy is moving, the listener hears the revelation of their own destruction.

Nesto's ears pricked up. There was a noise, faint as it was, coming from the backyard of the house. Once Nesto zeroed in on the sound he didn't waste second. He broke for the backdoor throwing it open and less than twenty feet away was one of Maududi's sons trying to escape via the backyard. The piles of trash back there prevented both a quick exit and provided sounds enough for Nesto to place the location of the movement.

"Stop," Nesto called out loud enough to be heard but low enough not to wake any neighbors. The figure in the dark spun around.

Nesto had been in enough firefights to know when a man was submitting and when he was intending not to submit. Pfft… Nesto killed the man instantly. Maududi's son never got off a shot with his pistol falling from his hand and adding itself to the trash pile.

Rolly and Aiden were standing on the small second-floor landing, shielding themselves from whatever dangers might be inside the lone bedroom on that level. Rolly thrust his chin down at the dead man on the stairs so Aiden would have a look. "Maududi's son," he whispered to Aiden.

"Maududi," Rolly called into the bedroom, "we know you're in there. We know about the plot, all of it."

Rolly and Aiden listened for a response. None came.

Rolly tried a different tact. "Maududi, your driver is dead and I'm looking at your son out here dead on the stairs. You have one son still alive. You can save him and yourself by surrendering now."

Again they waited for something, anything from Maududi. Again, nothing came.

Rolly whispered in Aiden's ear, "When I say the word promise, we go, OK?" Aiden nodded quickly in the affirmative. Rolly tapped him on the shoulder.

"Mr. Maududi, I promise…"

Before Rolly could get to the second syllable in the word, Aiden took one full stride into the doorway and dropped to a knee pointing his assault rifle into the room. Rolly lunged in upright and slammed into the frame of the door, also pointing his weapon.

Kneeling behind a musty, old club chair the cleric aimed an AKR rifle at the door.

Pfft Pfft…

Pfft Pfft…

Aiden and Rolly each fired two bullets into the chair. The caliber of bullet ensured each round would obliterate the meager defense. The seventy-one-year old cleric never got off a shot, nor would he ever again.

Both Aiden and Rolly were displeased the cleric chose to fight rather than surrender. He had information they needed and now they'd never get it from him. They had killed three. There was at least one son left. They needed him and they needed him alive.

The top level of the house consisted of one relatively small bedroom and one really small bathroom, too small for even a shower. Rolly and

Aiden made quick work of making sure there were no other threats on the second floor and broke down the stairs.

The moment Rolly hit the landing of the main floor and saw Nesto standing in so casual a stance he knew. Aiden leaped down the last three stairs and immediately came to the same conclusion. They had done the unthinkable, he had killed the second son.

Nesto could see the disappointment on Rolly's face. "He's in the back yard. He climbed out the casement window and I ordered him to stop but he drew on me. He's dead."

Rolly and Aiden bowed their heads in thought. What would they do now?

Nesto could see something was really wrong. "What?" Nesto pushed.

"The old man and the other son are also dead," Aiden explained.

Nesto knew what that meant. "Ugh…oh boy," he said of the dilemma.

Rolly clearly frustrated, glanced over at the dead man still sitting upright on the smelly, velvet couch. "Fucking morons. All four of ya'… Not one of ya' got off a damn shot. Now look at ya'."

Nesto was quick to get the group to refocus. "What now? We don't have much time here."

Rolly got the message. It was time to improvise.

"Aiden upstairs. Nesto down in the basement. I'll take this level… phones, computers, papers…two minutes. I wanna be out of here in two. Go!"

The three men sprinted around the house tearing apart drawers and closets looking for anything that might tell them of the whereabouts of that second suitcase.

Ninety seconds after Aiden ran up the stairs, he came down the stairs. He looked at Rolly with a tinge of disappointment, "Nothing," he said, "Not a thing. No phone, no computer, no notes…nothing. They're not even carrying their wallets."

Rolly knew they were in trouble. "Nothing down here either," he said in stunned surprise.

Nesto entered the forward room and having heard the report of what Aiden said and Rolly's reply, simply shook his head conveying he too had come up empty.

"What the hell? All of a sudden they're smart? They couldn't figure out how to get off a shot between them and now they're geniuses?" Nesto asked more to break the uncomfortable silence than as an act of brainstorming.

"Nah, they got lucky. Tonight was the last night they were never going to be staying here. There were no clothes in the drawer upstairs, furniture is shit, no computers, no nothing. That stuff has already been moved."

Rolly knew Aiden was right. He also knew they had to do something with the clock was ticking. Rolly looked at his watch, "Well, we gotta do something and we can't stay here. First thing we gotta do is drag that body inside."

Nesto and Aiden didn't speak a word. They moved quickly into the back yard and as quietly as they could, lifted the dead man off the pile of trash, and brought him into the back room of the house and laid him on the floor.

Rolly picked up where he left off, "Alright, the mosque. We'll break into the mosque. Now."

"Shit!" Nesto said in a bit of panic pointing to the man on the floor. "That's not the son, the second son. That's not the guy I followed today."

"You sure that's not the guy?" Aiden asked almost as an indictment of Nesto's memory.

Nesto had moved to the body lying dead on the stairs, "Fuck, that's not him either."

Aiden confirmed that the body Nesto was now looking at was indeed not him, "No, that's the mutt I followed into New York."

Rolly pointed at the same dead body, "Are you sure?" he asked of Aiden.

Aiden responded with great certainty, "Yes, I'm absolutely certain."

"Then the second son isn't here" Nesto said, pointing at the body they had dragged in from the yard. "He must have gone out with this mutt.'

"Fuck," Aiden said with an almost forlorn tone.

Rolly took over the conversation, "Fuck is right. But we can't worry about that now. We need to get inside that mosque."

Aiden played devil's advocate, "You're not going to find shit at that mosque. These guys are going to disappear on Monday and the last thing they're likely to do is leave anything at that mosque which would speak to anything. Whatever they need for their travel is close by. I won't argue that. But it ain't in that mosque. Maybe it's…"

As soon as Aiden said the words a light went off that only someone with his way of thinking could see. "No… no… I know. I know what we need to do no," he said enthusiastically. "Remember I told you the son stopped and picked up those two guys, the two guys he dropped off in New York by the UN?"

"Yeah," Rolly said with curiosity.

"The house, the house you idiots. The house where he picked them up is four blocks from here. If Maududi's shit isn't there, I bet there is something we can use anyway."

No one said a word. They didn't have to. They knew what they had to do.

Chapter 47

Take It All - Jersey City

"Alright, one more pass then we go," Rolly said as they drove by the house.

"Still no lights," Nesto informed them. They had driven by the house where Maududi's son had picked up the two men who he dropped off in Manhattan earlier in the day.

If Maududi's house was small, this one was smaller, but it was similar to the house they had raided just minutes earlier.

"Same plan," Rolly said as he parked the car two blocks from the entrance of the house. "Me, then Aiden, then you Nesto, we go in the same way." Rolly exited the vehicle first, taking his black duffle bag from Nesto before he disappeared.

Nesto and Aiden exited the vehicle next and as they had done less than an hour earlier, nodded to one another and went off in opposite directions.

Less than six minutes later the three men convened in the driveway of the house. It looked as if there was no movement at all inside the house. The house was still completely dark, no lights were on inside and no outside lights were shined that might shed light on the breach. It looked as if there was no movement at all inside the house. The three men checked their watches and nodded to one another.

"Quickly boys, quickly," Rolly whispered. They were off.

Aiden burst through the front door and it offered only token resistance. The three rushed in as they had done for years, leap frogging one another quickly and methodically to clear each room on the main floor.

"No basement," Nesto whispered as he made his way to the back of the house as fast as he could. He wasn't sure how the terrorist got out of the previous house without detection but he didn't want to lose another bad guy over a back fence if that's how he got away. "No yard," he whispered again.

Rolly pointed at Aiden, then himself. They were going to use the same attack they had just employed in the previous raid.

Aiden paused at the bottom of the stairs and steadied his breath. Rolly tapped him on the shoulder and Aiden pounded his feet up the stairs and dropped with Rolly following behind. Seeing no threat emerge, Rolly ran past Aiden leaping the stairs two at a time until he reached the landing above. Aiden didn't waste a millisecond and the two men arrived at the top step almost simultaneously. Once again they steadied their breath.

Aiden tapped Rolly on the shoulder. The signal to move being received, Rolly kicked in the door and Aiden rushed in and dropped to a knee. Seeing no movement Rolly rushed in pointing his weapon at any possible place where an ambush could present itself. The room was empty and both men felt relieved on the one hand and frustrated on the other. It appeared no one was in the house and that wasn't good.

Aiden, still resting on one knee with his weapon at the ready and comfortable at least enough that no one was in the room, flicked on a small flashlight. Rolly and Aiden looked around the room and what they saw sent chills down their respective spines.

Any person looking at the room could plainly see this was a bomb-making factory with spools of white wires and spools of blue wires. It was strewn with unopened boxes of bomb-making switches, discarded food wrappers, at least ten detonators, and twenty grenade hulls sitting like fruit in a bowl on an old desk with arm lamps and magnifying glasses. There were bits and pieces of old cell phones and clock components seemingly everywhere. Amongst the filth, smell of perspiration, and urine were pages of manuals all over the walls and floor having to do with electronics, explosives, and detonation. The manuals from which they were ripped were in a pile in a corner of the room.

It was a room full of propaganda magazines, fast food menus, and prayer books. It was a room full of evil and hatred. They could feel it on their skin as they tried with all their might from feeling it in the depths of their hearts.

This wasn't a half-destroyed, three-story walk up in Iraq. It wasn't a cement and sand, windowless house in Afghanistan. It was a tiny little bungalow in New Jersey. It was in and among other little houses and jam packed apartment buildings in an American city. A city from where, on a clear day, you could have seen the World Trade Center Towers just across the Hudson River.

Aiden and Rolly were sickened, furious, and a bit frightened. Something in the glare of the flashlight on the wires and clock fragments was the realization that they were all that stood between people going to work on Monday and not going home. All that stood between thousands of people going through their lives never knowing what might have happened and reliving what happened every day for the rest of their lives, perhaps even between peace and world war. It was an awareness they had not before experienced. While initially frightened, they became terrified. As they stared at the instruments of destruction, they had their training, their courage, their wits, and their honor on the one side. On the other side was everything else. They had to shake it off and keep moving.

"Grab everything you can find that might tell us something, papers, notes, anything electronic. We gotta get out of here," Rolly snapped. "Nesto and I will strip the first floor. Three minutes max, three minutes."

Rolly bolted down the stairs where Nesto had been providing security, picking up Nesto as soon as he hit the first floor landing. "Strip it. Anything you can find. We're outta here in three."

Nesto didn't waste a second throwing open the kitchen cabinets. He pulled from one of the cabinets a box of thirty gallon, green garbage bags and tossed one to Rolly.

Rolly looked around for a second. "Grab the box and take it up to Aiden. There's a fucking bomb factory up there and not much down here. Go help Aiden."

When he hit the second floor and entered the room a feeling of shock fell on him like a trance. Aiden recognized immediately that Nesto was experiencing what he had experienced only a minute ago. But they had to be out of there in less than two minutes so he pushed Nesto "C'mon, c'mon, c'mon. I know it's fucked up but we got ninety seconds to get out of this hell hole. Start packing."

Nesto knew he had to move and reflections about what the room was saying to him would have to wait. He began furiously rummaging the room for anything that might offer a clue. The two began shoving any papers they could find into the garbage bags taking, virtually no notice of each other and saying not a single thing to each other.

Two minute later they were gone. Twenty-five minutes later they'd be back at Fifty Two and a Half Barrow Street. Twenty-four hours after that they'd be in the fight of their lives. At stake, the fight would tilt the future peace of mankind one way or collapse into a condition altogether different.

Chapter 48

Barrow Street, NYC

It was after 3:00 am when Nesto came through the door at Fifty Two and a Half Barrow Street into the operation room and handed Katy one of the two green trash bags taken from the bomb factory. Rolly came in behind with the third bag and immediately dumped it onto a four-foot round conference table. Aiden, now no longer bolstered by the adrenalin rush of combat action, and still feeling the pains of the beating he took in Phoenix, arrived a few seconds later dragging only himself into the room and having trouble with even that.

Rolly seated and already rummaging through the bag newly emptied into the center of the conference table said, "Katy, c'mere. We took this out of a God damn bomb assembly house. We think the two guys who lived there are in Manhattan with explosives and we're looking for anything about who they are, who they work for or with. Anything that points this at the location of the damn suitcase. Anything at all that can tell us anything at all. One bag at a time."

Nesto pulled up a chair and began pulling individual shreds of paper from the pile. Aiden joined.

"Don't throw anything away," Rolly said to the group. "Place it on the floor and we'll go through everything twice, three times if we have to."

Aiden reached for a piece of what looked like a detonator switch attached to nothing but a few wires poking from it, "We gotta see if we can get prints off this stuff."

Nesto leaped to his feet and hustled to his jacket where his phone was pocketed, "I'll call the Doc and have him get over here and see what they can get."

Aiden held up a scrap of paper, "Well we know what the two guys were carrying. Here's a receipt for two pressure cookers." The paper in Aiden's hand did not disclose a revelation but rather a confirmation.

Rolly didn't skip a beat, "Katy, Aiden has a photo of a kid with a backpack and its' got a pressure cooker in it, one like the shitheads in Boston blew up at the marathon. There are two guys and each one of them has one of these bags. When we're done going through this stuff, hopefully with a positive ID on these scumbags, you gotta call Capps to relay the information. My guess is these guys are there for secondary explosions for the first responders' arrivals once the suitcase is let go. They're in Manhattan somewhere and if we can ID these two maybe they can scoop them up before they do more damage."

Katy never looked up. "Got it," was all she said and kept digging.

"What the fuck is this?" Rolly said as he studied a dog-eared strand of 8x11 papers in one hand while holding similar pieces of paper in his other hand. "Itineraries for airline travel for the cleric and his son. Maududi was supposed to fly out of Newark for Paris today at 11:40 am. One son was supposed to be on that flight with him."

"Was supposed to? What do you mean by supposed to?" Katy asked

"Well, your boy over there," Rolly said pointing to Aiden, "shot them. The son is lying dead on the stairs and Maududi is dead in a corner behind a ratty old chair. He ain't going anywhere."

A light went on in Nesto's head as he returned to the conference table to help with the search, "Doc's on his way. That reminds me. What about those guys? Shouldn't we have someone go out there and clean it up?"

"Why only one son?" Aiden asked brainstorming.

Rolly already had the answer. He had gotten it off the itinerary. "I can't tell you why, but I can tell you when. The other son is scheduled to fly out of Kennedy on Wednesday." Rolly's voice picked up a shot of energy.

"Forget the Doc. The son is flying out with two others; gotta be the backpack guys. They're all three booked on flight late Wednesday out of Kennedy for Brussels." He handed the pages to Katy. "Get on these two names. Anything you can find. Go!"

"Should I cancel the Doc?" Nesto asked.

"No, he can go over the stuff anyway. Maybe he can find other prints, other players." Rolly answered.

Aiden asked, "The question is: Was the son we killed the same one booked on that flight or is it the one that got away? And if it was the one that got away, is he gone now or is he going to go through with it?"

Rolly thought through Aiden's pertinent questions but before he could answer the doorbell facing Barrow Street rang; two short rings, two long rings, two short rings.

"It's the Doc," Nesto said as he hustled to the access buzzer allowing his entry.

Rolly continued with Aiden, "I don't know but we have to assume it's a go. These bastards are fanatics and the caliphate is their cherished prize. If they pull it off the family name goes in history books as the family name that is spoken with Muhammad. Nah, this is once in two thousand year stuff. It's a go; bet on it."

The Doc entered the room. "Whatya' got?" he asked.

"We need prints off this stuff," Nesto responded

"Not yet, Doc," Rolly interrupted. We need you to go out to Jersey City to 2350 Central Avenue; it's a twenty-five minute ride from here. There are four dead bodies in the house and we need prints and ID's."

The Doc inquired, "Am I cleaning up?"

"No. The world is already on fire from the Muslim killings in Michigan and we can't risk anyone seeing four more dead bodies coming out of there. Just get their prints for now. We'll clean it after Monday."

Nesto, playing devil's advocate, jumped in. "What if someone else finds the bodies? Wouldn't it be wise to clean it tonight rather than risk it?"

"No I don't think so," Rolly responded. "Go Doc, while it's still dark. We need the names as soon as you have them."

The Doc disappeared without saying a word.

Rolly continued as soon as the Doc was out of the room, "I don't think it's worth the risk tonight. First, these guys are booked on a flight in less than eight hours. There was nothing in that house, nothing. No, they're already gone and no one is going to be looking for them until they don't show up in Paris late tonight. With Paris being six hours ahead, the flight they're scheduled to be on won't land until late at night, which means they won't come up missing till Monday. Second, I don't want to risk Gafar getting wind of their deaths. I'm sure they've gone black. Any wind of a problem coming out of Jersey City might scrap the whole thing."

"Anything on those guys yet, Katy?" Rolly called over to Katy who was furiously typing on her laptop.

"No, nothing," she responded without looking up. "No hotels, nothing yet. I'm looking for their phones, if they're on any lists."

The time flew. One hour. Then two hours. They went through a second trash bag of items all of which proved to be just that, trash.

Just as Nesto was dumping the third bag onto the conference table Rolly's phone rang.

"Yeah Doc. Say again. Spell it," Rolly grabbed a pen and wrote a name on a loose paper. "Thanks, Doc. Great work."

Rolly leaned over Katy's shoulder and placed the paper beneath her, "Qasim Maududi, the dead son."

Rolly returned to the conference table and as soon as he sat down Katy already had something on Maududi.

"That's the son scheduled to leave out of Kennedy on Wednesday, the one with the two backpackers."

"So the one scheduled to leave today with the father is the one that got away." Nesto correctly reasoned.

"Doesn't tell us much," Aiden chimed in. "Tells us the prick is out there. Tells us to keep digging."

"Wait a minute," Katy said into her laptop screen, "Wait a minute." All three stopped what they were doing and waited for Katy to expand upon her comment.

"Hey, I got a Qasim Maududi booked on a flight from Philly to Brussels for Wednesday. He booked it twenty-five minutes ago and he cancelled today's Kennedy flight. I don't see anyone else with him. He's going out alone it looks like."

"Philly? Why Philly?" Nesto thought aloud.

Aiden had a sense. "He's still a go. There was nothing in the house to identify him so he thinks we don't know he was there and that he's in on this. He's still here."

Katy followed up, "Nothing on the two backpackers. Nothing anywhere, nothing. Shit!"

"Relax. You can't think clearly if you're pissed off. Keep looking, kid." Rolly wanted to tell her to take a break; they could all use a break. Rolly knew it but he pushed her a little anyway. "Go back to the beginning and start walking it forward. Try to clear your head and start over."

Rolly was impatient but he knew she was burnt. He knew they all needed a rest. "You know what? We all need some sleep, same as always, four hour shifts." Knowing Aiden was still hurting badly he said, "Aiden, you and Katy first. Nesto and I will pull the rest of this crap in the meantime."

Aiden stood up immediately. He knew his body and he knew they were better off if he had more strength. He also knew Monday was coming fast. Everything was coming fast.

Katy resisted, "I'm OK."

Aiden beat Rolly to the punch. "You're not OK. It's 4:00 am, you're frustrated and tired. Do what you're told."

She wanted to stay and keep searching but complied. She made a note on her legal pad, stood up, and left the room. Aiden followed her. Nesto and Rolly continued rummaging through the pile of trash on the conference table.

When Aiden and Katy were out of earshot, Rolly softly said to Nesto. "Six hours, those two look like death. We'll give them an extra two hours and wake them at ten." Nesto nodded his approval.

Chapter 49

Believe It - Barrow Street

Rolly and Nesto could hear her footsteps flying down the hundred and twenty-five-year-old wooded stairs and there was anger in her feet pounding. Katy, still in her underwear and tight, plain white t-shirt, burst into the situation room. Her hair was a wild mess and if one looked close enough she still had sleep crude in the corner of her right eye. Neither Nesto nor a heavy-eyed Rolly took much notice. They had been, for six uninterrupted hours, organizing, separating, and segregating the trash. They hadn't learned a thing and they wanted desperately to stop looking at and speculating about each item. Both badly needed some sleep and that they hardly noticed her exceedingly pronounced feminine form was proof of their diminished capacity.

Katy ripped into them, "Ten o'clock. It's fucking ten o'clock. Ten o'clock. You let me sleep till ten o'clock? This is about to explode into a million pieces and I'm friggin' asleep? What the hell were you guys thinking?"

Rolly smiled at his infuriated partner, impressed with her hutzpah and passion. He would never tell her as much but there was a purpose and determination about her he really liked. "I can tell you what I'm thinking now, what's with the hair? Get a brush or a comb. Maybe a tooth brush."

Nesto saw how Rolly was disarming Katy. Rolly had disarmed him a thousand times. He was a professional at disarming fire and brimstone types. He thought he'd play along, "Jesus Katy, put on some clothes. I'm still at an impressionable age here. It's embarrassing."

Katy would have none of it, "This is funny?"

Rolly didn't want to quell Katy's desire to do something positive here or want her to ever think he was even the slightest bit capable of making light of the situation. "Alright, take it is easy. Listen Katy, I know you want to get your teeth into this thing but you're the most important person we've got right now. Let me rephrase that. You're the most important person this country has right now. We can't have you at half speed. You need your wits, all of them. We have less than twenty-four hours before that suitcase goes off. That extra two hours of sleep might make your mind just clear enough to find the needle in the haystack. What you find may be the difference between a shitload of deaths and those people going home to his or her family. If those two extra hours cost us, it's on me. Nesto, why don't you get some zzz's. I want to go over with Katy what we've done and what she has here to dig through."

Nesto was exhausted. He wanted to affirm to Katy what Rolly had just said was spot on. But if it was spot on, he knew he needed to be sharp himself. He got up from the table, touched Katy on the shoulder, and went out of the room for a shower and some sleep.

"I'm sorry," Katy said to an equally exhausted Rolly, "I shouldn't have cursed at you. I just know how little time we have and I was losing it."

Rolly appreciated the deference. "Hey, it just means you give a shit and that's the most important thing, so no worries. We were there once, but we've been through a million fights and aside from strength of principle, the strength of mind has ended most of them."

Katy didn't know what to say feeling a new level of camaraderie. She knew however long she was going to be working with these men, indeed however long she had been working for the protection of her country, what Rolly Byrnes had just taught her she would never forget.

Rolly for his part needed rest. "OK, we've separated this crap into three parts. Here is anything non paper. This is receipts anything paper; newspaper articles, manuals, etcetera. This small pile is anything with handwriting on it. I'd suggest you start with that stuff. Aiden will be down in a second to make himself available to you. Use him; he's a lot smarter than me. He might be the smartest guy you'll ever meet. Use him. Good luck."

Rolly dragged himself up the stairs.

Katy sat down with the trash. She still had her determination, her hutzpah, and her purpose. Only now she also had a clear head and a crushing desire not to let the Rolly, Aiden, and Nesto down.

Not five minutes after Rolly left the room Aiden appeared. His still swollen face had begun the healing process, which as it progressed through the early stages actually looked worse.

He looked at Katy, who had by now put on some clothing and combed her hair a bit, "You look rested," he said to her to break the ice.

"You look terrible!" she said back, while sympathetically pointing to her own still blackened cheekbone. "Your face, it looks horrible."

"Gee, good to see you too," Aiden said playfully.

She was glad to see him. "I'm sorry. Coffee?" she asked.

"Love some," he really did desperately want some coffee.

While Katy walked into the kitchen to pour him a cup of coffee, Aiden sat down at the conference room table and started thumbing through the clearly separated piles of trash. He knew Rolly and Nesto had segregated it and didn't want to disturb it until Katy had brought him up to date on where they were.

Katy returned with two cups, placing one in front of Aiden who scooped it up immediately and gratefully sipped it. When he could clear his lips he asked Katy, "How are you feeling? Did you sleep OK?"

"Yeah, I slept OK, too OK, six hours. I gave Rolly and Nesto a hard time about going past the four hours, but he wouldn't hear it."

"Did he give you the 'you're the most important guy, we need your brain, and you're our smartest guy stuff?'"

Katy's eyes lit up and her tone took on a hint that she knew she had been played, "Yes, yes he did. He said that exact thing."

"Yeah, he gave that speech to me once in a firefight in Afghanistan. We were trapped on a friggin' hill for nearly forty hours. When night fell and watches were handed out, he allowed me to sleep an extra hour or so while he, as exhausted as he was, stood my watch by himself. I regained my mental focus and figured out a way to get us out alive." Aiden looked her deep in the eyes. She looked back into his. "Whatever he tells you, believe it. He's the best leader I've ever known. And he's incapable of bullshit."

Aiden pointed to the piles on the table. "What do we have here?"

Chapter 50

The Hourglass - Barrow Street

Frustration began to set in for the pair. For Aiden, three hours of combing through the trash on the conference table had yielded nothing but a single name scribbled on two separate pieces of paper; the handwriting of which he couldn't make out and which meant nothing to him.

For Katy, three hours on the computer hacking email accounts, trying to find a connection to someone, anyone, from someone, anyone, who might help them find the second suitcase yielded the same…zero.

They had always been aware of the time but now they began to feel the sand in the hourglass escaping grain by grain.

Katy went intermittently between cursing her computer screen to begging it to deliver something. Suddenly she cracked, slamming her hand down on the desk and with more than a little whininess in her high-pitched voice, she cried, "C'mon!"

Aiden recognized the signs of being mentally blocked. Frustration brings it on and it's the most damaging thing to puzzle solving. Your mind starts to narrow itself and finally you are reduced to seeing only one thing. You get fixated on it to the exclusion of every other thing, a near hypnotic quality to the single object takes over and a trance rolls over.

Aiden knew they had become wedged into that kind of futility, the enfeebling mental blockade where they were far less likely to discover anything useful, mostly because they were trying to find it in the useless.

"Alright, we need to step away. It's 2:00 pm. Order some pizza's." He pointed to a cork board hanging on the wall to Katy's immediate left. "There's a menu there from Famous Ray's. Call over there and order two, no Rolly's gonna be hungry, order three. And make sure to order one pepperoni. I'll go get the boys. Make it carry out. While they're getting themselves together, we can get some fresh air. It's only two blocks, but it'll give us a chance to get our eyes off this thing. After we eat, the four of us can recalibrate."

Katy felt a small wave of panic come over her. She really didn't want to walk away from her computers and they were nearly out of time. But after what had happened in the airport where she had done exactly what Aiden told her to do in and it saved her life, she knew now not to question the judgement of the men who knew what deadlines really were and what pressure really was. She picked up a prepaid phone and dialed Famous Rays.

Sixty seconds after Aiden left the room he hurried back into it, "Did you order the pizzas?"

Katy nodded. "Two regular and one pepperoni"

"Good, let's get the hell out of here before Rolly gets here. He can be an absolute monster before he has a coffee."

When they hit the cold November air Aiden stretched his arms above his head as if he had just awoken. Katy looked at him in amazement for what appeared to be an incredibly cavalier posture. She was tight as a drum and couldn't imagine being any other way given the circumstances.

Aiden noticed her noticing him. "It's taken me years of practice to fake being calm," he smiled. "But this I know. It's the smallest thing you find when you put aside looking for the biggest thing, that gets you out. Let's walk."

She had no idea what he meant but she acted like she understood.

Chapter 51

The Forger - Barrow Street

They had slept. Their bodies had healed a bit. They had eaten. They still had nothing. Worse perhaps, two more hours had escaped with nothing they could use.

Rolly tried to seem upbeat but it was a hard sell, even to him. "Alright, let's go over it again."

Nesto was thumbing through a propaganda pamphlet when his posture got rigid in his chair. "Hey, let me see that piece of paper."

"Which one?" asked Aiden.

"The one with the name written on it you couldn't read."

Nesto had everyone's full attention and their prayers as well. His eyes were shifting back and forth between the pamphlet and the loose paper. His eyes made several passes over each to make certain he was seeing what he was seeing. He held the loose paper up in the air. "I know who this is." Everyone was locked in on him now. "His name is Jihad Ahmed Diyab."

Aiden was confused and hopeful together at once. "Jihad? That's his name? Jihad? Can I see that?" Aiden asked as he extended his hand to Nesto and studied the paper. "There's no way that says Ahmed Diyab. It's not even close Nesto."

"No, Aiden, my dear boy. The writing is Abu Wa'el Dhiab. That's the name written on the paper. The guy here goes by both. And yes, he's referred to as Jihad."

Aiden looked at it again. "OK, you got it. The Abu threw me. Well done."

Nesto went on as he read from the English language terrorist recruitment propaganda magazine. "He's a real asshole. Get this; he's a former Guantánamo detainee." Nesto glanced over at Rolly. "Your boy in the White House snuck him out of Gitmo in one of those the middle of the night moves. Apparently he's living in Uruguay."

Katy who had been typing the name of the terrorist into her databases interrupted, "He was living in Uruguay."

Rolly knew what Katy said was going to take this conversation in a whole new direction. "What? Whatya' mean: was?"

Katy anticipated the question. "He's gone missing. Apparently following a trip to Brazil he disappeared. Brazilian authorities say they have no record of Jihad Ahmed Diyab. Authorities there are searching for the guy and their national airline told employees to be on alert."

Katy kept reading aloud from her screen. "Jihad Diyab, also known as Abu Wa'el Dhiab, was released with five other Guantánamo Bay prisoners into Uruguay in 2014. It was part of a program organized by socialist President José Mujica to help the president empty the military facility of detainees. Having staged various hunger strikes while in detention, Diyab suffers from poor health and cannot walk without a limp. He speaks very limited English and no Spanish or Portuguese.

Believing they'd soon be looking for Jihad, Aiden opined, "That'll make it difficult for him to travel in the region unnoticed."

Katy kept going, "Ugh. Columbia is warning this guy may be traveling on a fake Syrian or Moroccan passport. It follows an admission by the government of Brazil that they have no record of the man entering the country despite Uruguayan authorities insisting he went to Brazil. Uruguayan Minister of the Interior, Eduardo Bonomi, insisted he did not pass through any official registry. He added that Diyab had tried to enter Brazil previously but was denied entry due to his record as a documented jihadist. Qatar also rejected him for the same reason. His whereabouts Columbia insists is now Brazil's problem."

"Nice," Nesto added sarcastically.

Katy kept reading, "The White House is aware of the disappearance but insists it should not be cause for concern. The White House spokesman said of Jihad, he'd be crazy to associate to get back into the fight".

Rolly spoke over Katy, "Yeah, crazy. When he shoves a suitcase full of radioactive isotopes up the president's ass maybe they'll think differently. God I hate these morons in the White House."

Katy wasn't finished. "According to his dossier Jihad was arrested for his ties to numerous jihadi groups, including "Libyan Islamic Fighting Group (LIFG), Lashkar-e-Tayyiba (LT), Ansar al-Islam, Harakat al-Mujahidin (HUM), and Harakat ul-Jihad-i-Islami (HUJI). He is described as an associate of several other significant al-Qaida and now ISIL members."

"He got around, huh?" Nesto interrupted.

Katy was rolling, "And get this; his specialty is forgery and forging documents. According to this, DHS thinks he may be in possession of stolen Syrian blank passports and an original government machine to make official passports."

"You got his dossier that quick?" Aiden asked.

"Hey, that's my job," Katy assured him.

"Impressive."

Rolly was circling the wagons. "OK, he's a bad guy. He screams that he's likely part of this. His name was in a bomb factory but what does it mean? What's the connection?"

"Maybe he's providing travel docs," Nesto guessed.

Aiden squashed it. "I don't think so. They booked flights on airplanes using their own U.S. passports. It'll be far safer to travel as Americans after the case goes off than Syrians or Moroccans."

"OK 'Miss I-can-hack-into-anything,'" Rolly said to Katy with a bit of hidden admiration. "See if you can find Jihad or Abu booked on flights anywhere on the earth in the coming days. He's on the no fly so I doubt he'd be stupid enough to try but look anyway. Maybe his time in Gitmo dulled his senses."

Rolly shrugged his shoulders to Nesto and Aiden. Both knew there was zero chance a guy, a master forger with a lifetime of trade craft and a thousand year caliphate hanging in the balance, could possibly be so dumb. But they also knew, despite the odds against so abject a stupidity, they had to look anyway.

"And get us everything you can find on this mutt."

All three men looked at their watches. It was 5:45 am.

Chapter 52

The Passenger - Barrow Street

*M*ostly men take no note of passing time…mostly. Then there are moments when every surrendering minute screams out to be noticed.

If they had felt frustrated by the clock ticking away earlier in the day, it was as a calculus of poor advance. Now it had become a calculus of inertia and they felt panicked. Their lack of movement on discovering the whereabouts of that suitcase, three hours stalled, terrified them. No one wanted to look at a clock or a watch.

Rolly looked at his watch, he had to. It had just broke 8:00 pm.

"Anything?" Aiden asked Katy.

"No, sorry. I'm doing the best I can. I've looked at every airline in the world, every hotel, motel, hostel, boarding house. He's not anywhere."

"Keep looking," Aiden encouraged.

Nesto speaking to no one in particular, "He's traveling under a different name."

"Duh, ya' fuckin think?" said an obviously agitated Aiden.

Nesto was the least cynical of the three men but he didn't like being spoken to in that way. "Hey, fuck you. I'm thinking out loud here."

"Then think of something more than that shit. It's fucking meaningless. My fucking barber could have come up with that shit."

"Fuck you, Aiden. I haven't heard anything from you in two fucking hours. What would your barber say to that?"

Rolly knew high strung men in high stress situations often get testy with each other but he needed focus. There was no time for diversions. He had to stop it, "Hey, hey…knock that shit off. We got a fuckin' job to do and we're not getting it done. And we'll never get it done if we start arguing like a bunch of friggin' wash women."

Aiden immediately knew Rolly was right. He also knew he was wrong for snapping at Nesto. "Sorry bro. I think I'm just getting frustrated and it's making me an asshole."

Nesto also knew Rolly was right. He knew, as smart as he was, Aiden's brain was operating on a much deeper analytical level than his own. If his blockage was resulting in high anxiety he could only imagine how the lack of movement was affecting Aiden. He accepted Aiden's apology. "It's OK. Its' all good. I'll try not to think out loud."

Now that he had reigned in the arguing, Rolly wanted to refocus attention.

"Alright, let's go all the way back to the beginning and start looking through this crap one piece at a time. Katy is there anything new on Jihad? I don't mean about where he is. Is there anything at all that we don't know, anything about him from his time at Gitmo, anything at all?"

Aiden was still a little embarrassed about his behavior. His eyes were bothering him a little and his cracked rib was barking from being sedentary in a chair so long a time. He needed a short break to gather himself. "I'm gonna get a breath outside. I'll be back in a minute." He stood and walked over to a sofa where he had left his windbreaker and slowly limped his way to the door.

Katy responded to Rolly's question saying, "Gitmo? Not really. I've been reading his file for the last three and a half hours. By all accounts he was pretty much a loner. He couldn't walk so he didn't participate in any physical activities. He was really quiet and reports have him as a near model prisoner. He didn't abuse the guards or threaten the U.S. as the others had."

"Not once?" Rolly asked. It was commonplace for Gitmo prisoners to make blustering claims as to when and how they were going to return with a vengeance and annihilate America, Israel, infidels, and non-Muslims who would not submit to Allah.

Katy thumbed through her notes and scrolled through computer pages. "Ugh..um, here it is. One time he threatened a guard. Actually he tried to attack the guy for picking up a book that Jihad always had in his hand wherever he went."

"The Koran?" asked Nesto.

"No, that's just it. It was a pretty obscure Islamic novel no one ever heard of. Actually, if you can believe it, it was a romantic novel."

Aiden had heard the exchange between Nesto and Katy from the bottom of the stairs. He forgot about his ribs and his eyes and his embarrassment. He bounded up the stairs and burst into the room while ripping his windbreaker off and throwing it in the direction of the sofa. It missed its target by a mile and landed on the floor three feet away from the couch.

"The book, what's the name of the book? Jihad's identity. He's a master forger and he was willing to risk punishment when someone just touched that book. He needs an identity. He's looked at one book for a decade. Something is in it or someone in it kept him going. I'd bet my life he's in that book, his new name. He's in that fucking book!"

It was well known that no one ever questioned Aiden's instincts. Besides they had nothing else.

"What is the name of the book?" Rolly urgently inquired.

Katy had already been searching Jihad's Gitmo file for the incident. "It's called *Saladin and the Assassins*."

"Assassins? Jesus, how apropos." Aiden pushed, "The author, who is the author?"

"Um, ugh, um…a guy named Jurji Saidan."

Aiden rushed to a second laptop and began typing. No one knew what he was doing but they knew it was purposeful. Nesto and Rolly stepped aside so that Aiden and Katy could play.

"Ok, look for Jurji Saidan on any flights into Brazil or out of Uruguay."

Rolly and Nesto knew then where Aiden was going.

Katy began furiously typing and scrolling, "Nothing."

"OK, try this name, Hasan Fatimid."

Katy repeated the process, "Nothing."

"Ah shit," Aiden said, admonishing himself, "the guy's one of the bad guys."

"Bad guys?" a confused Katy asked.

"Yeah, a bad guy, a bad guy character in the book." Aiden responded to Katy then returned to talking to himself. "The star, the hero. Who's the fucking Islamist hero, you idiot?" he said as he poured over the text of the book.

"There you are you magnificent caliph bastard. Try this name Imadin Saladin."

Katy once again repeated her search for flight bookings when she dropped her hands to the desk and stared in amazement at the screen as if she was discovering her own sight for the first time. "Holy shit. There he is. An Imadin Saladin left Rio de Janeiro, Brazil on Tuesday for Vancouver, British Columbia, Canada."

"Aiden, you fuckin genius!" Nesto championed. He leaped over to Aiden and the two exchanged demonstrative high fives, the kind of high fives professional baseball players exchange at home plate as the homerun hitter has rounded the bases after tying a game in the ninth inning in game two of the World Series. "You can holler at me any damn time you want!"

"I'll remember that," Aiden said smiling at Nesto with forgiving affection.

Rolly knew there were innings left to play in this game and games left to play in the series. He needed Katy to step up to the plate and he needed to make sure everyone knew the other guys were now still at the plate. "Where is he now?"

"Give me a few," Katy returned.

She went to work on the business of locating where the forger had been and more importantly, where exactly he was now. Less than a minute had passed. Katy had it, "Imadin flew from Vancouver to Ontario on Wednesday. He flew from Ontario to Indianapolis also on Wednesday. He then flew from Indianapolis to Newark on Thursday. That's it."

"Son of a bitch!" Rolly surmised, "That's why his name was in the bomb factory in Jersey City. One of those back pack scumbags must have picked him up in Newark on Thursday."

In an almost depressed voice, Aiden offered, "The guy on the couch. The guy on the couch in the cleric's house, the first one I smoked. Could it have been him?"

You could feel every bit the air coming out of the room. The three men exchanged looks as if they knew they were right back where we started, right back to fearing the clock and thinking the worst.

Without turning her head away from her computer screen Katy broke the silence, "No, you didn't shoot the forger in Jersey City."

Everyone's head whipped in the direction of Katy. She was everyone's hope, the room's oxygen, "Imadin Saladin is currently booked in a hotel in Stamford, Connecticut. He's reserved two rooms at the Sheraton Stamford."

"Great work Katy!" Rolly cried out with an almost religious halleluiah.

"There's more," Katy went on

"More?" Aiden interjected.

"Yes, more. An Imadin Saladin is scheduled to address the fourth annual meeting of world religious leaders tomorrow morning at the UN. Guess who spoke at the last three meetings?"

No one answered. They were in no mind for guessing games.

"Maududi, our Jersey City Cleric.

Guess who set up the annual conference?" She looked around at the men waiting for her to disclose what she knew.

"That's right, one Hannah Gafar."

"Fuck me," Rolly said with his words nearly inaudible as they mixed with all air escaping his lungs.

Katy shed more light, "Apparently she set this thing up four years ago for religions of the world to come together in peace. Do you believe that?"

Aiden provided the flavor. "Yeah, it makes perfect sense. This will be the fourth meeting of its kind. Everyone will accept is as normal. Different religious leaders meeting on behalf of world understanding, blah blah blah… All at the behest of the White House. Patient fuckers."

"What? What the fuck? What balls. He's gonna walk from Gitmo into the UN with the intent to blow up the fucking place?" Nesto balked.

Aiden knew better, "No, he's not stupid enough to think he could get inside the UN. The suitcase is most effective if its let go into the atmosphere. He's not going let it go inside of it. He's going to let it go in sight of it."

Rolly picked it up from there. "The backpackers provide the carnage twenty minutes later when the first responders show up and it's all caught on camera."

Aiden finished it off. "It's claimed all over the Middle East to be Allah's retribution on the West, Christianity, America, hatred of Islam as shown in the murders of Muslims in the Michigan forest. This along with the perceived American vulnerability witnessed in the internal American conflict we're now seeing viscerally played out on televisions all over the world. Illustrated and documented by the other killings blamed on Right Wing Extremists, the condemnations of which the Pavlovian left wing, main street media has played right into and has levied on their own citizens, bolstered by the stupid liberals regurgitating it all in the White House. Throw in the race riots, cop shootings, and the burning of cities like Ferguson and Baltimore. It makes us look like we wouldn't piss on each other if we were on fire."

"Fuck. That's some long-term thinking there," Nesto said to no one in particular.

"Well, if you were stuck in Gitmo for more than a decade you'd be accused of long-term thinking," Rolly concluded.

Aiden summed it up. "This thing has been planned for seven hundred years. They were just waiting for the infidels to be so stupid."

"What next?" Katy innocently asked, bringing it back to all four of them that they still had a suitcase, bad guys out there with bad intentions, and a job to do…a very dangerous job to do.

Chapter 53

The Dupe - Barrow Street

Rolly knew the difference between a soldier and a warrior was that most soldiers on any battlefield are targets and it's the warriors who are targeting them. It was time to decide what to do here.

They knew it would be Jihad carrying the case and they knew where he was. They knew they had no time to kill without threatening eternity. Rolly was thinking one thing great leaders always think; how to get the initiative and keep it.

"Well, we gotta go to Stanford now, right now. Get your stuff boys we are going to take Jihad tonight. If we're lucky, the two backpack assholes will be there too. I'm going to call the President; you go gather your things. We leave in twenty."

Rolly left the room. He went outside through the courtyard and out onto Barrow Street. He didn't expect many to be out walking the cold November Greenwich Village streets on a Sunday night. A couple, shielding each other from the cold and walking tightly together, hustled past. Rolly and the male nodded a greeting at each other as the couple crossed in front. They disappeared.

Rolly dialed the prepaid phone he had given the president. The president answered, "Rolly?"

"Yes, sir," Rolly gave the president a second. The president said nothing.

"Are you alone, sir?"

"No," the president responded.

"Please go somewhere where we can talk. I'll wait," and Rolly disconnected the phone.

Two minutes passed and Rolly's phone rang.

"OK, I'm alone."

"Sir, we've located or at least I think we've located the second case, who is carrying it, and where they are planning to drop it. We believe it's at the Sheraton in Stamford, Connecticut right now and we believe we've identified the carrier. He's a guy that you recently let out of Gitmo, the forger who escaped Uruguay. I'm sure you're aware of the guy."

"Shit," the President screamed into the phone. "How the fuck did he get into the country?"

"Sir, with all due respect, he's a master forger who's been creating travel documents for terrorists for decades. What did you think he would do?"

Of course the president knew he was being rightly scolded but he didn't enjoy it. "Watch your tongue Mister."

Rolly wasn't intimidated. "Look sir, frankly you should care less about my tongue than what I'm telling you and about what is going to happen."

Rolly wasn't going to get into an argument with a guy he had no respect for. As far as he was concerned he was in charge. "Here it is. Listen carefully. The suitcase is to be let go sometime tomorrow morning, somewhere as close to the U.N. as they can get it. The carrier has forged documents, passport, and ID papers showing he is to be a speaker at a conference there."

"Speaker for what? What conference?" the president asked.

Rolly didn't like getting off track. "Some fuckin' annual phony world conference for religious peace. Ironic, huh? I don't know. It's been going on for four years and they bring in religious leaders to talk about love and shit. It was set up by Gafar. It's a ruse. A four years in the making Trojan horse."

"Ah, damn. Are you sure about this?"

Rolly knew the president was hoping somehow it might be a mistake. Rolly didn't have time to smooth over his humiliating deflection.

"Look sir, it's real. You've been played. You're a dupe."

The president got agitated quickly and his voice rose with each word, "I told you to watch your fucking mouth when you talk to me!"

Rolly couldn't believe the president was so shallow that even now he was worrying about the wrong damn thing. Rolly was about the right thing. Whether it was his legacy, the humiliating press he'd receive or justifying the collapsing policy he had long pursued, Rolly didn't care a wit. Rolly lived his entire life on the straight line and he despised politicians for spending their lives blurring it.

"Fuck you, you idiot. Let me tell you something. I don't give a shit about your feelings or how you think this will look or how it will affect your stupid fucking legacy. So shut the fuck up and listen."

Rolly took a breath so to calm down and to see if the president would signal a direction of the conversation but none came.

"You're gonna have to bring the FBI and NYPD in on this…in a big way. They're gonna need to be organized by rush hour tomorrow, people on the rooftops, all over the place near the UN. I don't know what else they may have planned for the area except this. They have two guys who will be carrying backpacks. We know they were dropped off in New York. The forger booked two rooms at the Sheraton so we think they may have all taken different routes to Stamford, but we're not sure. If we can't cut them off tonight we'll let you know. If they're not there we'll send you a photo of the backpacks to this phone and you can pass it along to the FBI.

"Do you want me to call Tim Cooney over at the FBI? I'm sure he can get his guys there in minutes," the president offered.

"No, we don't yet know if the carrier is there. If he is there, we still don't know if the case is there or if its somewhere else and the carrier is to pick it up in the morning. The FBI might spook the thing and they have… um …er…lets' say behavioral constraints, legal ones."

Rolly hated talking about the gray lines, but he measured the legal line against the number of people likely to die in a world war.

"Listen, we're gonna be on these guys in an hour. As soon as we know what's there or who is there, I'll call you and we can put the FBI and the NYPD in motion. I'm calling ahead so you can prepare to get things moving tonight if we have to. Sit tight and be ready. We'll get back to you in a couple of hours. Out."

As soon as Rolly disconnected the phone he could again feel the cold stinging in his right hand. He hustled back into the house.

Aiden and Nesto were standing ready to go. Rolly grabbed his things and the three disappeared.

The president walked from his residence into the Oval Office. He hit the button which automatically connected him to the head of the FBI.

"Tim, the president here. We have a situation. Hold on, I want to bring in a third party who can explain in detail what I'm about to tell you and give context to what's happened so far."

The president hit the conference button and dialed a number.

"Tim, can you hear me?"

The FBI Director quickly responded, "Yes sir, I can hear you."

"Good. I usually have the secretary set up conference call."

The two men could hear the intended party's phone ringing.

"Carter Capps here."

"Mr. Capps, the President here. I have the FBI Director on the line. Are you alone?"

Chapter 54

Lower Manhattan NYC

If flying a plane was needed, Aiden was your man. If driving a car fast was called for, Nesto was best to employ behind the wheel. Nesto could drive through a jungle at a hundred and five mph and still avoid the trees.

Getting out of lower Manhattan was the worst of it. Fifty Two and a Half Barrow Street was only a block from the Hudson River and fifty-six blocks from the West Side Highway and only five traffic lights between here and there. Traffic lights Nesto fully intended to ignore. On a weekday, if it was a good day, it would take two hours or more, perhaps much more to travel the forty plus miles from lower Manhattan to the Sheraton Stamford. On a Sunday night in November, if there was no road construction work to slow Nesto down, he was determined to get there in less than fifty minutes, well less.

Just as he'd hoped Nesto made the drive in fifty-five minutes. He turned into the parking lot of the Sheraton and drove immediately up to the front of the hotel where he dropped Rolly off at the front door. Nesto took the car around to the back of the hotel and waited for Rolly to open the rear door entrance. It was 9:50 pm on the east coast.

Rolly lit a cigarette outside of the hotel and made sure the front desk agent saw him do it. He took a minute to observe any activity that might be going on inside the relatively contained lobby. Satisfied that Jihad had not posted a guard in the lobby or outside of the hotel, Rolly tossed the unsmoked cigarette onto the floor, doused it under shoe and went inside. He went directly to the front desk clerk and asked for a room, preferably a room on the ground floor.

The hotel had plenty of available occupancy so the clerk was able to accommodate their new guest. She gave him a room key and bid him a restful night.

Before leaving the house on Barrow Street Katy had pulled up the hotel's blueprint of the Sheraton Stamford and each of them committed every inch of the facility to memory. They could walk it blindfolded. They knew where every entrance and egress was. They were not going to allow the forger or anyone with him to escape.

Rolly thanked the girl at the counter and started walking away. He started walking away from the front desk when he stopped and turned, "Oh, is there a pool?" he asked.

"Yes," the pretty clerk responded, "It's just through those doors."

"Can I look at it?"

"Sure. Its closed right now for use but you can certainly have a look."

"Thanks."

Rolly had no interest in the pool of course; he just wanted to get to the back entrance of the hotel without drawing any attention to himself while doing it. He went down the small hallway walking past the pool to the rear entrance and opened the rear door to let Aiden and Nesto in.

"OK, just as it looked. There's one girl with a small office just behind the counter. Give me ninety seconds and then move."

Rolly returned to the lobby and walked up to the far end of the counter holding up a map of Stamford in his hand. "Excuse me. Can you help me with some directions? I have to wake up early and go to a meeting at this hedge fund office and I'm a little confused."

"Oh sure," said the clerk as she made her way to the edge of the counter where Rolly had spread out the map.

Rolly pointed to the map with his finger. "You see here?"

The clerk leaned in close.

Before she could raise her head, Nesto and Aiden rushed into the lobby. Dressed in all black with ski masks covering their faces and assault rifles pointed right at her; they scared her near to death when she saw them.

Before she could make a sound Rolly had swung around her and cupped his hand over the clerk's mouth. He leaned on her with such force that he pinned her motionless to the counter. You could see the terror in her eyes.

"We're not here to hurt you," Rolly whispered gently into the petrified clerk's ear. "We have to get out of this lobby. You and I are going to walk together into the office behind us. OK?"

The clerk nodded that she understood. Rolly nodded to Aiden and Nesto to go into the office ahead of the clerk and him. Aiden and Nesto backed into the office while keeping their rifles trained on the lobby in the event someone should come in.

"OK, move slow. We are not here to hurt you. We are here to help you. Move slowly."

The clerk did exactly as she had been instructed. Rolly kept his hand over her mouth until they got inside the office and he could close the door but he really didn't have to. Something told the girl that what Rolly was saying was true. Perhaps she wasn't afraid, or perhaps she was, but she was not going to try to escape this man's grip.

Once inside the office Rolly closed the door behind them, keeping his hand over her mouth long enough for the clerk to see Aiden pointing his assault rifle at her forehead. "You see that man with the gun?"

The clerk nodded as she had before.

"He will shoot you if you scream. The gun has a silencer on it. No one will know your dead and we'll be gone. I'm going to ask you some questions. Understand?"

Again she nodded. Rolly slowly withdrew his hand from her mouth. The woman stood still, unable to take her eyes off the six foot four inch giant of a man with the gun aimed directly at her.

"Good, sit down…please," Rolly instructed her. She did as she was told.

"What is your name Miss?" Rolly asked her.

"Kathy, Kathy Brewer."

"OK Kathy. Can I call you Kathy?" Rolly asked in an attempt to disarm her. She nodded that he could.

"Kathy, I'm so sorry to put you in this spot, but it was necessary. We couldn't take a chance that you might set off a silent alarm or something."

The girl wasn't buying the apology yet. Rolly went on, "My name is Rolly Byrnes. This is Aiden Palmer and Nesto Suarez. We're agents, American agents. We're not law enforcement. We're a different kind of agent. We're pretty sure there are at least three terrorists staying here in two separate rooms. They are planning something terrible against the people of the United States and they're planning to do it tomorrow. What I just told you is top secret information and I could be hanged just for sharing that with you. We're going to take them out of here and we need your help. I don't want to tie you up but I will. I need you to tell me what rooms they're in and we need a master key."

The girl looked up at Rolly. She shifted her eyes to Aiden and Nesto, who had taken off their black ski masks and had trained their weapons down to the floor, and then back at Rolly.

"Are you talking about Mr. Saladin, Imadin Saladin and his people?" she asked.

All three were confused as hell. Either she had phenomenal recall of her guest's names or he had been a guest for a long time.

With a tilted head and a scrunched inquisitive brow Rolly responded to the question "Yes, that's exactly who we're talking about. How do you know him and why do you ask?"

"He checked out of here twenty minutes ago. I was processing the room when you came in. He's gone Mr. Byrnes."

Nesto plopped down into an office chair, put his gun in his lap and stared at Rolly in disbelief. Aiden punched the desk top. "Shit!" was all he could muster.

"Did he say anything? Did he give any indication of where they were going?" Rolly asked the clerk.

"No, I'm sorry he didn't."

Rolly kneeled down on one knee almost in a position one might if he were proposing marriage. "Listen Kathy, a girl is going to call you in a minute. Her name is Katy Quigley. She is a CIA operative and she's going to ask you questions about Mr. Saladin and his people. Tell her what you know. Don't speak of this with anyone, not the police, not the hotel. Not even your husband. Many lives are at stake tomorrow and any leak of this could have terrible consequences that might contribute to the deaths of American citizens. The FBI will come looking for you tomorrow or the days immediately after. Until then talk to Quigley and no one else. Clear?"

The clerk nodded in the affirmative, her eyes tearing up in a combination of relief and disbelief. She would never imagine herself in the middle of something like this, but she was glad it was over.

Rolly tossed his head at Aiden. Aiden took the que and ran out of the room first with Nesto scurrying out after. "Thank you, Kathy," Rolly said to the clerk as he too disappeared.

Aiden was a fine athlete, but Nesto Suarez was faster afoot. Despite Aiden exiting the hotel first, Nesto was first to the car. Nesto jumped into the driver's seat turning on the ignition as Aiden piled into the front passenger seat. Rolly, the slowest of the three, arrived a few seconds behind and dove into the back seat.

As soon as Rolly's door slammed shut Nesto burst out, "What the fuck, Rolly? They knew we were coming!"

Aiden was already analyzing what had just happened. "That's four times we've been compromised and we've been wicked careful since Brussel's. How could..."

Before Aiden could finish his thought Rolly was already talking into his phone. "Katy, Jihad is gone." Katy tried to ask questions but Rolly needed her instead to get busy. "He's gone. Somebody tipped him we were coming."

Again Katy tried to speak but Rolly cut her off abruptly. "I don't have time to explain. I need you to get Gafar's phone, any calls she made or received, anything in or out. I also need you to call the Sheraton and speak with a girl named Kathy Brewer, she's the desk clerk and expecting your call. We need anything you can find out about Jihad and his crew. Get descriptions of the people, backpacks, the car they were driving, anything else that might place where they went. Get CCTV feeds for the last forty-eight hours starting with the last hour. We need that car they're driving, Katy. GO!"

Rolly turned his attention to his driver, "They're out in front by a half hour, Nesto. I'm sure they're careful not to break speed law. Chances are they're heading into the city, run 'em down before they get there, Nesto. Go!"

Nesto stomped on the gas pedal like it had stolen his mother's purse. The car jumped and the tires screamed.

While dialing a number on his prepaid phone Rolly followed on Aiden's analytical track, "How could? How could? I'll tell you how could."

Before he could explain to Aiden what he knew his call was answered. "They're gone. They're fucking gone. Did you call anyone? Did you call anyone?"

The president immediately went into full panic, "Just Tim Cooney at the FBI to give him a head's up on tomorrow."

"Fuck! What the fuck is wrong with you? I told you not to call anyone until you heard from me. Now the bastards are on the fucking run."

"Well, maybe they will shut it down and try to run," the president said, trying to grasp at the straws that turn into silver linings.

"Are you fucking kidding? These fuckers are trying to start World War III and they've got one chance. They've been praying for this for seven hundred years and planning for it since you and Gafar walked into the White House. You think they're gonna run and hide when the caliphate is just around the fucking corner?"

The president went silent and Rolly kept going. "Well, call Cooney and tell him Jihad is out there and he has the UN in the crosshairs. He's going by the name Imadin Saladin and he's got two guys with him. Tell him to call me and I'll brief him on what he's looking for."

The president tried to squelch Rolly's ire, "I already had him briefed."

"What? Whatya mean, briefed?"

"I hooked Carter Capps into the call with Cooney," The President responded.

Rolly lost it, "Capps! Capps? You fucking idiot. Capps called Gafar as soon as you finished with him." Rolly had an incoming call. It was Katy and she was more important to him than the president. At this moment a loaf of stale bread was more useful to him than the president. "I gotta take this call. Don't do anything. I'll call you back in an hour. Don't call anyone…A N Y O N E!!!!"

Rolly took the call, "Yeah Katy."

"Rolly, Gafar received one call and made one call in the last two hours."

"Let me guess. She took a call from Carter Capps and called the Sheraton Stamford."

"How did you know?" an amazed Katy asked.

"Never mind. Get on the girl in the hotel. Maybe she can give you something we can use and call me if you learn anything. Go."

Rolly looked deeply at Aiden who had been listening and watching Rolly's back seat turmoil and who by now himself knew Capps was the leak. "How could? The president is a fucking moron, that's how could."

Speaking into the back of Nesto's head, who by now was as much trying to control the hundred and five mile an hour four-door missile down Interstate 95 as he was trying to drive it, Rolly said, "Get 'em, Nesto. Run 'em down."

Chapter 55

Square One - Barrow Street

Nesto came through the door first at Fifty Two and a Half Barrow throwing his jacket at the sofa in total disgust. Rolly came in behind Nesto, shoved a chair to the ground, cursed beneath his breath, and threw his jacket across the room. Aiden dragged himself in and threw himself on the sofa. Exhaustion and frustration are to the wits as three to one.

"Anything?" Rolly asked of Katy. Rolly and the others knew she didn't have anything new because if she had she surely would have called them immediately, but he asked her anyway.

"No," she began, "As I told you, they drove out of the Sheraton in a Ford Five Hundred and the car was found abandoned a half a mile away. There's nothing after that and nothing on the cameras in the hotel. We only have a still photo of one guy at check in but nothing after."

"Great we're back at friggin' square one," Nesto lamented.

Aiden tried to assuage the group. "Well not exactly. We have them ID'd. We know it's the U.N. We flood the area with FBI, CIA, DHS, NYPD, and anyone who can load a damn gun. This prick shows himself we should have him…should."

Rolly thanked Katy for the coffee she handed him and dialed his phone. The president answered.

"Tell me something good, Rolly."

"Can't do it. They swapped cars and disappeared. I need to talk to Cooney. We gotta flood Midtown Manhattan with his people."

"Perhaps we should cancel the conference and shut down the area," the president returned.

"No good. Then we lose him. Maybe he drops that case outside your door in three days or in Seattle or Boston. No, we need that case. He's determined to do this. Immortality is on the line. We know what his plan is and we need to cut him off, now, now, now."

The president knew Rolly was right. As dangerous it was, he knew losing them to caprice was the worst option. "OK, I'll have Tim call you in a minute."

"And don't call anyone else."

The president wished he could punch Rolly in the face and had he the chance he would. "God damn it, alright, you don't have to tell me twice, for Christ's sake."

Rolly wished he could punch the president in the face and had he the chance he would. "Yeah, I do. Out."

Rolly looked at his watch. He felt compelled to remind himself that the clock was always ticking. Saying to Katy, "Stay on Gafar. This bastard is still readying this thing and he may try to coordinate with her to see what she knows."

When the warrior knows there's a battle to be fought and he can make no plans for it, he feels helpless. For a moment everyone felt a deep sense of helplessness that Jihad had taken the initiative and they needed to take it back. But how?

Nesto wanted to break the malaise. "What the hell do we do in the meantime?"

"There's not much we can really do, Nesto. He's gone under until he wants to come up. We've never seen the guy," Rolly admitted. "The FBI can APB him and the backpacks. They'll have to take it from here, I guess."

They were spectators now. There was a peculiar fatalism in the futility. It had an insulting anti-climax to it.

"I don't like this Rolly," Aiden said. "I don't like this at all."

"What can we do Aiden?" Rolly asked rhetorically. "Hey, we stopped them in Phoenix and put a lot of bad guys down for the dirt nap. We exposed Gafar and the State Department Director's email breach, we followed them here, we got them ID'd. We did good."

Aiden wasn't prepared to let it go; perhaps it was vanity of some kind. He knew the men in the room were the best players on America's team and he hated it that the best players were going to be sidelined for the final plays of the game. Or maybe it was that on some baser level he felt outplayed, outstripped, and beaten. Whatever it was it had a bad taste. "Maybe so, but I don't like deferring."

Rolly knew exactly what he was saying, knew what he was feeling. "I know man, but what is needed now are eyes and guns, lots of eyes and lots of guns. The FBI and the NYPD can provide those things better than we can. The CIA can follow the trail after and if they need us they can call us."

Rolly turned to Katy, "That doesn't include you, Katy. You're way ahead of everybody. Keep digging."

Rolly's phone rang and he answered it abruptly, the frustration of being marginalized, still wearing away at his core. "Byrnes"

The FBI director was on the other end of the line and wasted no time. "What are we looking at?"

Rolly looked at his watch, he had looked at it eight times in the last ten minutes. This glance however left him with a sinking feeling. A combination of all the things Aiden and Nesto were feeling overlaid with that this thing had minutes left, not days. He felt sick, vomit sick. It was 3:45 am.

"Tim, we have three hours, five max. This is what we know…"

Chapter 56

Waiting - Barrow Street

There's patience and then there is waiting; patience implies strategy, waiting implies luck. Warriors despise luck.

You could hear the ticks echoing from a million lizard-like clocks in the room. Each tick whipped away like ants on monotonous, unrelenting lightning fast tongues, one after the other it whipped and swallowed. Clocks are always enemies, especially when they're enemies at the gate.

None of the four could sleep a wink, none of them felt at all tired. It wasn't adrenalin, nor was it excitement, it was dread and it was terror. A dread for the possibility of a very bloody morning, and terror for the possibility that a generation might soon be losing itself in a violent war, still another violent war, set up as a lie. None of them could assuage the fears of the other.

Katy hadn't taken her eyes off of the computer screen, nor had she said a word for over an hour. The three men dug through the trash they had taken from the bomb factory in Jersey City, hoping against hope that something would leap out of the pile of crap which might help them. If anything in that pile of bad guy shit had legs it would've stood up by now. They had almost no hope, but "almost no hope" isn't the same as zero hope.

Aiden peeked at his watch and then out the window. Night had begun its ritual of stepping aside for the day. "So dawn goes down to day. Nothing gold can stay."

"What?" Nesto felt compelled to ask. He looked at his watch and pinched it between hid thumb and forefinger in the hopes it might have gone from an acid-throwing fortune teller to a le Jeune timepiece since he last checked it a few seconds ago.

"Ah, it's something my father used to say a lot just before he left the house for work. It's a Robert Frost thing. I'm not sure why I thought of it other than the sun is coming up."

Everyone in the room turned their heads towards the window. No one knew exactly what Aiden meant, but in the supplanting of streetlights by sunlight somehow they knew exactly what he meant.

Rolly checked his watch. It was 6:45 am. "Turn on the two TVs there Katy, will ya'? We might as well keep an eye on the world from here. See if the CIA can find the needle and if the FBI can block and tackle."

Katy turned on the two televisions from her desk seat using a single remote control.

"Gimme Fox News on one and CNN on the other," Rolly requested. Katy complied.

The next twenty-five minutes were an excruciating blur of silent contemplation. Every image on the television screen injected itself into someone's contemplative subconscious, spitting out a different depth of empathy, of fear, of loathing.

A three-minute business segment on Fox News caused Rolly to think about how the value of physical possessions was going to plummet around the world and how military stocks would enrich the cynical and callous who were so uncaring as to profit from war. He thought about all the war he had seen.

A commercial on CNN for Cialis brought about Aiden to a place where he thought about how humans can be so attuned to lovemaking and so devoid of love at the same time. He thought about all the war he had seen.

Nesto watched a Fox segment on Syria where a former CIA agent, turned pacifist, was presenting a statistic about how more than forty-five thousand people a day were being displaced worldwide by Middle East conflict and how Syrian children hadn't been in school for half a decade. Nesto thought about how they would be another generation of stupid people waging battles of hatred and destruction upon one another. He thought about all the war he had seen.

Katy hardly lifted her head from the computer screens and keyboards. Not really knowing exactly what she was looking for, she went over every email she had looked at the previous days. She poured over every connection Asidilov had made, every trail Atta had left, every possible loose end Gafar might have left uncovered, every hacked Secretary State Department email which landed in Moududi's inbox, every sent file and deleted file. If that bomb was going off at 8:30 am, she was going to keep trying to find a way to stop it. She thought about all the war she had never seen and she was damn determined to keep it that way.

Rolly's phone rang and he answered it. The FBI director didn't have much time and he said so. Rolly put the phone on speaker, "You're on speaker, Mr. Cooney. I thought the team might want to hear this."

Katy stopped what she was doing for the first time in over an hour. They all drew close in so they wouldn't miss a word.

"That's fine, Rolly. Call me Tim…please. Men, I want to thank you for all you've done. The president is proud of you and he thanks you too."

The reference to the president's pride in them brought nothing of value to the room.

The director continued, "I just thought you should know what has been brought to bear as a result of your efforts. We have a hundred and forty of our top FBI agents on the ground, twice as many NYPD. We have repositioned two satellites and have seven drones flying overhead. We've placed instruments strategically which can detect any radioactivity with a half mile radius and can detect any radioactivity which is in motion. We have more than ten bomb-sniffing dogs surrounding the UN. If this bastard farts we're gonna smell it before it leaves his ass."

"Great work, Tim. I'd hate to have you guys after me. We're here if you need us."

"Thank you, gentlemen," the director said to conclude.

"God's speed, sir. Out." Rolly said and ended the call. He looked at his watch. It was 7:18 am.

The commitment to the fight, as well as the mobilization, was impressive to say the least. Rolly was proud of the FBI and the NYPD, many of them now knew what they were trying to prevent. They were in the spaces where if they failed to stop the suitcase from going off, they themselves would suffer first. He thought of the NYPD, Port Authority Policemen, and New York City Firemen running up the stairs of the Trade Center on September 11th. He loved each and every one of them. He wished he could tell them so.

Nesto felt comforted, "Well, it sounds like they've got the thing surrounded anyway."

Aiden concurred, "If that maggot bastard pokes his head out of his hole he's going to get it blown clean off."

"Good. The fuck head," Katy angrily said as she made her way back to her screens and keyboards.

Rolly was oddly silent. He wasn't a praying man, but he was praying hard. Thinking about those cops and FBI agents got him to thinking about the people; the innocent people, they were trying to protect. People who may never go home again and it was eating at him in the worst way. He had seen enough to know that when the first bullets fly in any battle, the last great idea gets obliterated, so too do the lives of innocents near it. He had been is so many fights thought won which ultimately were lost, so many advantageous fighting tactics thought perfect which had to be improvised, so many fortresses thought impenetrable which turned out to be burning huts and had heard of so many military geniuses thought to be infallible who led his men into cluster fucks. He trusted nothing and no one except the people in the room with him. But it almost didn't matter at this point who Rolly trusted. He was learning a new lesson.

Preparing for a fight is the first lesson learned about warfare; he excelled at it. Waiting to get into a fight is a hard lesson to learn; he excelled at that too. Waiting for a fight you can see coming but cannot influence; this was new. The last thing a true warrior learns about, as it turns out, is himself and Rolly felt like he was failing badly.

The morning slowed again, now moving like a snail. Rolly had written a thousand scenarios in his head. Nesto set himself to imagining every possible conversation he could have with his wife. Aiden made self-promises that changes to his life would be made. Oh, it dragged and dragged and dragged. The waiting or not knowing while waiting, became a new type of tension. The tension for which there is no training to rely upon, no motivational speeches to get behind, the tension in the watching from the sidelines. It scares the self out of the warrior and each man felt what fear had been like for everybody else.

It was the hardest thing, the fear of waiting. They sat. All four were silent but for Katy's fingers punching her keyboard, watching TV and pulling apart small pieces of a dead man's garbage.

As the minutes died off one by one, their fear increasingly transformed into a peculiar resolve that they were out of the fight. Their thoughts narrowed further still into wondering who would end up dead. The countless people unlucky to have been caught in the blast radius or absurd terrorists whose absurd names would be misspelled in the never again seen sit reps and in after-action reports obscured in files and which would then get buried in locked titanium vaults in the basement of a building in Langley, Virginia.

The FBI had the numbers, but the absurd terrorists had the initiative. To The Three Ravens the outcome was fifty- fifty.

They were staring at the televisions but couldn't hear a word being said on either screen. They were simply waiting for the break in news alert or a call from the FBI that no alert would be necessary because they had neutralized the threat. Each man constantly checked their watches. Rolly was the last to do so. It was 8:43 am.

Chapter 57

Improvising - Barrow Street

Katy threw her head back and rubbed her tired burning eyes. Having lost track of time she leaned forward to look at the small clock in the lower right hand corner of her laptop.

She stood and stretched her arms into the air as if rising from a bed, "Geez, 8:52 am. Eight minutes to nine."

She had no idea that verbalizing the time could have jolted the three men so fundamentally. It's one thing to internalize fear; it's another when the reason for your fear is visiting your internalization from the outside. Each man looked at his watch and contemplated the world as the world knew it and the brevity of minutes before it would be no longer the same world.

Katy never turned around to take notice of the fact that she was not alone, "I have to pee," she said aloud. At that moment it occurred to Katy that she had just announced why she needed to use the bathroom and how uncouth it must have sounded to the men. She lowered her head and left the room.

After a few moments Katy reentered the situation room fully intending to apologize for her tacky announcement. She walked into the center of the room and gathered her thoughts. Just as she was about to speak she looked up at the television screen.

"Ahhhh! Ahhhh! Ahhhh! It's him. It's fucking him, there, there," she screamed, pointing at the television and gasping for air.

All three rushed to her side and looked at the screen, "What? What are you saying? Where?" Aiden urgently asked.

On the television screen a financial reporter was standing in front of the New World Trade Center discussing how the new president elect might influence the commodities markets.

"There! Right there," Katy ran to the screen and pointed. "There, down there in the lower park, by the benches, the three guys. One guy is using his phone to film the other guy talking. The guy talking, look in his right hand, look at the cane, he's got a cane! The guy holding the phone, look at the backpack and the third guy has the same backpack. It's them, it's Imadin. They're not at the U.N. They're at the Trade Center!"

Aiden ran up to the TV, "Holy shit, Rolly. Katy's right. Those are the two guys the cleric's son dropped off by the U.N.!"

Rolly and Nesto joined Katy and Aiden at the TV.

"Fuck," Rolly said and then went directly into leadership mode. "This prick is taping a statement. They're improvising. They correctly assumed if we made them we made their plan. They're moving it to the Trade Center. Let's move!"

Nesto was already moving before Rolly ordered them to move. "Son of a bitch. These guys are only five blocks away. We can get there faster on foot."

Rolly cancelled the thought of running, "Negative. Start the car Nesto. We might need some long guns. Let's go! "

Within seconds the three men were in the car with duffle bags of weaponry. Within two minutes they were a block away from the Trade Center and a minute later they pulled alongside the park where they had seen Jihad filming his final charge. Rolly jumped from the front passenger seat, Aiden from the backseat and both began feverishly turning their heads in all directions. With the car still running and the car doors not yet closed, they both stood and easily surmised Jihad and the backpackers were nowhere to be found.

"Fuck, where did they go?" Rolly asked Aiden as if he might know.

"They could have gotten far, the fuckin' guy can't walk. Security is wicked tight since 9/11 and there's no building you can get into down here," Aiden said, while keeping his head on a swivel.

"OK. We agree they're outside, but where?" Rolly kept spit balling, "Where's the most foot traffic?" Aiden looked around. "Here, right here where the trains let out. The path train from New Jersey too."

"Fuck, where's the next most heavily trafficked area?"

Rolly's phone rang. The phone was on the dashboard of the car so Rolly sat back down in the passenger seat and put the phone on speaker. Aiden leaned in so he could hear.

Katy went straight into it, "Rolly, I just picked up an email sent to the dead cleric from someone in Iran about Imadin. Seems the plan is to get Drake and Wall Street. President-elect, Ronald Drake is meeting at his building at Forty Wall Street in an hour and a half with his incoming cabinet members. Before he goes into the meeting he intends to give an impromptu presser on the top step of the Federal Hall Building on the corner of Wall and Broad Streets. The presser starts in fifteen minutes."

"Great work, Katy," Rolly said into the phone. "I know the building. We're three blocks from there."

"Wait. Rolly, there's more. Apparently there is a plane due to land in Newark, New Jersey in twenty-seven minutes. The plane is carrying the Israeli Prime Minister and he's coming to meet with the president-elect in a top secret meeting at Drakes's home tonight. The plane is probably starting its initial descent as we speak. They're going shoot that plane down."

"What?" Rolly screamed into the phone, "How the fuck do they even know about the Prime Minister's fucking plans?"

Aiden looked directly down at Rolly, "They have our State Department emails hacked. Any flight like that would be coordinated through State."

Nesto began punching the steering several times screaming in unison with each punch, "Fuck! Fuck! Fuck! It's the son!"

"What? What are you saying, Nesto?" Rolly asked urgently.

"Christ, it's the cleric's fucking son. The one that got away, the one I followed Saturday. Remember I said how weird it was that he pulled over by the marshes and there was a rest stop only a mile up on the right from where he pulled over. He wasn't walking that fucking dog. He was leaving the shoulder-fire stinger in the fucking grass and using the dog as cover should anyone ask him why he stopped there. A fucking dog, I should have figured it out. Fuck!" Nesto punched the steering wheel one more time.

Rolly stood up, "Nesto, the spur is easy the way you drive. You can get there in twenty. Go. Go get this prick."

Nesto looked at his watch as he threw the car in gear. The Lincoln Tunnel was five to seven minutes away and if there weren't any traffic accidents or emergency road work going on, he'd get there in slightly less than twenty.

Before Nesto could lean on the gas, "Wait, Nesto!" Rolly screamed, "We need our bags. Pop the trunk."

Nesto popped the trunk as ordered. Aiden grabbed his black duffle and Rolly his. Aiden slammed the trunk and slapped it twice with his palm. Nesto hit the gas and was gone.

"Katy, call Tim Cooney. Tell him everything you just told me and anything else you know. Tell him what's going on. Maybe they can divert that flight. Go, now!"

Chapter 58

Financial District
New York City

Aiden and Rolly sprinted through a small park in front of 17 Battery Park Place, overlooking the Hudson River. They continued going east along Vesey Street and up onto Broadway before taking measure of where they were. They were surprised by their luck that they were only a single city block north of Wall Street.

Sprinting south along Broadway they stopped directly in front of Trinity Church, which sat at the very western end of Wall Street. From this slightly elevated ground they could see north and south on Broadway and east down Wall Street. If the backpacks were moving anywhere this would be the best vantage point.

Trinity Church is the grand Lady of New York churches. The elegant steeple with a long and storied past, built in the very late 1600's by Great Britain, it holds the distinction as the first Anglican Church to grace the city. Resting very near the southern most point in Manhattan Island, and at the western most end of Wall Street, the oldest church on the island looks down on the preeminent capitalistic acreage. The church and grounds originally maintained a vital place as civic center, cemetery, meeting place and prayer house for a young, but fast burgeoning, trading post between The Netherlands, Great Britain and the New World.

Nearly a decade after its completion, Britain's Queen Anne would ensure its perpetuation when she bestowed upon it more than two hundred surrounding acres. Fifty years later, the Anglicans erected St. Paul's Chapel where it remains today, smack in the middle of a piece of earth which could not at the time possibly foresee itself as the financial epicenter of the nation -- the world's most powerful nation, and a nation under dire threat this very morning. But there she was this quiet morning receiving her tourists from around the world. And as she had for nearly three centuries, her local residents looked to pray before heading to off to their respective workplaces.

Rolly and Aiden were feeling pretty good about their chances. The corner of Wall and Broad was the perfect spot to detonate the suitcase. Wall Street was only three blocks long, with two connecting streets, Broad Street and Exchange Place. Federal Hall, the building the President Elect was due to conduct his impromptu press conference, was just over a hundred and twenty yards from where they stood on the corner, keeping it close and in plain view. The only disquiet for them was the partially obstructed view in front of the New York Stock Exchange.

Rolly and Aiden were hopeful that they had a good enough line of sight from where they were standing vigil. If their targets, Imadin walking around with a cane and the two back packers that Aiden could identify, were mulling around anywhere on Wall Street they'd be visible to them.

As they scanned the streets looking for Imadin and the backpacks containing the pressure cooker bombs, they tried to appear like a typical tourist. Rolly pointed up at the more than two hundred foot church steeple and rationalized the target's value. "I'm surprised they didn't target this instead of the U.N. Look around this place. Federal Hall is the place of Washington's inaugural address, an historic Western Christian Church, and the damn New York Stock Exchange. They get all of it, including the new president and his cabinet as a fucking bonus."

Aiden couldn't agree more. "Well, I'm sure they chose the U.N. because they could build come-and-go access. There was no way they could anticipate this new president being here a few years back. But you're right; this is the mother lode."

Rolly reached into his black bag and took out a small pair of binoculars, pointing the lenses up at the church steeple and then around at the skyline. Pointing to a wire mesh trash can a few feet from where they were standing, "Grab that street map there, Aiden. Look like a tourist."

Aiden immediately picked up on what Rolly was doing. Lifting the map out of the trash can, he unfolded it and held it as tourists were likely doing all over Manhattan.

As soon as Rolly saw Aiden doing his best tourist imitation he brought the binoculars down to the street level.

"Aiden, 12:05, two blocks, southeast corner Wall and Exchange Place. Backpack."

Rolly handed the binoculars to Aiden and took the map from him, "See him?"

"Yeah, I got him."

"Ok. If you go down to Broad Street there and make a right, then take a left on New Street, you can get behind him. I'll find the other mutt and Jihad. Go."

Aiden handed the binoculars back to Rolly. Walking quickly east down Wall he made a right onto Broad heading south, all the while pretending to be on the phone getting directions. Just in front of the New York Stock Exchange he crossed to the eastern side of Broad and made his way to the next corner, New Street.

New Street was anything but new and hardly a street. It was one city block south of Wall Street and ran parallel to it east to west. In one of Manhattan's most congested areas it was a remarkably desolate New York City street. Thin enough that if you didn't know better you would think it a back alley rather than a city street. It was the delivery area for the buildings during the day and served to facilitate trucks and construction containers. Only a Yugo could pass through should there be a truck with its wheels half on and half off the sidewalk and during business hours and this was always the case.

If one was wearing a Zegna necktie you used the front of the building, if you were wearing stained Timberland work boots you went in through back doors on New Street.

The street had only two shops, a small coffee shop and a faded old shoe shine store, both of which hadn't been updated in fifty years. The breakfast joint was frequented by clerks, maintenance people, and doormen who thought to grab an egg sandwich on their way to work. No Wall Street bigwig had been in the shop since the Jimmy Carter administration.

When Aiden turned onto New Street he could see how unpopulated it was for people afoot and took off flying as fast as he could.

Nesto was flying as well with every bit of his driving skill on display. Red lights meant nothing and he moved in and out of traffic like it was choreographed. He had gone from Broadway in lower Manhattan, racing along the Hudson River to 23rd Street and West Street in under five minutes. On a bad traffic day that stretch of West Street might cost an hour, but he was helped by the fact that during the morning rush hour most drivers were heading downtown and he was driving north heading away from normal Monday morning traffic patterns. He hadn't expected it to be too bad but he was gratified for an open lane.

In less than a minute he'd be inside the Lincoln Tunnel heading west beneath the Hudson River to New Jersey. If his luck held out it'd be only ten minutes to the terrorist with a stinger missile and the prime minister on his mind.

From where he stood, Rolly couldn't make the other backpack nor was there any sight of Imadin and his catastrophic suitcase. Reporters were now starting to set up microphones at the top of the stairs of Federal Hall. Most of the Wall Street folks paid no mind to it since five out of five business days' news reporters and microphones from agencies from all over the world could be seen in front of or very near the Stock Exchange Building.

Rolly didn't like it. No one knew what they were setting up for but once they realized the newly elected president would be making his way to the makeshift podium everyone would naturally gravitate to the area. A swelling crowd would make finding the bad guys all the more difficult.

Rolly was getting antsy. He had a good view of Wall Street but there were two cross streets he couldn't see well as he searched from his elevated position. He was sure in order to cause maximum damage one backpack would be south of the Federal Hall building and the other would be just north of it. If he was right, and he was sure he was, this meant the other backpack had to be close to where he was standing. He couldn't stop thinking to himself where the fuck did Jihad go and more importantly, who had the deadly suitcase?

Nesto was still having good luck and thrilled that he hadn't yet encountered or seen a patrol car. He chalked it up to the necessary police presence demanded by the FBI at the U.N. in Midtown, a building entirely on the other side of Manhattan and three miles away. He hit the Lincoln Tunnel and busted through it at better than ninety miles an hour. When he exited the tunnel on the New Jersey side he would be six minutes away from his target and several minutes from the prime minister's plane arrival time.

Aiden turned the corner intersecting New Street and Exchange Place and peered east again to Wall Street. Exchange Place was the side street connecting New and Wall Streets and was quite short, maybe a hundred and fifty feet with its' entire length spanning the office buildings on Wall. His man with the backpack, one of the men he had followed into Manhattan a few days earlier, was standing on the corner of Exchange Place and Wall Street looking west one block back at Federal Hall. He was stalking the president-elect, waiting for his chance at his own martyrdom. Aiden looked behind him checking to see if anyone was back there who might be unfriendly. He was amazed that, at just after 9:00 am there was no one walking on New Street or Exchange Place. He started towards his man.

Nesto made it through the eight thousand feet of tunnel in seconds and thought to himself, 'I got this, I'm gonna get there.' He started thinking about which markers might help him remember where the cleric's son might have gone into the high grass and what he might face in the tall weeds and marshes once he got there.

"Fuck! No... no ... no, not now!" seeing as soon as he exited the tunnel he was smack into the back of an infamous New Jersey traffic jam.

Rolly ambled downhill from Wall and Broadway to the wealthiest street corner in the world, the meeting of Wall and Broad Street. Stopping as a billion visitors had before him, he looked up, half in amazement and half feigning amazement, at the towering bank buildings and brokerage houses surrounding him. These were the places where JP Morgan and John Rockefeller once sat and concocted their vast fortunes.

Staring down Wall Street, Rolly picked up the first backpack. He knew by now Aiden was only feet from it. Rolly thought to himself, 'Think, dammit. Where's the shithead with the second backpack? Where should it be placed to cause the greatest damage? Think!'

Aiden was a mere ten paces from the backpack. The man carrying it was a fanatic so he was to be treated with great care, but as Aiden drew nearer he could see that he wasn't more than twenty years old, if that, and a little guy, barely five foot six. In an instant Aiden supposed him to be a radicalized dupe, only trained for this one task of martyrdom. His had a single task, to place the bag on the ground and detonate it when people began to flee the area and the first responders began to arrive on the scene.

Aiden knew instinctively he could take him. The question was could he take him without alerting the other two, one of whom was carrying a years' worth of contaminated Wall Street shutdown and who knows how many thousands of innocent deaths.

Aiden walked up behind the boy pretending again to be on the phone and lost. "I'm heading out onto Wall Street," he argued into his phone, "Don't tell me I don't know how to read a street sign."

Aiden walked right past the boy with the backpack and stepped out onto the Wall Street sidewalk. "I don't see it," he barked into the phone. He turned back towards the boy with the pressure cooker full of nails and shards of twisted metal inside it, "Excuse me," he said to the neophyte terrorist as he got within two feet of him, "Can you tell me where the Brown Brothers Harriman building is?"

Aiden, with a big country smile on his face and with his six foot four inch frame, crowded the boy enough to get him to take a step back. From here he was out of the line of sight by any angle other than the one behind him, the one Aiden came from.

"No," the boy said angrily as he tried to walk around Aiden's uncomfortable advance. Before the boy realized what was happening Aiden dropped his own bag and had, in a single undetectable move, put a pistol to the boy's temple. With his free hand, Aiden removed the backpack from his shoulder and pinned the boy against the building, pushing the gun tighter to the boy's head. "Easy boy, I will kill you if you make a sound."

Aiden went right into it, "You speak English? Do you know what I'm saying to you?" he asked the boy in a very soothing voice. The boy nodded that he knew what he was being told.

"I don't want to kill you but I will if you don't do what you are told." Aiden pointed to in the direction from where he just came, "Turn around and walk that way slowly. When I say stop, you stop. If you don't do exactly as you are told I will kill you. Understand? "

The boy nodded again.

"OK, move slowly."

The traffic heading onto Route 3 from the tunnel was at a dead stop with two of the three lanes closed forcing a merge. Nesto stopped and got out of the car to see what was ahead. With the two lanes completely shut down that left only one lane open. He jumped back into his car and before he could make a move his phone rang. He hit speaker on his phone and veered his car left driving directly over the cones the work crew had placed down on the road and into the blocked off lanes. It was open space now. He was driving in the construction zone but he was moving.

Katy blurted into the phone with more than a bit of joy in her voice, "Nesto, they were able to divert the prime minister's plane. He's safe!"

"That's great news but this isn't over. That fuck in the weeds doesn't know that and he's gonna shoot down the next thing he sees. I've got less than ten minutes to get there. Out!"

Katy never saw that coming, but of course Nesto was right. This fight wasn't over by a long shot. She sat still for a moment thinking about how Nesto could give a hoot about who might be in peril, that anyone was in peril compelled him. He never skipped a beat.

She thought about what Aiden and Rolly might be doing and sat for a second longer. She thought how she had come to love, respect, and admire all three of these guys and her eyes swelled and she fought back the tears.

"Fuck this!" she said as she leaped from her desk chair.

While the uncountable cars sat frustrated in a dead stop on Route 3, Nesto was again hitting speeds near one hundred miles an hour. He could feel their eyes on him and he could almost hear the stuck drivers cursing him as he blew by.

Three miles at that speed closed in a hurry and Nesto could see a man up ahead in a yellow vest with a hand held stop sign. Between the man with the sign and the line of cars to the left of the man was a space maybe five inches wider than the sedan Nesto was driving. To the man's right and directly in front of Nesto sat a massive work truck with an enormous steel bumper. On the front side of the truck Nesto could see black smoke from the tar mix and smelt it burning as the road crew was filling potholes. Beyond the work crew there was open highway.

Nesto was determined to fit his car through the space and do it at ninety miles an hour. He needed that guy with the sign to move out of the way and the guy looked like he wasn't going to budge. Aiming the car directly at the stubborn construction crew sign bearer, Nesto pressed harder on the gas. It was a game of chicken now and one Nesto was sure wasn't worth dying over for twenty-six dollars an hour. If he side swiped the cars in the traffic line that would be bad enough but if the road crew kid stood his ground he was going to be killed. Five hundred feet turned into one hundred feet in a flash and the road crew kid still hadn't surrendered his ground. A hundred feet became twenty faster than that, twenty feet to six feet in the blink of an eye. Six feet to the kid diving under the work truck took less than a second.

The only thing Nesto hit with his car as he passed through at nearly one hundred miles an hour was the outer edge of the last yellow cones. When he hit the open road he glanced at his watch.

Rolly still hadn't seen any sign of either the backpack or the suitcase. 'How hard can it be?' he asked himself, 'The guy has a bad limp, he should be easy to find.'

'What would be a smart play?' Rolly looked around for a clue. 'OK… help…where's it most likely that the help would come from? There's Water Street and then there's Broad Street. Water Street is covered with the other guy so it has to be Broad.' Rolly turned south on Broad Street.

They had walked exactly one block back in the direction Aiden had come and before they reached the corner Aiden ordered, "Alright, stop." The young terrorist did as he was told.

Aiden got up close to the man, "Make a right here onto New Street, walk five paces and stop."

Aiden wanted to ask the kid about the suitcase. He didn't expect the kid to tell him the truth but maybe he would give away something he could use.

Just around the corner, behind the Brown Brothers Harriman building, there was a half-filled construction container. Aiden's plan was to get the kid behind the other side of the container to interrogate him for thirty seconds, after which he would put the kid under with a blow to the head, secure his hands with plastic ties, and dump him in the dumpster. He'd put the backpack in a second construction container so if it went off it would be a contained blast. It wasn't an optimum solution but they had no time with Drake taking to the mic any second and it was the suitcase they were really after.

Aiden softly ordered the kid, "Slowly, very slowly. Go."

The moment they turned the corner the kid took off running. He was quick but he didn't have a chance as he tried to make a run for the construction container thirty feet away on the far side of the street. The kid drew a gun as he reached the container but before he could even get off a shot Aiden had put two bullets from his silencer into the back of his head. He fell and crashed into the side of the container dead before impact. Aiden rolled him over, he was dead alright. The bullets had passed through the back of his head and out through the top of his skull.

Aiden threw the back pack into the dumpster. When refuse companies dropped a container onto New Street they placed them as close to the building as possible often blocking the entire sidewalk so the cars and delivery vans could get down the street. In the case of this dumpster there was just less than two feet between the container and the building. It would be considered a bad drop but it was a fortuitous drop for Aiden since he was able to drag the kid between the container and the wall and still have room to search him out of sight.

Moving fast Aiden bent over the kid and began going through pockets hoping to find anything that might help. When he was done searching the kid he was going to toss him in container and move on after Imadin.

Rolly was baffled. Surely the second backpack would be near, it only made sense. They could do enormous damage to fleeing visitors, Wall Street employees and first responders at both approaches to Federal Hall. He continued down Broad Street heading past New Street. With the first backpack already established to be on the other side of the block, there should be zero chance the second backpack would be on New Street as well. As Rolly passed New Street he turned his head to peek down the road in the event Aiden was somehow stuck there.

Aiden was on the far side of the container still hovering over the dead terrorist so he was out from Rolly's line of sight. What Rolly did see though was the second backpack and it was heading rather quickly towards Aiden's position. Rolly didn't know it at the time but the second terrorist had been tucked in a doorway on the north side of New Street the whole time. The plan was for one terrorist to detonate on the Wall Street side of New Street and one to detonate on the Broad Street side of New Street. When Aiden had run by the second backpack he never saw the guy and the terrorist had no way of knowing Aiden was stalking his co-conspirator. They simply passed each other unwittingly.

Rolly made his way along New Street as fast as he could without spooking the terrorist who was nearly three quarters away down the block. If the guy made him too early Rolly would have to kill him from a distance, a prospect he didn't like. Killing him would only increase the possibility that the suitcase with the dirty bomb might get wind that they were there and just let it go.

Rolly increased his speed thus closing the gap more rapidly but he was still not yet in the best position to take the guy. He saw the two construction containers and was hoping, just as Aiden had hoped, to take him as near to the dumpster as possible. Fifteen feet he said to himself, fifteen feet and I'll grab him.

They hadn't gone nine feet further when Aiden appeared raising the body of the dead terrorist over the side of the container. Aiden never saw the second terrorist who was slowing his approach and hugging the wall so to obscure any view of him. The second terrorist had seen Aiden shoot and kill his partner and thought he'd exact some revenge before detonating his backpack. Rolly saw the terrorist raise his arm and aim his pistol at Aiden's back. Still Aiden didn't see him, but Rolly did and drew his pistol.

"Hey!" Rolly screamed from twenty feet away and closing.

The terrorist turned his head for only millisecond to see who was behind him and then fired a shot at Aiden at the same time Rolly fired a shot at him. Three men went down. The dead kid fell into the dumpster and both Aiden and the terrorist fell to the ground.

Rolly ran right past the terrorist to where Aiden was lying. He didn't need to worry about the terrorist on the sidewalk. Being perhaps the finest sharpshooter in the world, he knew with certainty the guy was dead. It was his brother he was worried about.

"Dude, you alright?" Rolly called to Aiden as he flew to his aid.

The bullet fired at Aiden had hit him in the hip. The slight turn of the terrorist's head back at Rolly had delayed and altered the shot, giving Aiden a tiny window to push forward into the container.

Aiden could tell that it was a flesh wound. He was hurting but he had been hurting since he got nicked by the bullet in Huron Forest and had the tar beat out of him in Phoenix. He considered himself lucky to be alive and still in the fight. "Yeah, I'll be alright. Any sign of Imadin?"

Rolly looked at the wound and into Aiden's eyes. He was good to go. "No, but at least we don't have to worry about the fuckin' backpacks. C'mon, lets' put this piece of shit and his luggage in the dumpster with his buddy."

Aiden struggled to his feet with Rolly's help. In thirty seconds they had the terrorist going over the green wall of the container just as they heard the reverb of the microphone coming from Federal Hall. The president-elect was very near his appearance.

The urgency usurped the pain and Aiden looked at Rolly. Pointing to Exchange Place, "I'll go this way. It's a shorter distance. You circle around back and we'll meet at Federal Hall."

Rolly never said a word and took off running.

Nesto blew through the EZ Pass lane onto the four mile spur between Route 3 and the New Jersey Turnpike. He was less than ninety seconds from where he had seen the cleric's son coming out of the high grass with his dog. As he approached, he slowed his vehicle down significantly to look for an entry point, somewhere where the eight foot high weeds had been pressed down. Nesto had tracked bad guys in the woods, over mountains, through deserts and house to house for a decade. If there was bent grass in a sea of grass Nesto would find it.

'There, right there!' Nesto hollered to himself internally. It was barely perceptible but there were a few bent weeds. Letting the car roll to a stop he grabbed his assault rifle, pistol, and black, eight-inch blade and exited the car as quietly as he could. Making his way the ten feet hunched over as he kept along the highway shoulder, he arrived at the entry point pausing to listen. There was no sound. As he broke through the weeds and pushed in a few feet it was clear that the terrorist had been very careful not to disturb the weeds lining the highway but once through those first few feet the bent weed made the path clear.

Five more yards in Nesto looked at his watch. Three minutes. He wanted to move slower but the time was near. Actually, he would much rather not move at all. In the tall grasses the one in motion is at an extreme disadvantage. 'This prick thinks he's gonna fire that thing in three minutes. Let's go,' Nesto thought to himself as he moved along the beaten path.

Three more steps in and Nesto saw blood. It wasn't a lot of blood but it was absolutely blood. Nesto had seen enough of it to know and judging by the brightness of it, the blood was fresh.

Another step and the cause of the bloodletting became clear. The terrorist had stabbed the dog that he had with him a few days earlier. Nesto surmised that the guy didn't want the small poodle barking or running out on the highway, anything that would give him away, so he killed the dog. 'What a fucking prick,' he thought to himself. A few feet away lay the dog and, miraculously, he wasn't dead.

He leaned in and extended his hand to gently touch the dogs head but something in the movement of the grass told Nesto to duck. He never saw the blade as it went into his back just above his left side shoulder. He was lucky. The terrorist could have shot him. The terrorist had a handgun but thought the noise would give him up so he chose a knife. He chose to fight it out with one of America's most dangerous warriors. That was a mistake.

Nesto didn't know yet what had happened but the force of it knocked him to the ground and the shock to his arms caused him to release his knife and his pistol fell out from behind him. Both were now in the mud and useless to him.

Nesto had been in hand-to-hand combat many times during his tours in the Middle East. His training was the best the world had to offer and his instincts were razor sharp. His martial arts skill was mature and effective. He knew how to use his opponent's aggressiveness against him. He wheeled around just in enough time to side step the next thrust of the knife. As the assailant recoiled and thrust the blade again, Nesto pushed it further along in the direction it was heading rather than blunting it. The defensive technique of using lunging motion and weight against him sent the assailant off balance enough to allow Nesto to slam his fist into the back of the attacker's head knocking the guy to the ground.

Nesto could see into the cleric's son's eyes; there was desperation in his look. The terrorist could see into Nesto's eyes; he could see only confidence. Nesto bent down and removed his blade from the holster. The pain in his shoulder was excruciating and he was losing blood. The two men stared at each other.

A police siren could be heard fast approaching from the south and a plane could be heard fast approaching from the north. This was going to be over in seconds, both men knew it.

As Nesto had rightly predicted, the terrorist didn't know the plane carrying the prime minister had been safely rerouted to Kennedy Airport in New York. To him the prime minister was on that plane and that stinger missile was only feet from where he was standing. The only thing standing between him and immortality was this infidel. He lunged at Nesto with the knife. This time Nesto blunted the thrusting arm while dropping down and stabbing the terrorist in his thigh twice and then driving the blade of his knife into the man's chest, puncturing his heart as his body collapsed downward. The man died instantly. Nesto fell back into the muddy marsh. He looked up as the airplane passed unknowingly over him on its way to its' final destination, the landing strip at Newark International Airport in New Jersey.

Just seconds later a New Jersey state trooper burst into the weeds and pointed his pistol at Nesto, "Your hands, show me your hands," he screamed at Nesto. The trooper had been dispatched to find the crazy driver who nearly crashed into a work crew at a hundred miles an hour on Route 3. He couldn't have known he'd find the man who prevented the downing of a passenger jet. Nesto threw up his right hand. His left hand simply wouldn't cooperate with the officer. "The dog, make sure you take the dog with us," was all Nesto said to the astonished trooper.

Rolly flew back down New Street turning right on Broad Street and heading towards Wall. He looked around frantically for Imadin and the case. "Nothing...'Fuck!"

There was a speaker at the podium in front of Federal Hall prepping the ever burgeoning crowd for the President Elect who was to speak momentarily. He ran past the New York Stock Exchange towards Federal Hall. When he made it to Wall Street he turned right and picked up Aiden who was lumbering in his direction as best he could. They met in the middle of Wall Street a hundred feet south of Federal Hall and just north of The Drake building. Both men were spinning like tops hoping to get a glimpse of Imadin and the suitcase. Aiden threw up his hands and Rolly just shook his head no.

A bustling throng emerged in front of The Drake building as Secret Service agents came out first. Next two cabinet members exited the building, than some additional Secret Service agents and finally the president-elect appeared.

The podium at Federal Hall was fifty or so yards from The Drake building. The entourage began its slow march with cabinet members and the president-elect moving along to shake hands and stop to chat with well-wishers.

Aiden grabbed Rolly's arm and pointed in the direction of Trinity Church more than two hundred yards away. "There. Up there! There he is!"

Both Rolly and Aiden drew their pistols and started running towards the church.

"Gun!" One of the Secret Service agents yelled as he tackled Aiden. Rolly made it only another two strides before he was tackled to the ground by three more quick agents.

Jihad as it turned out had gone inside Trinity Church with the suitcase. It never occurred to Rolly or Aiden to look for the Islamist terrorist in one of the oldest Christian churches in America.

Rolly and Aiden struggled to be heard over all the secret service agents screaming. Despite screaming their credentials and begging to be heard, it took nearly a full minute for either man to get up off the ground and another several seconds to be set free.

Jihad was now at the top of the hill down on one knee. He had seen the disturbance and was moving to get the device out of the case as fast as he could before the melee could be sorted out.

Rolly and Aiden, along with several Secret Service agents, broke for the church.

Jihad was crouched behind the base of a lamp post and there were just too many scrambling pedestrians in the way to get a clear shot. It wasn't that Rolly and Aiden wouldn't gladly exchange one life for Imadin's, there just wasn't a shot to be had. They knew it was futile but they kept running towards the case in the hopes something would go wrong up there.

People scrambled in all directions. The president-elect and his cabinet members were whisked back into The Drake and made their way towards the basement of the building.

Rolly was still more than a hundred yards from Imadin. The concentration of the terrorist on his unfathomable intention superseded his attention to the oncoming assault. He was only a few seconds from detonating and there was nothing the on rushers could do but die within sight of it.

"Stop!"

Rolly heard it too. It was a familiar voice but Rolly didn't place it because of all the screaming voices.

Imadin reached down for the pistol at his feet and spun toward the female voice and threw the gun barrel in front of him. It was too late for him; a bullet hit Imadin just below his lower lip. The bullet passed through the lower part of his brain stem, killing him instantly.

There was no way the shooter could have known what a perfect shot had just been made and what it meant for world peace. Katy kept running towards Imadin with her pistol pointed at him.

"Gun!" someone screamed.

Before Katy could get to Imadin, a New York police officer tackled her. In the fall her head slammed into the lamp post just where Imadin lay dead leaving her semi-conscious.

It took several seconds for Aiden and Rolly to make it through the hysterical crowd of men dodging through the scurrying vendors and fleeing business crowds. While Rolly had his gun drawn and pointed at Imadin in the event he was not yet neutralized, Aiden made his way to Katy's side. She was bloodied and dazed, but alive. Imadin was not so fortunate.

A sense of utter relief came over the two men. There was an incredible amount of noise all around them. They could hear none of it. People were running seemingly in every direction. Police and Secret Service agents were barking orders at each other and at the confused crowds of people. Sirens could be heard approaching. Somehow to Rolly and Aiden at that moment the world had gone utterly silent.

Katy's body sharply contorted as she regained some consciousness. Aiden gently restrained her in the event she had been seriously injured whispering, "Easy, it's over. You got him. It's over."

Rolly, resting on one knee next to his longtime partner and his battered and heroic new partner lying in the street, looked up into the New York sky. He felt gratified that their targets had not done the unthinkable. He felt gratified further still that he had not heard the explosions of a passenger jet, accompanied by what would surely have been by now a sky full of low flying F-16's and swirling helicopters. He knew Nesto had stopped the attack and hoped his friend was still alive.

At that moment he couldn't help but notice the cross atop the Trinity Church steeple and wondered if it was coincidence.

The End

About the Author

Ed Kirwan is a father of four children and proudly hails from the streets and playgrounds of "The" Bronx, New York. He spent more than two decades working in the financial services industry for various Wall Street firms before building his own company. He is a life-long devotee of the stage, with a particular predilection for European and American tragedy, and the author of the play, Dying Twice; a play of death and life in mysterious ways.

Made in United States
Orlando, FL
30 March 2023